MAR   2023

Peach AND Plum

Rule at School!

For my Ridgeview Elementary teachers,
who taught me well.

About This Book

This book was edited by Andrea Colvin and designed by Carolyn Bull.
The production was supervised by Bernadette Flinn,
and the production editor was Marisa Finkelstein.

Little, Brown and Company
Hachette Book Group
1290 Avenue of the Americas, New York, NY 10104
Visit us at LBYR.com

First Edition: February 2023

Little, Brown and Company is a division of Hachette Book Group, Inc.
The Little, Brown name and logo are trademarks of Hachette Book Group, Inc.

The publisher is not responsible for websites (or their content)
that are not owned by the publisher.

Library of Congress Cataloging-in-Publication Data
Names: McCanna, Tim, author, illustrator.
Title: Peach and Plum : rule at school! / Tim McCanna.
Description: New York : Little, Brown and Company, 2023. | Series: Peach and Plum ; 2
Audience: Ages 6–9. | Summary: "Peach and Plum get separated by a new substitute teacher
with new rules" —Provided by publisher.
Identifiers: LCCN 2022019866 | ISBN 9780316306300 (hardcover) | ISBN 9780316306409
(trade paperback) | ISBN 9780316347358 (ebook)
Subjects: CYAC: Graphic novels. | Stories in rhyme. | Peach—Fiction. | Plum—Fiction.
Schools—Fiction. | Teachers—Fiction. | LCGFT: Graphic novels.
Classification: LCC PZ7.7.M41264 Pk 2022 | DDC 741.5/973—dc23/eng/20220525
LC record available at https://lccn.loc.gov/2022019866
ISBNs: 978-0-316-306300-0 (hardcover), 978-0-316-30640-9 (paperback),
978-0-316-34735-8 (ebook), 978-0-316-34756-3 (ebook), 978-0-316-34772-3 (ebook)

PRINTED IN CHINA

APS

Hardcover: 10 9 8 7 6 5 4 3 2 1
Paperback: 10 9 8 7 6 5 4 3 2 1

Peach AND Plum

Rule at School!

FRUITDALE SCHOOL DISTRICT

Tim McCanna

L B
LITTLE, BROWN AND COMPANY
New York Boston

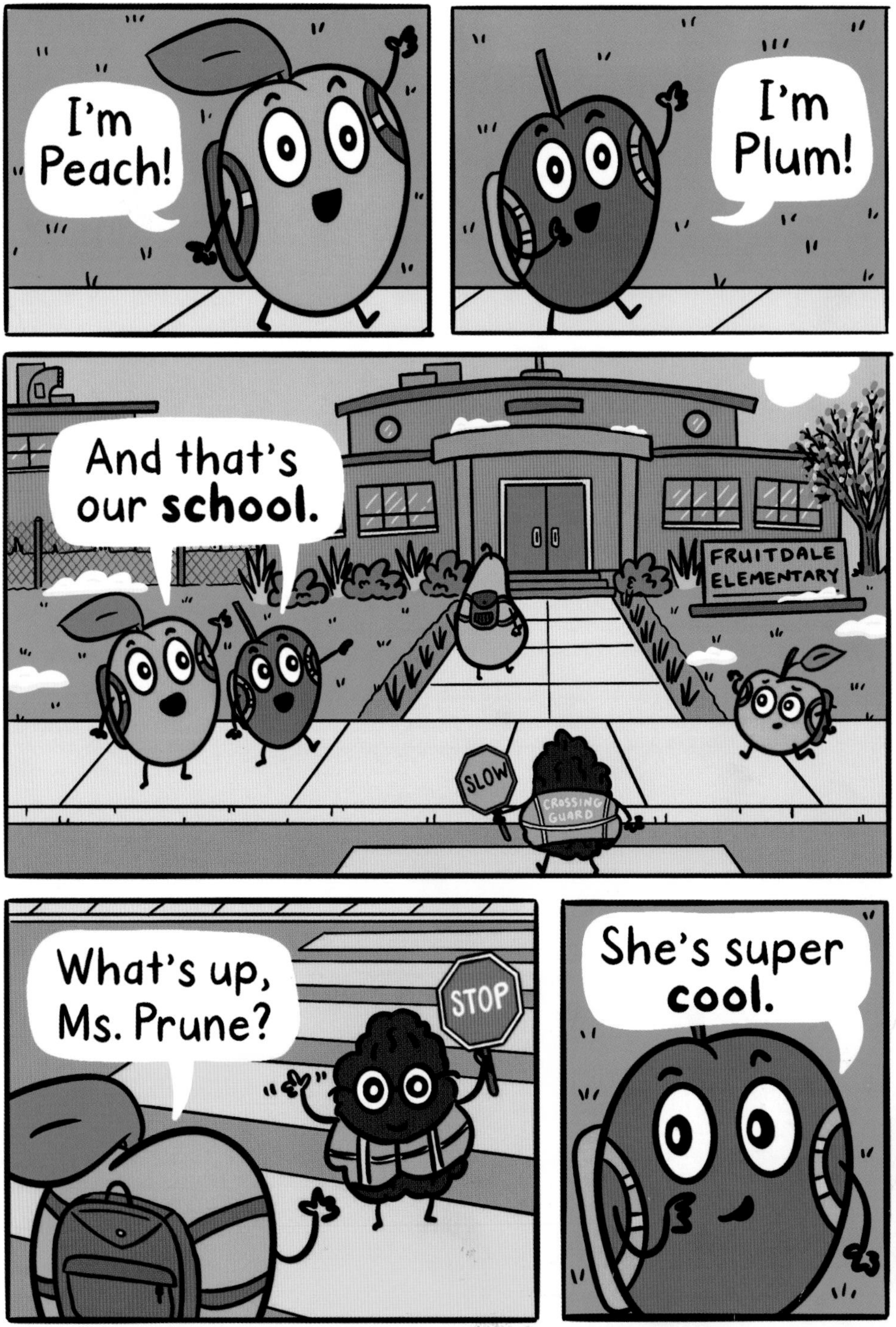
I'm Peach!
I'm Plum!
And that's our **school**.
FRUITDALE ELEMENTARY
SLOW
CROSSING GUARD
What's up, Ms. Prune?
STOP
She's super **cool**.

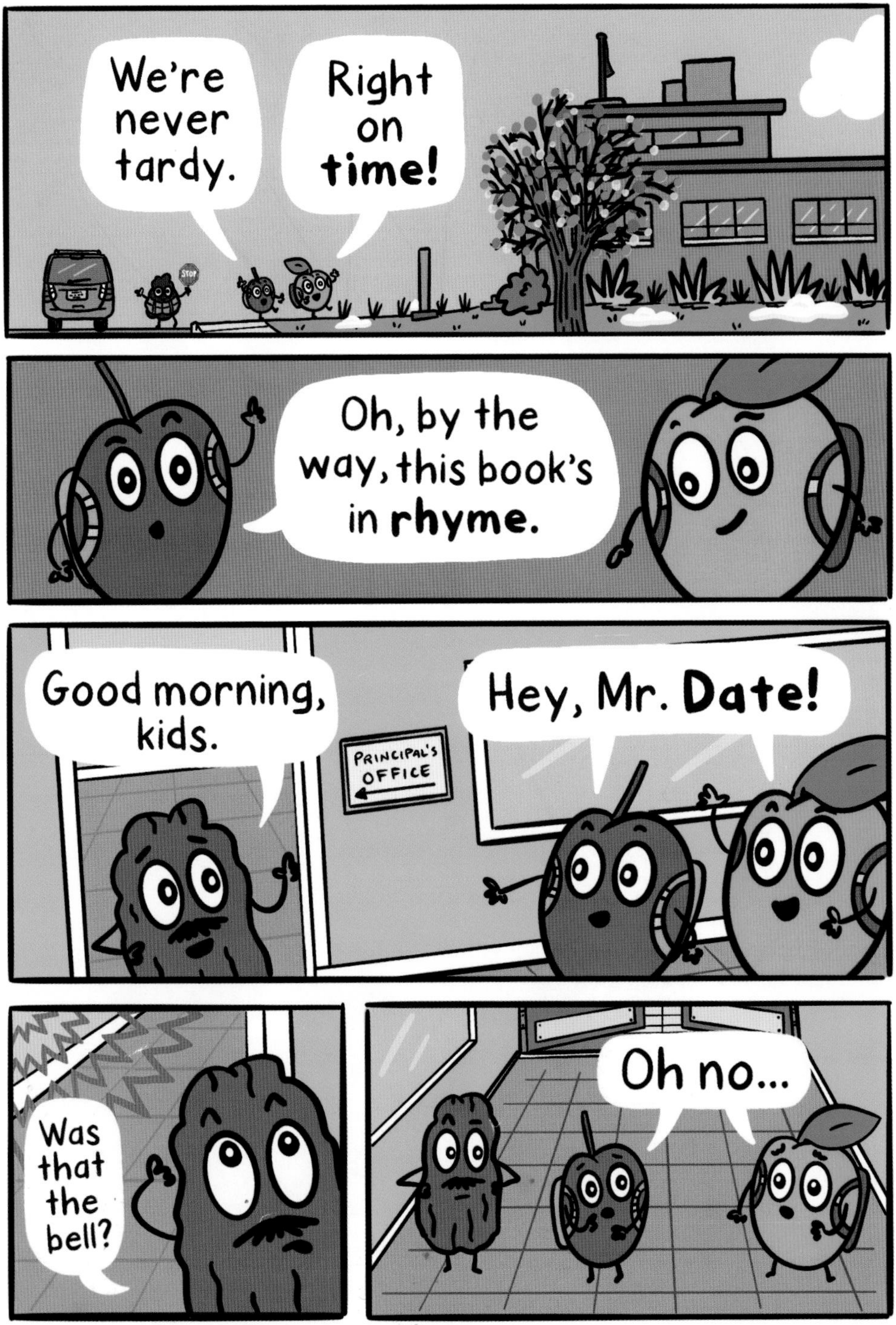
We're never tardy.
Right on time!
Oh, by the way, this book's in rhyme.
Good morning, kids.
Hey, Mr. Date!
PRINCIPAL'S OFFICE
Was that the bell?
Oh no...

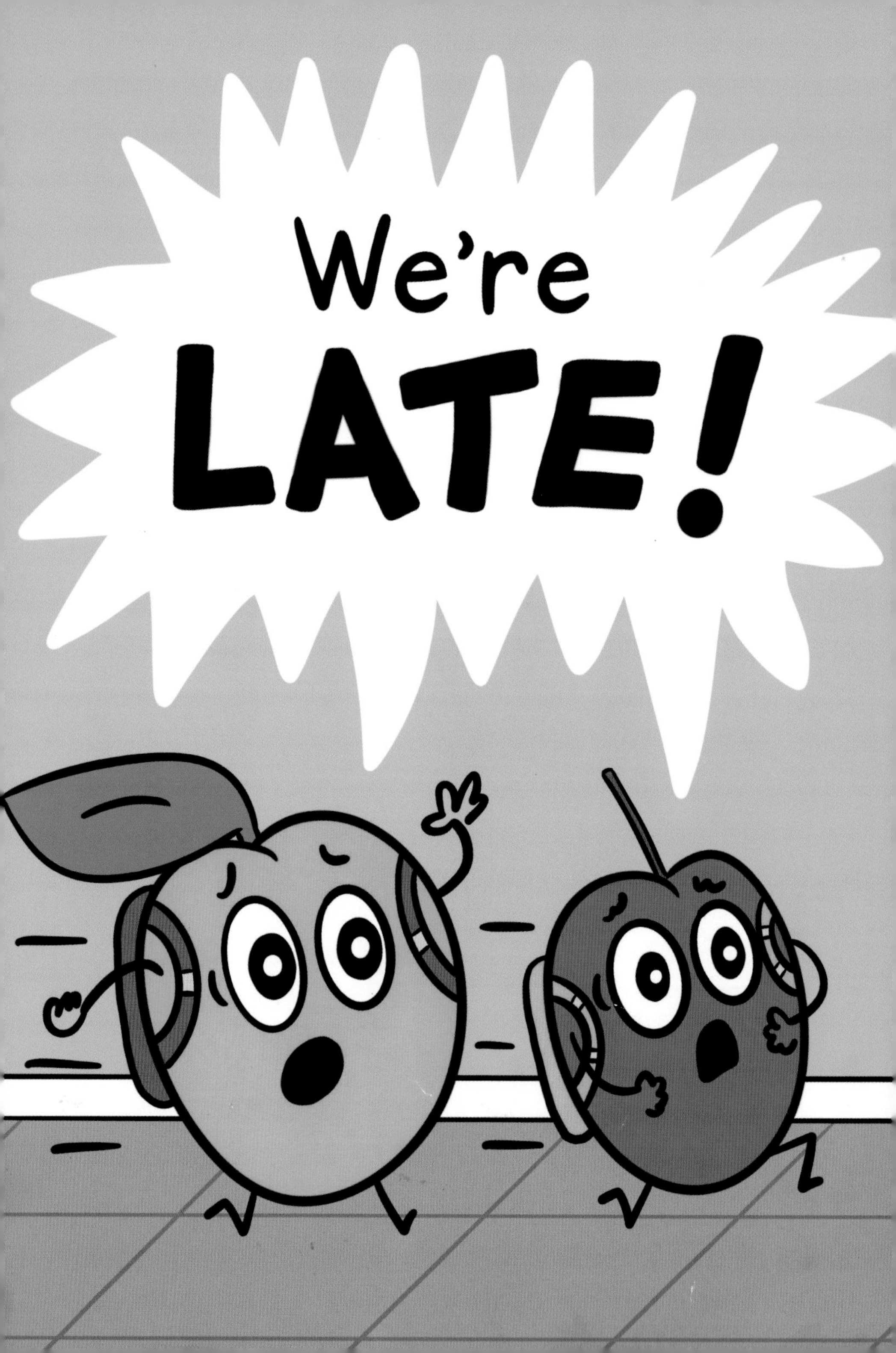
We're
LATE!

CONTENTS

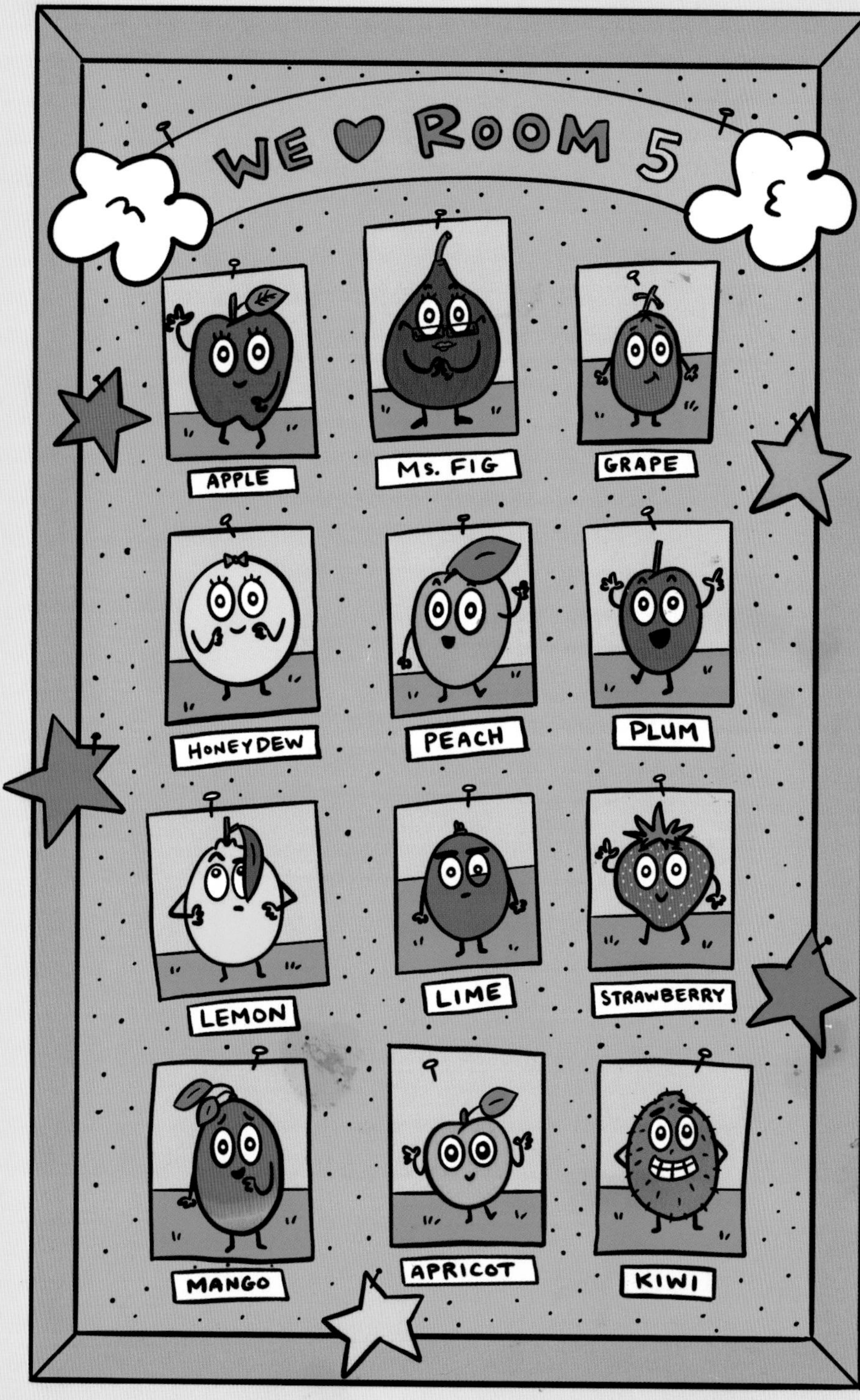

WE ♥ ROOM 5
APPLE
Ms. FIG
GRAPE
HONEYDEW
PEACH
PLUM
LEMON
LIME
STRAWBERRY
MANGO
APRICOT
KIWI

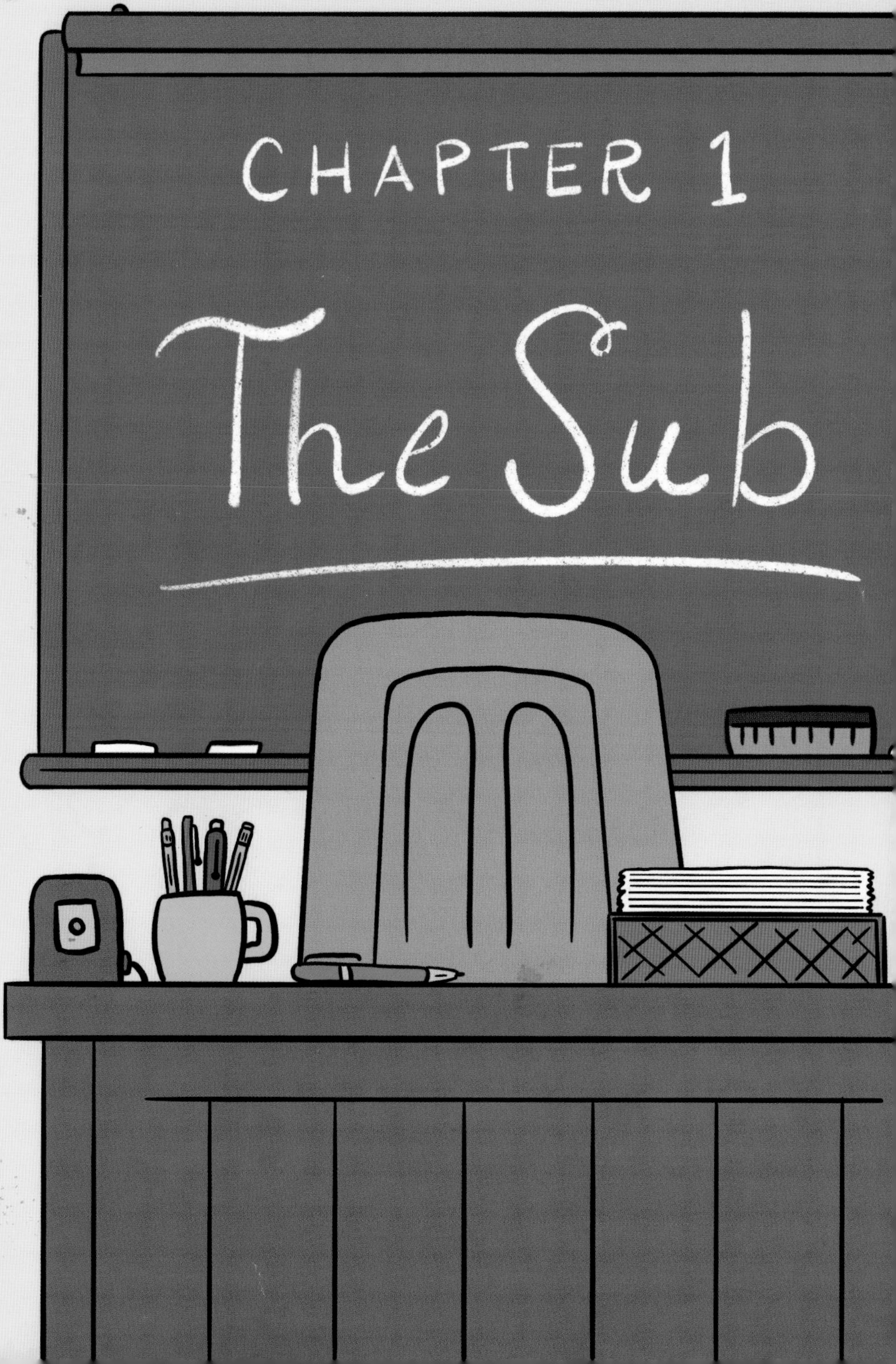
CHAPTER 1
The Sub

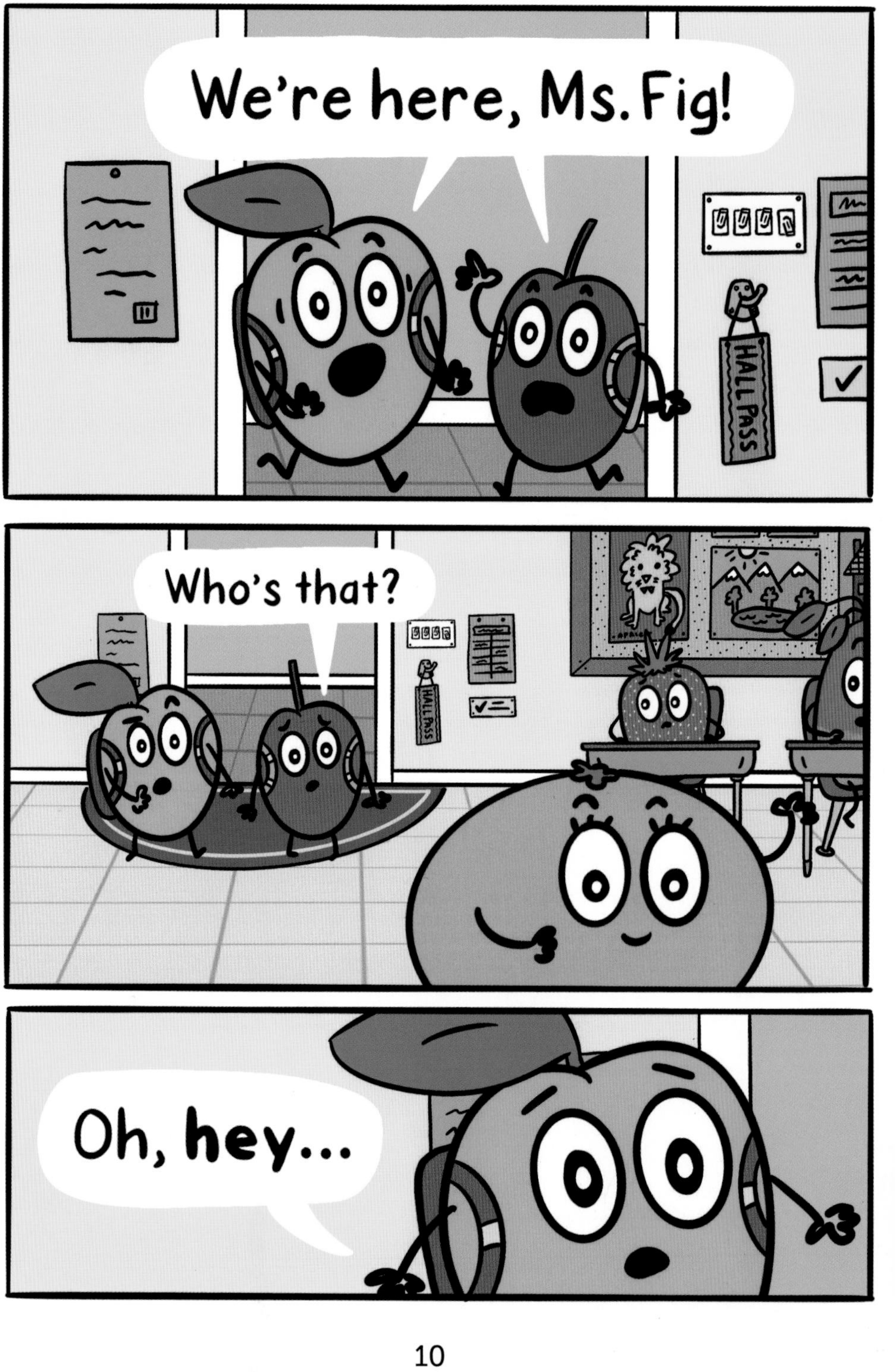
We're here, Ms. Fig!
HALL PASS
Who's that?
HALL PASS
Oh, hey...

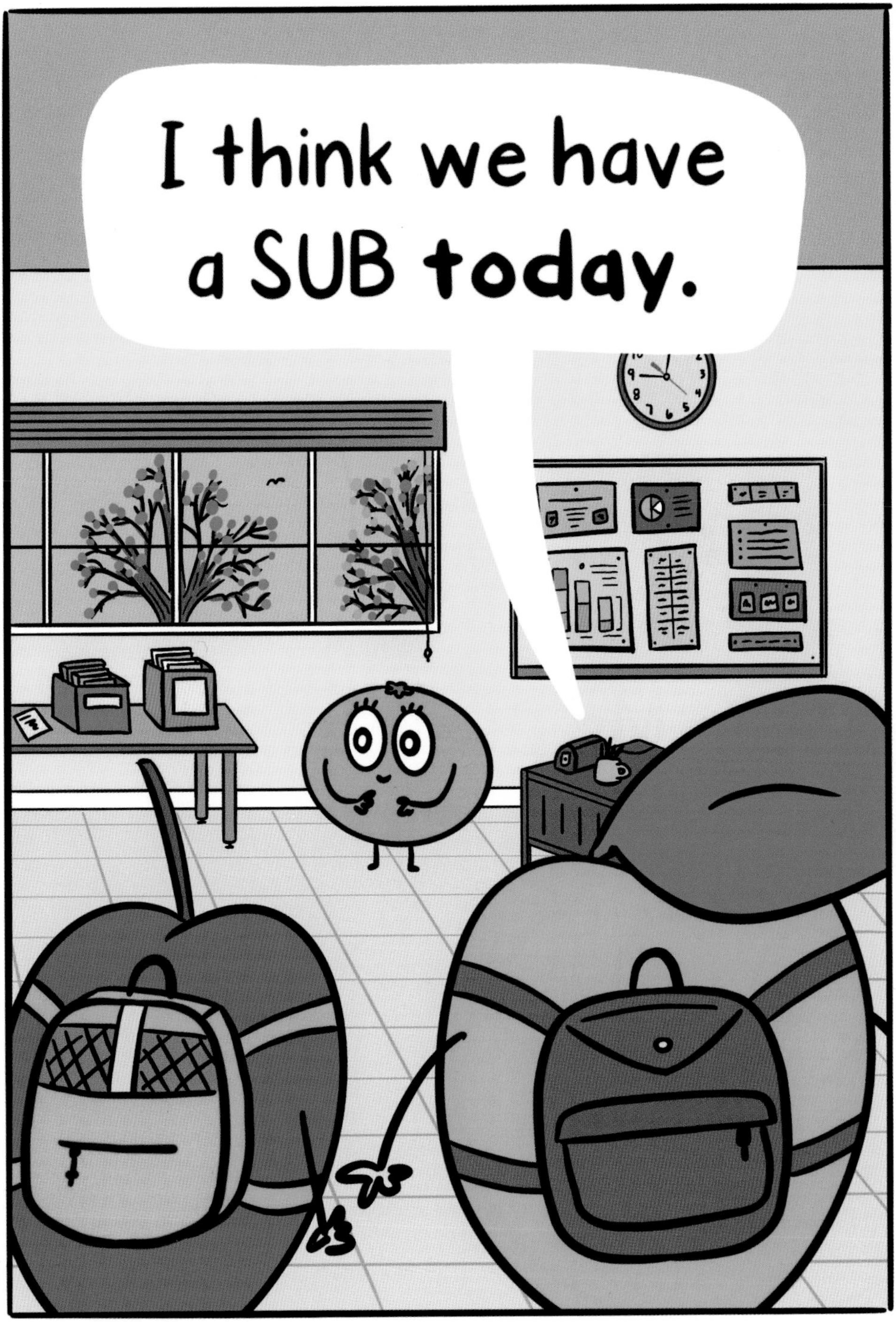
I think we have a SUB today.

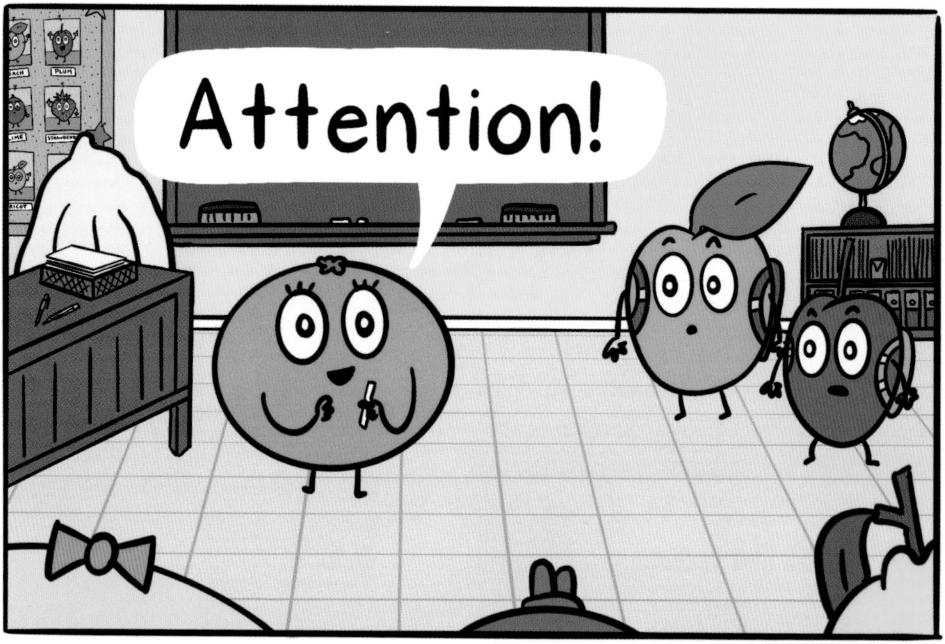
Attention!

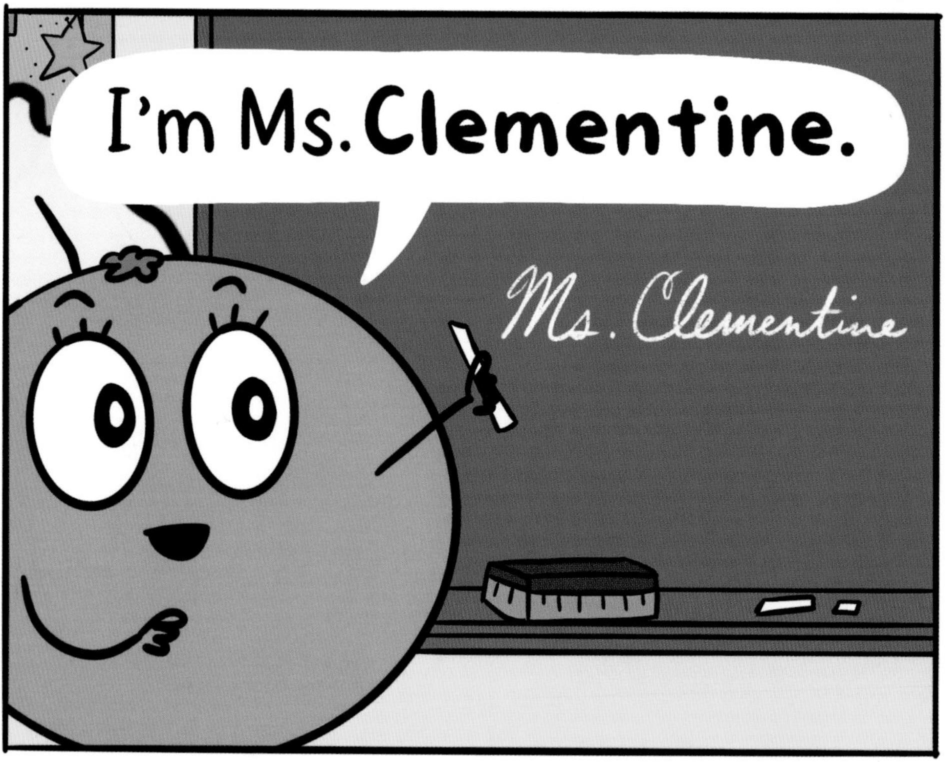
I'm Ms. Clementine.
Ms. Clementine

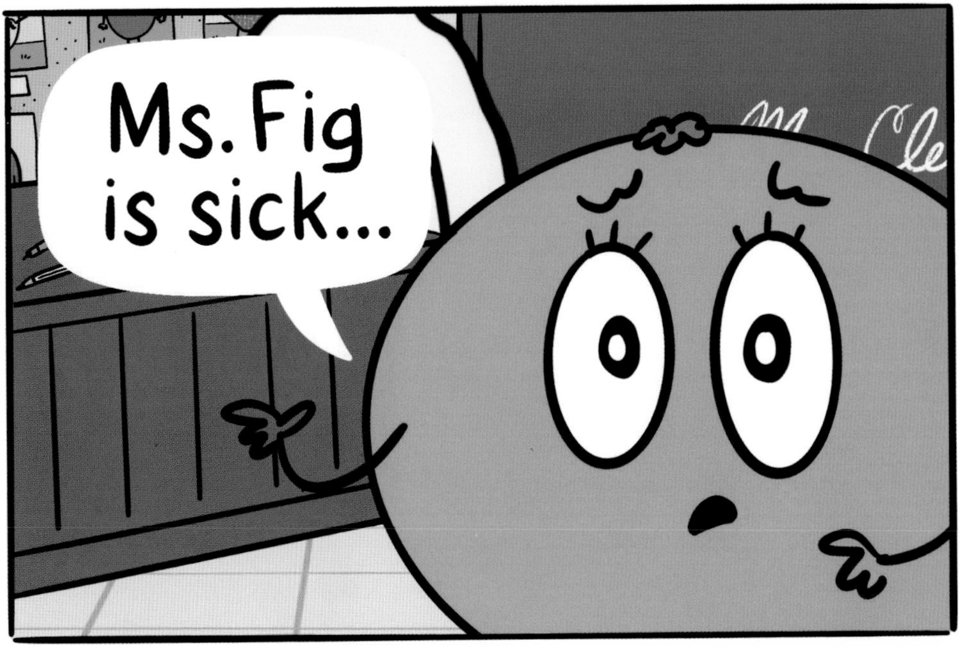
Ms. Fig is sick...

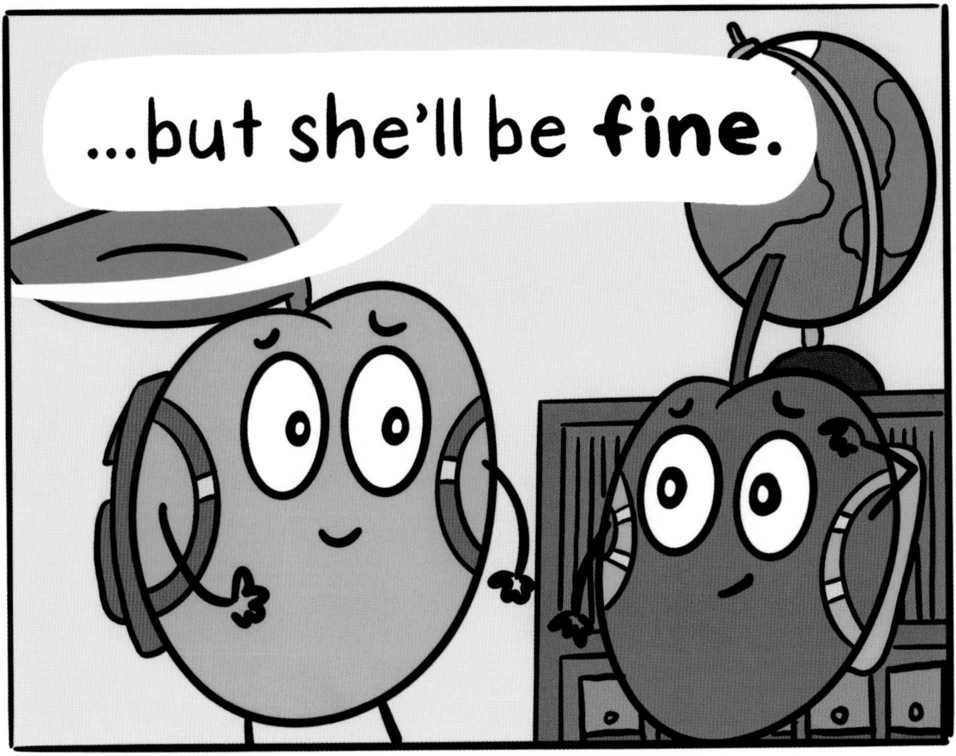
...but she'll be fine.

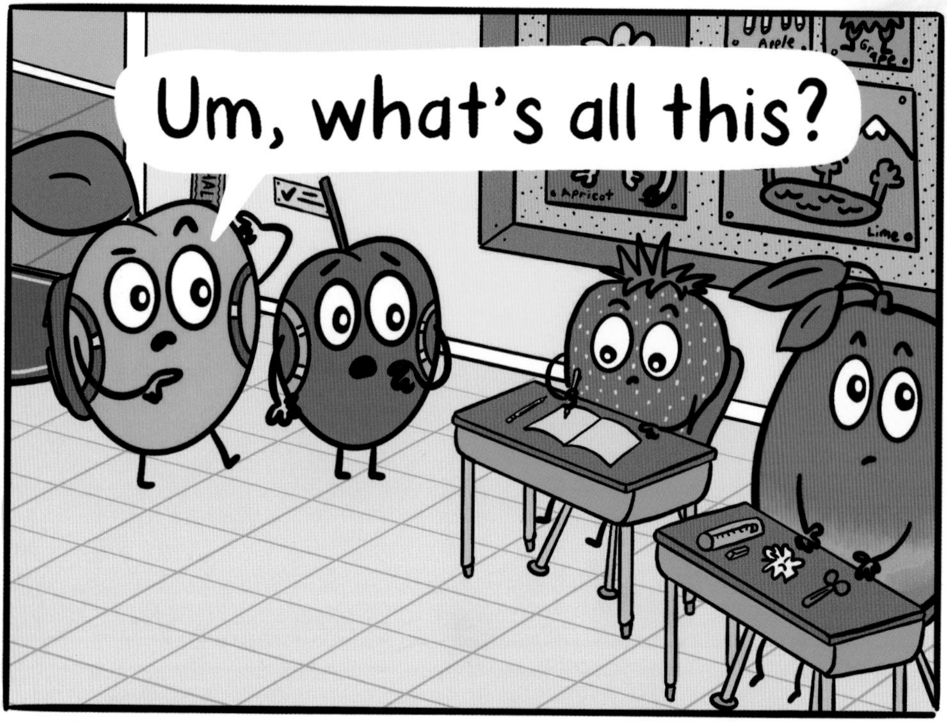
Um, what's all this?
Apple
Grape
Apricot
Lime

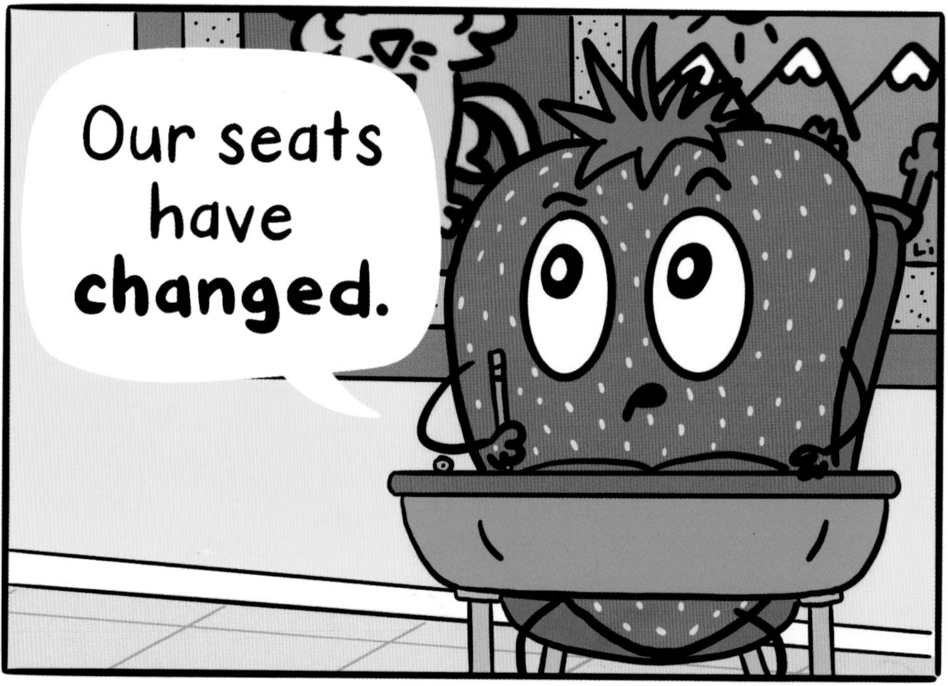
Our seats have **changed.**

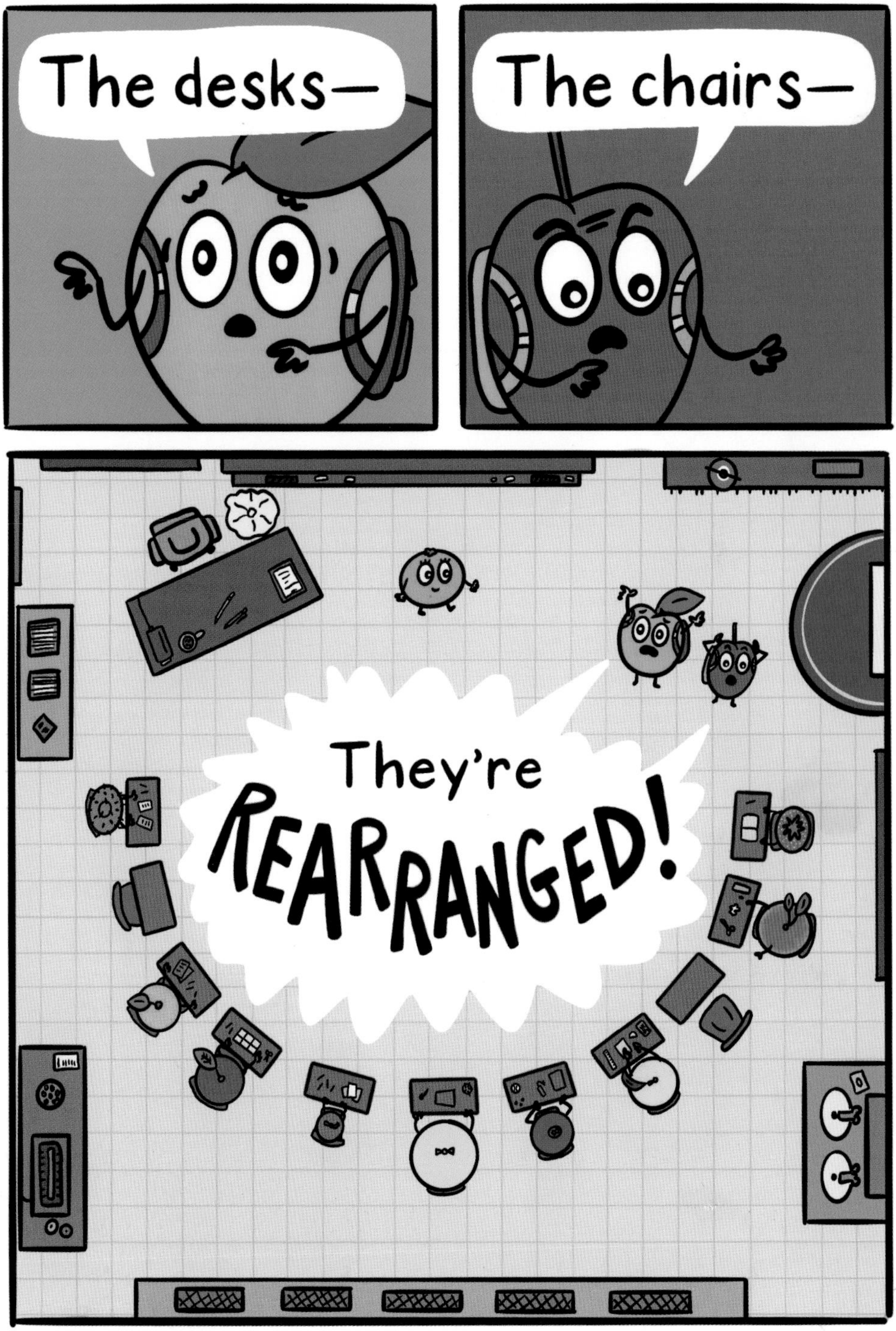
The desks—
The chairs—
They're
REARRANGED!

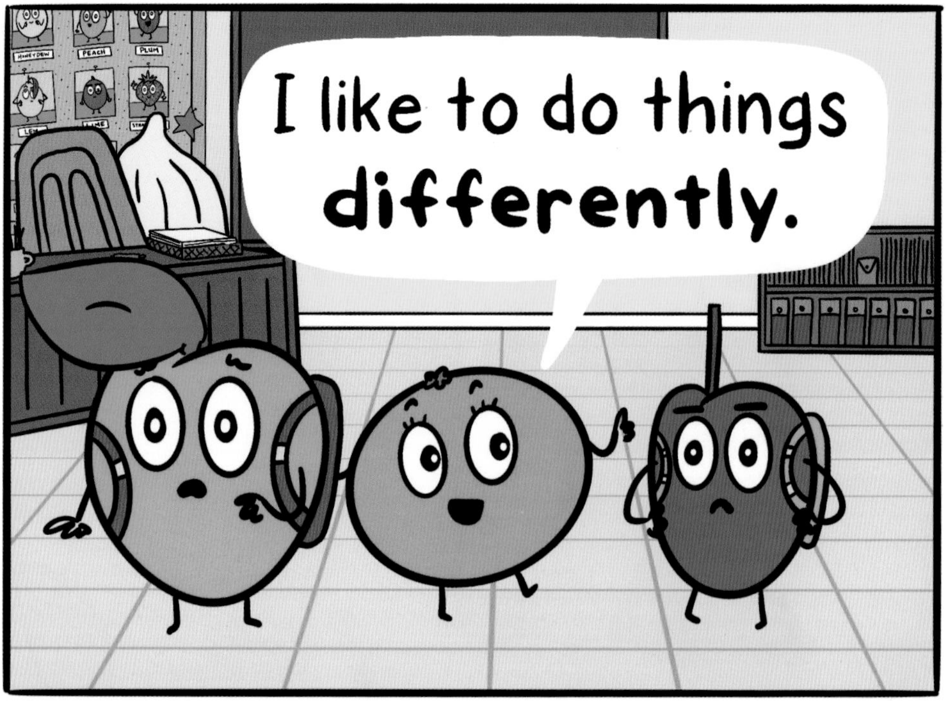
HONEYDEW
PEACH
PLUM
I like to do things **differently.**

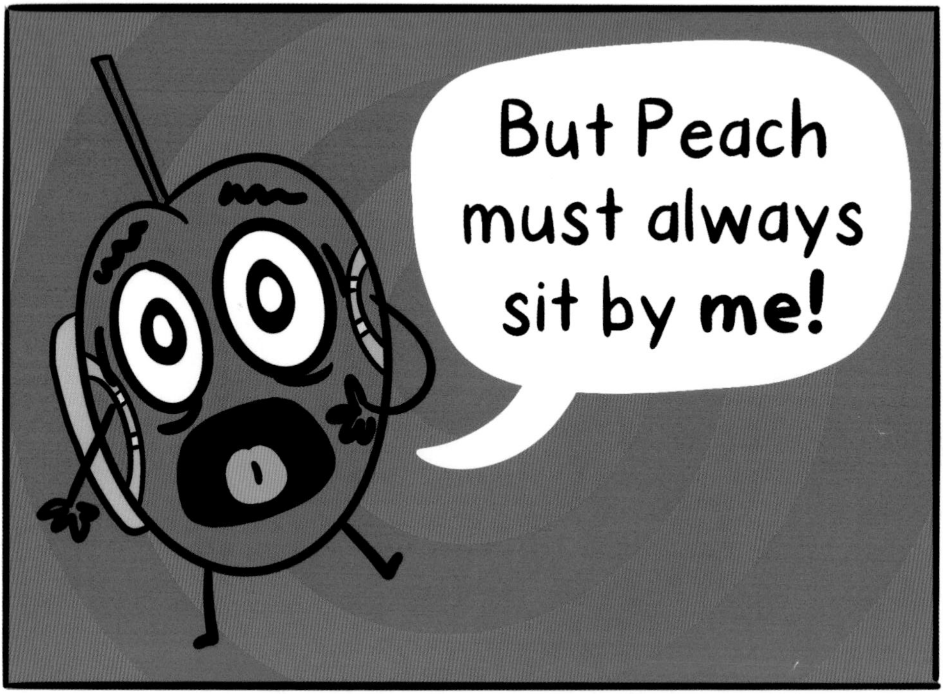
But Peach must always sit by **me!**

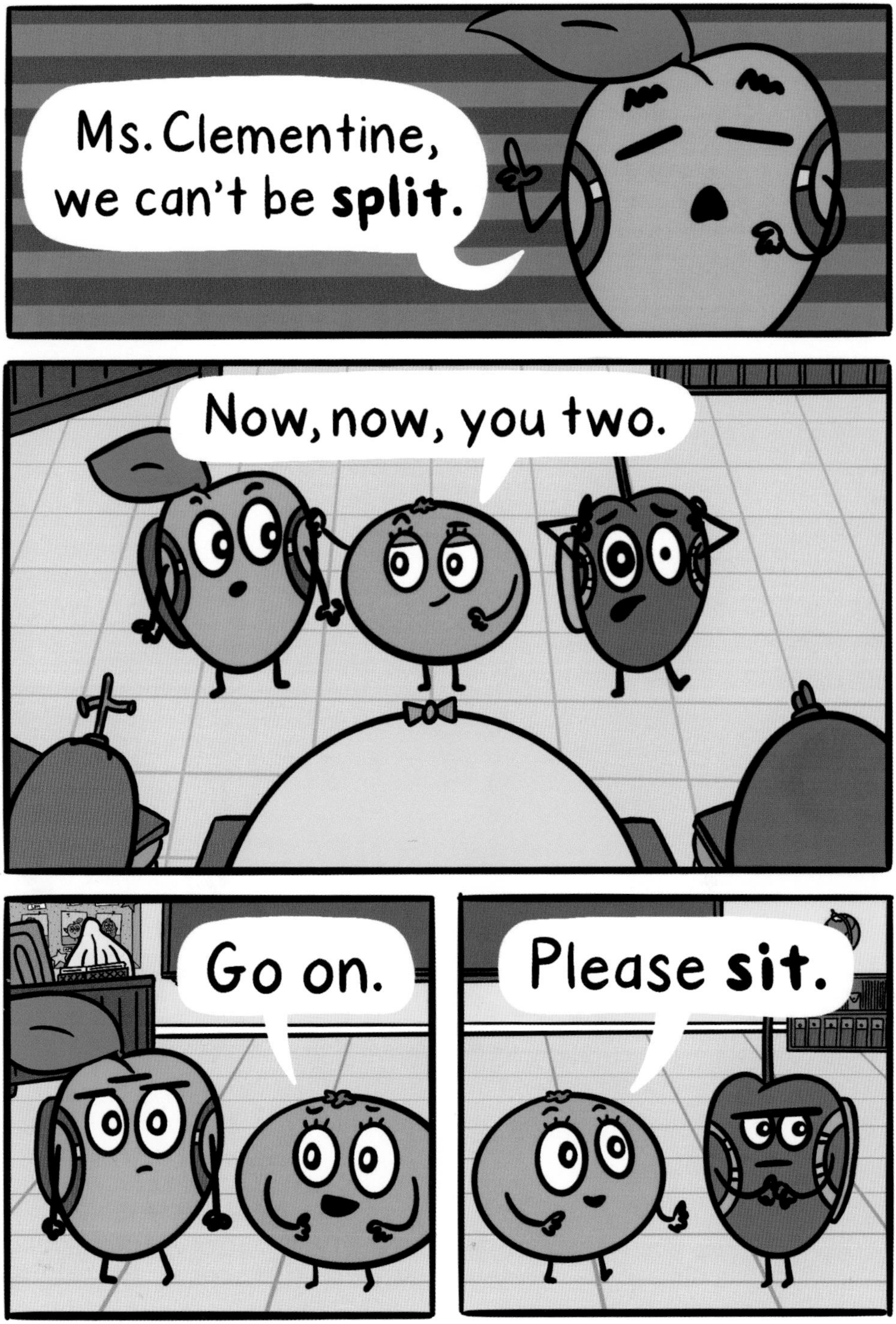
Ms. Clementine,
we can't be **split**.
Now, now, you two.
Go on.
Please **sit**.

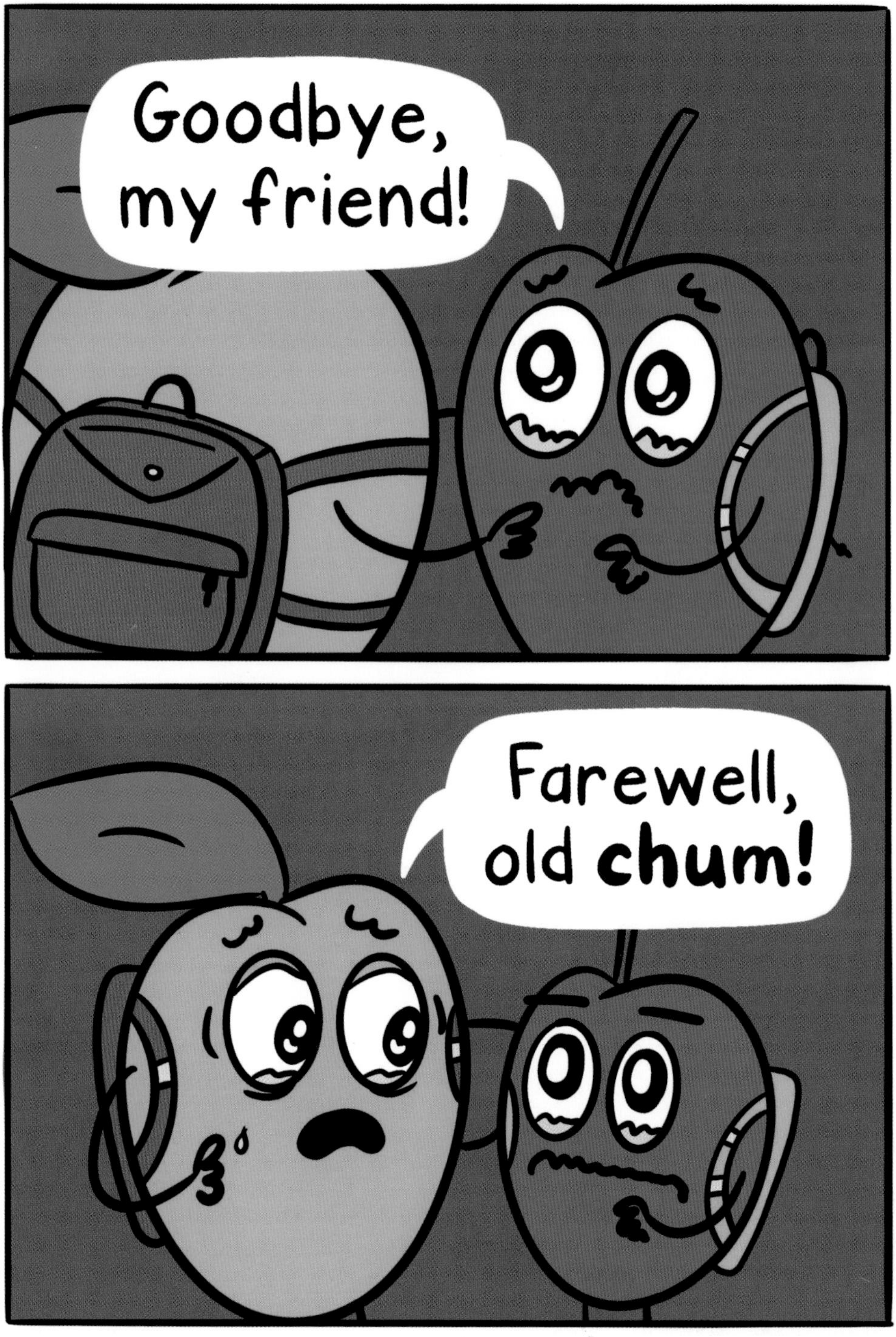
Goodbye, my friend!
Farewell, old **chum**!

Is this the end for Peach and **Plum?**

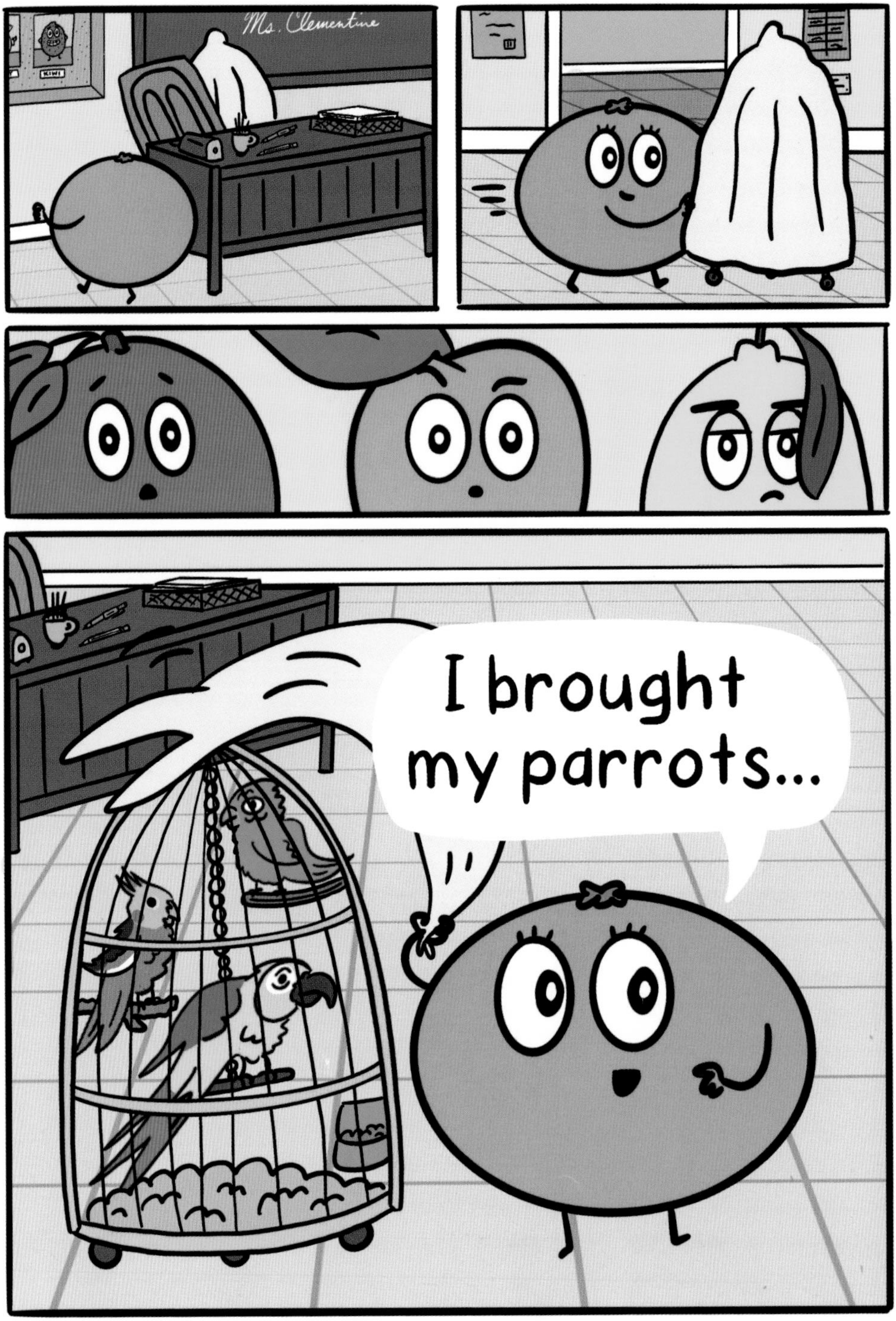
Ms. Clementine
KIWI
I brought my parrots...

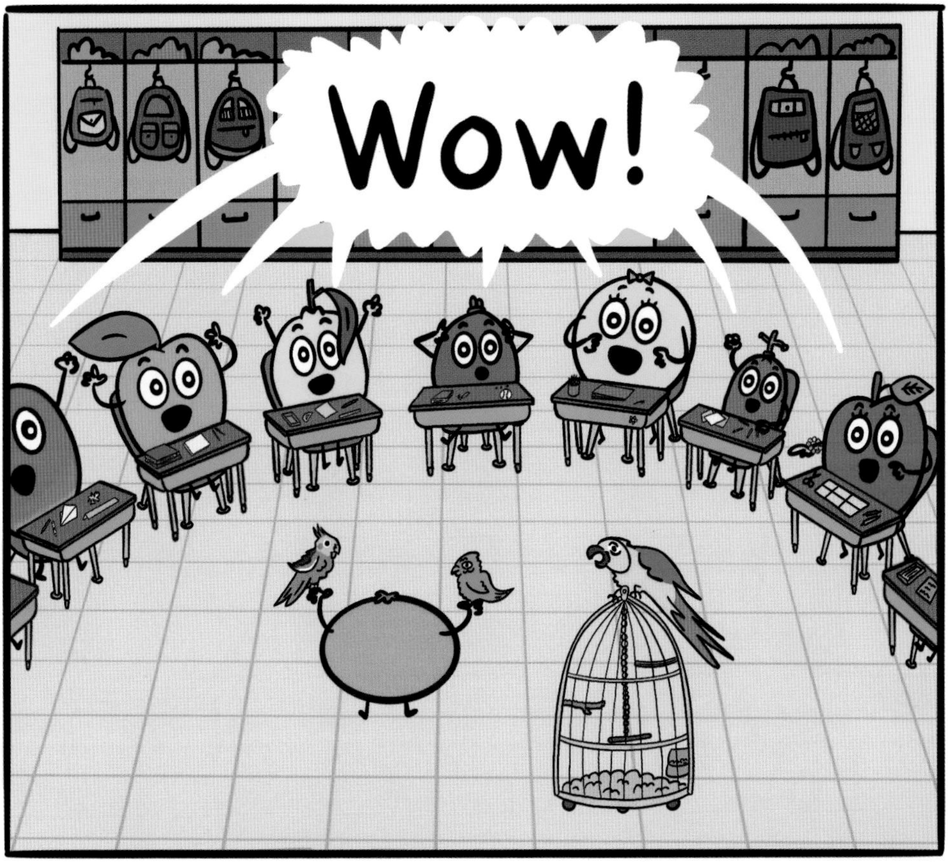
Wow!

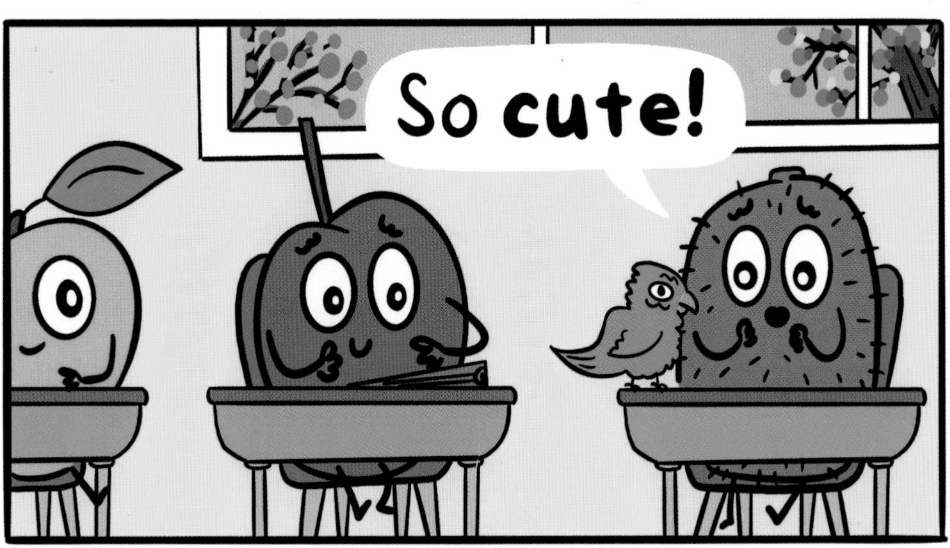
So cute!

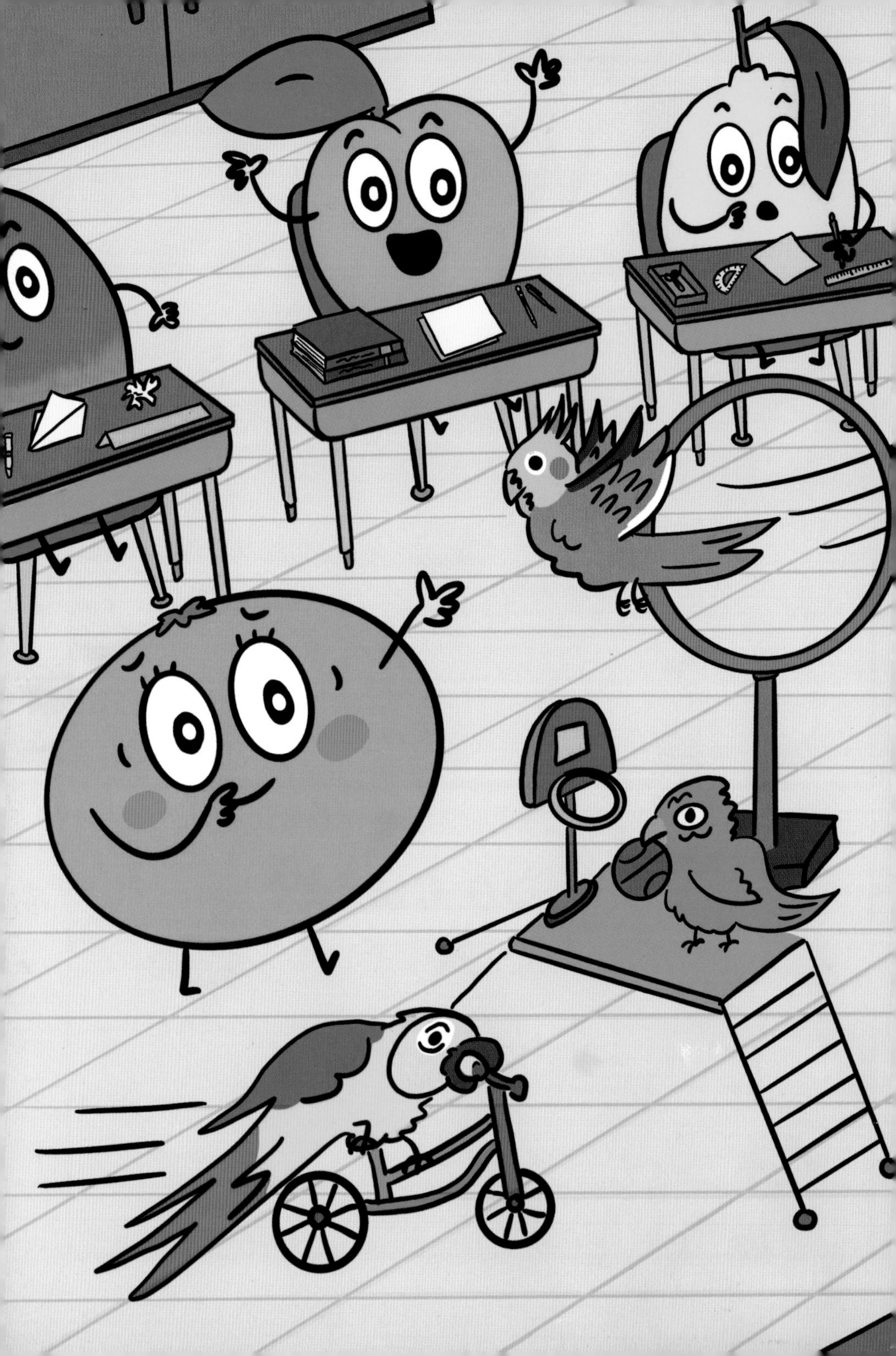

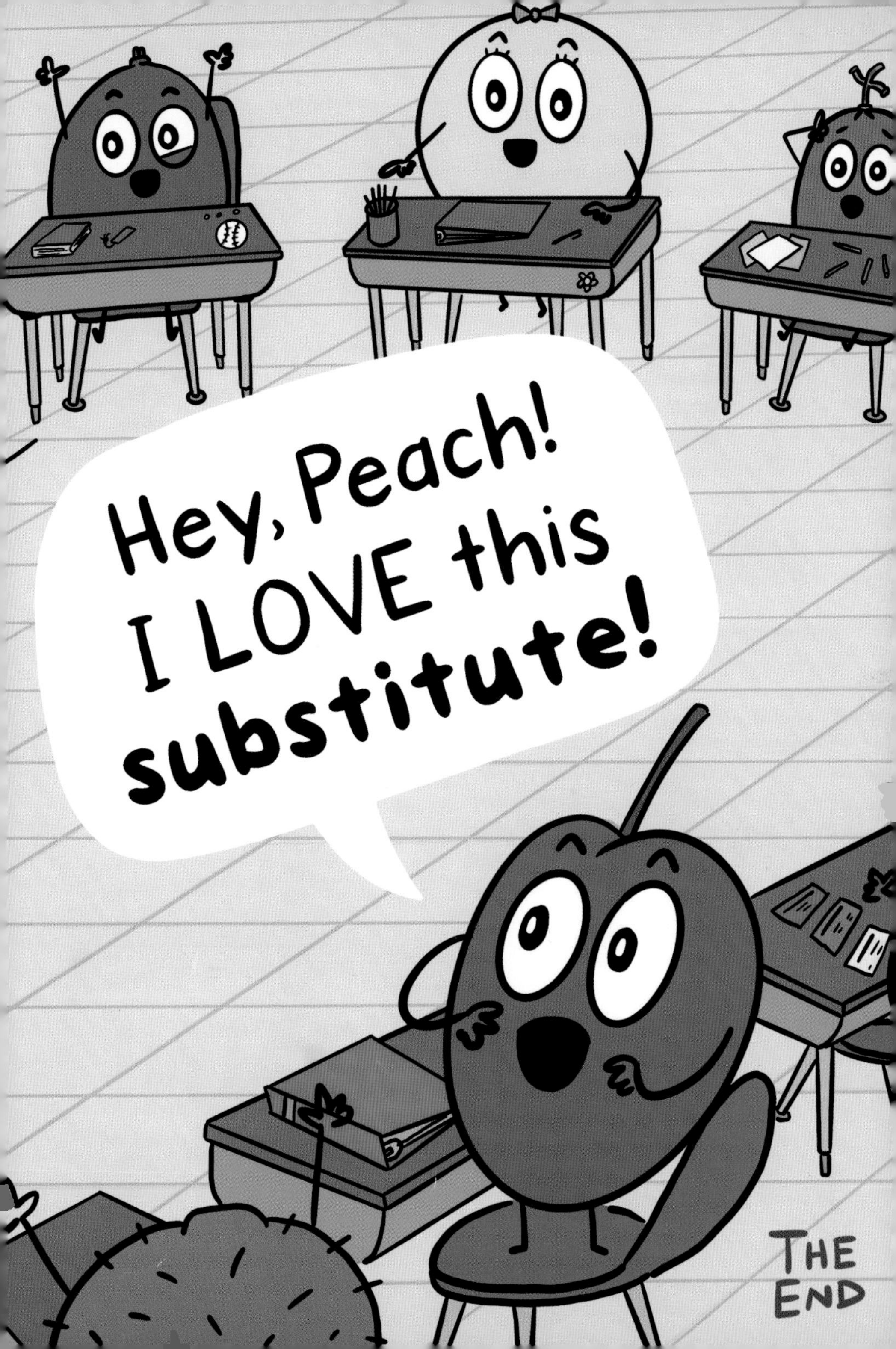
Hey, Peach! I LOVE this substitute!
THE END

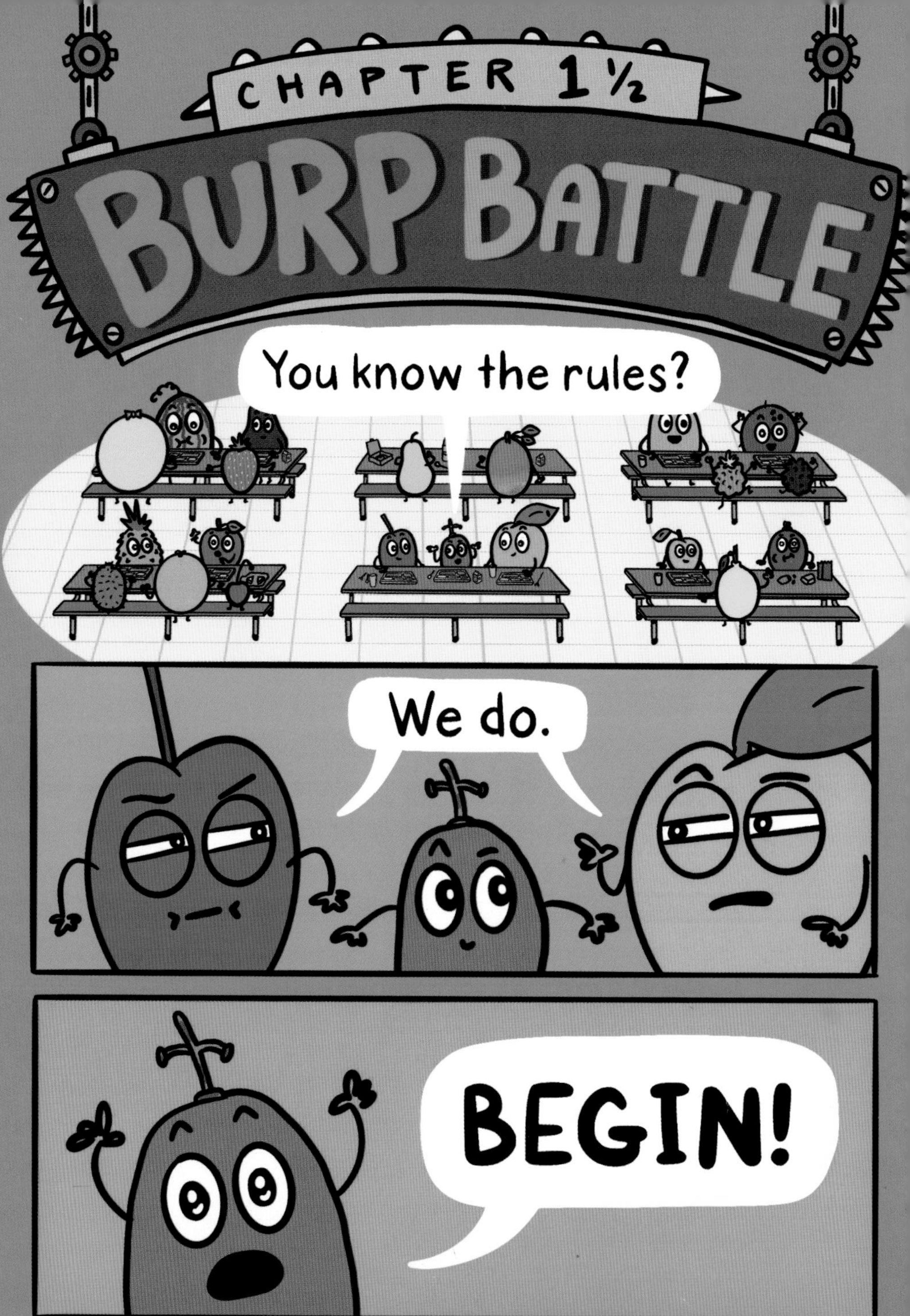
CHAPTER 1½
BURP BATTLE
You know the rules?
We do.
BEGIN!

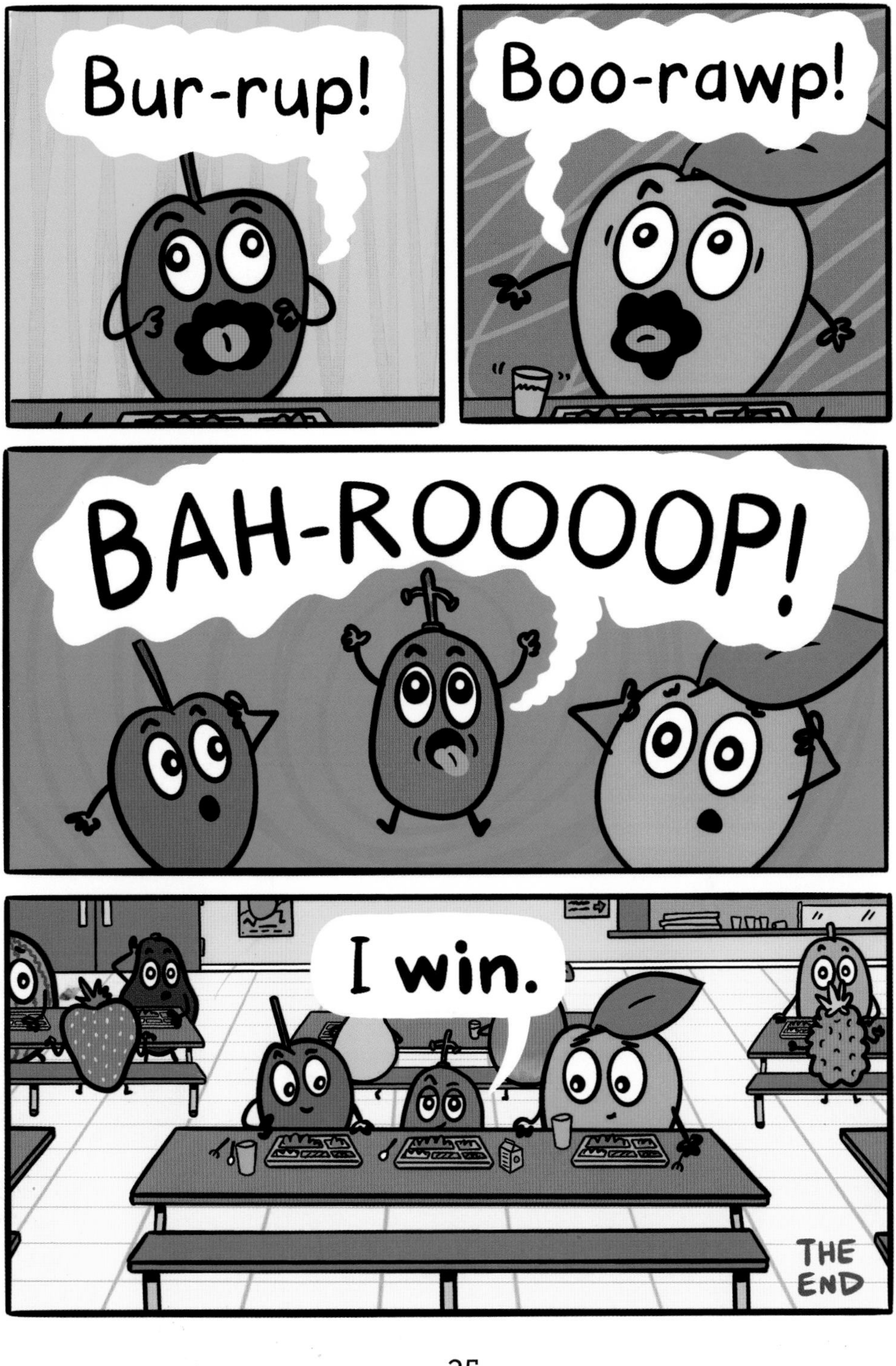
Bur-rup!
Boo-rawp!
BAH-ROOOOP!
I win.
THE END

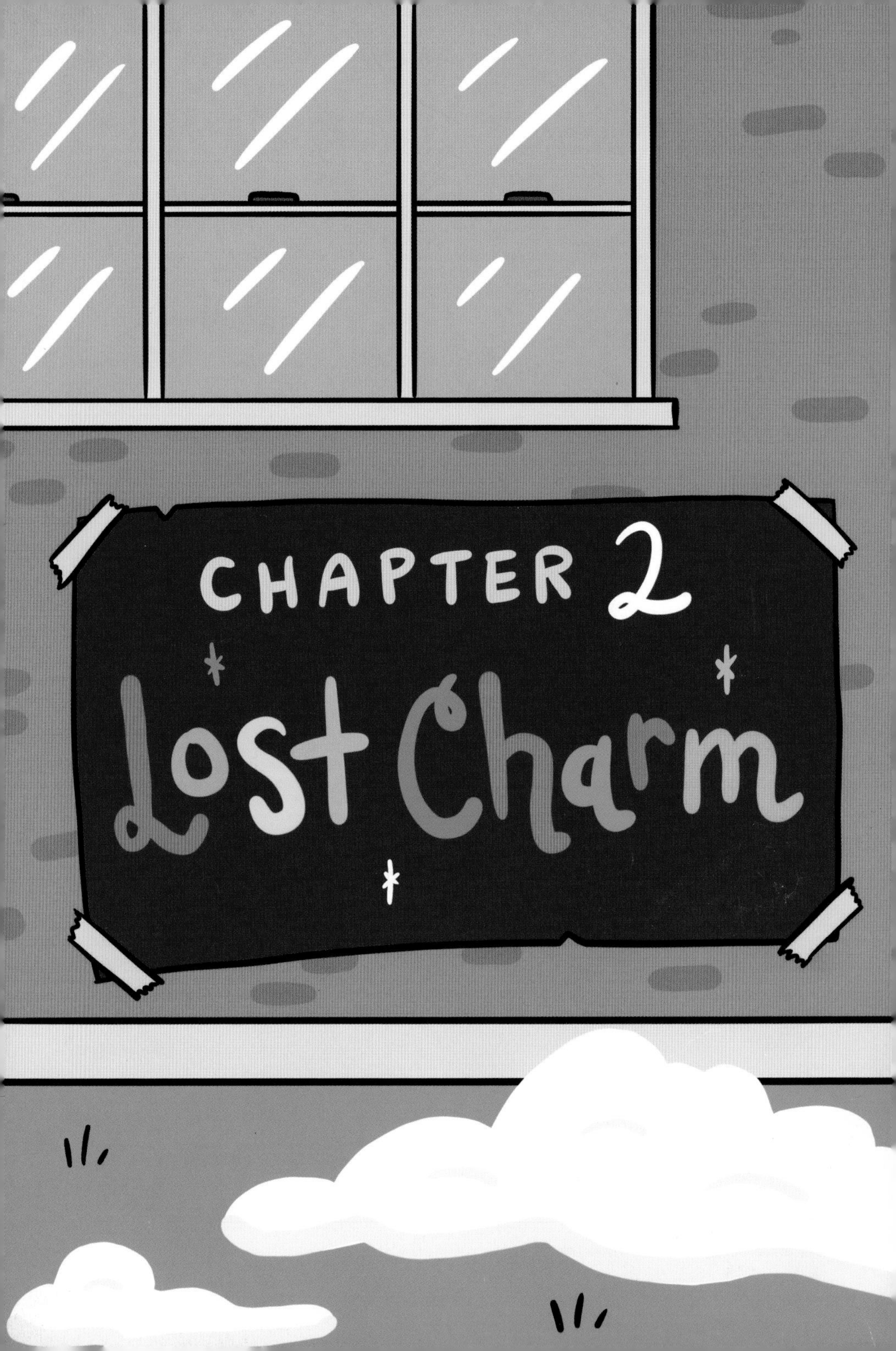
CHAPTER 2
Lost Charm

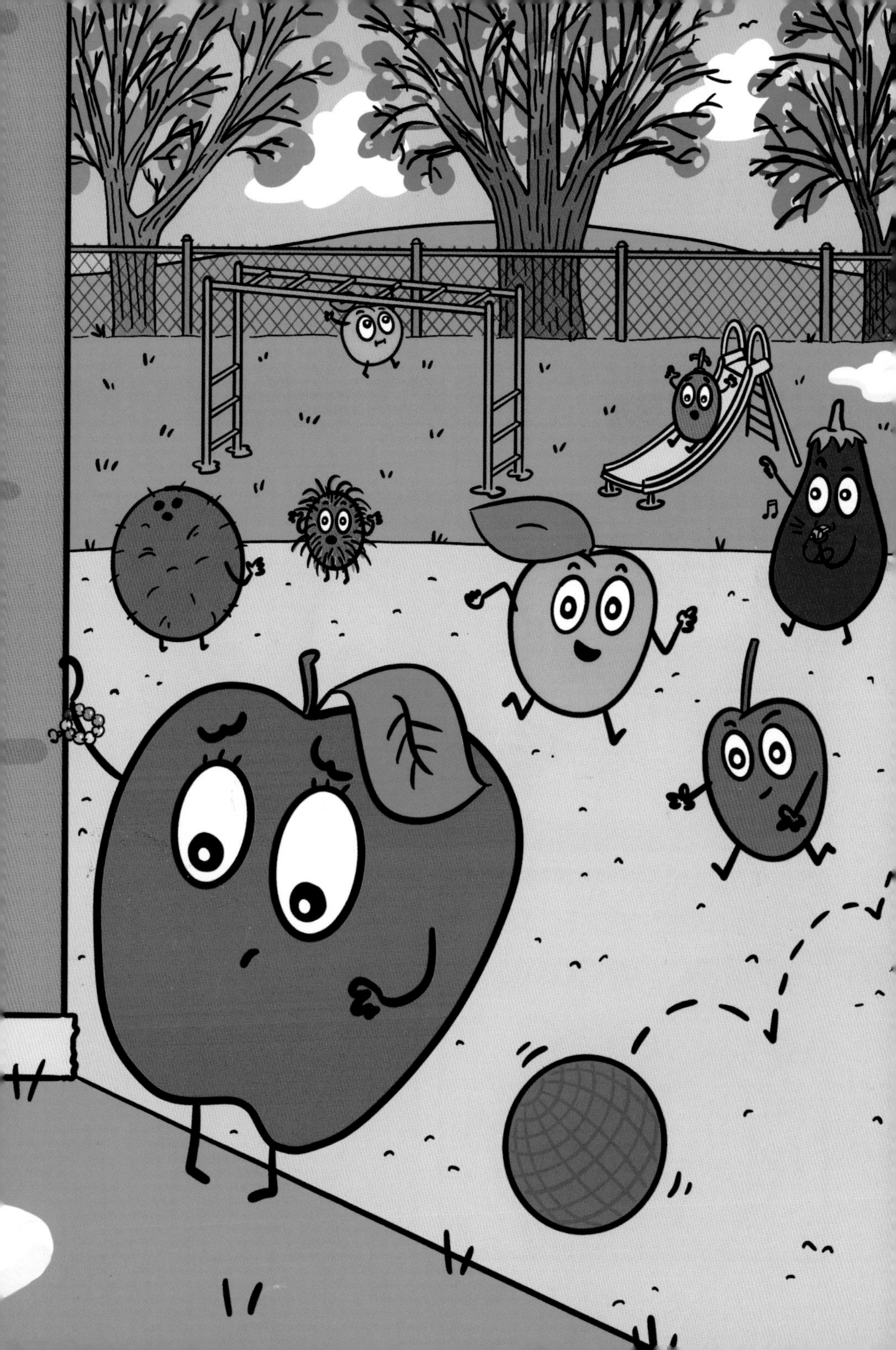

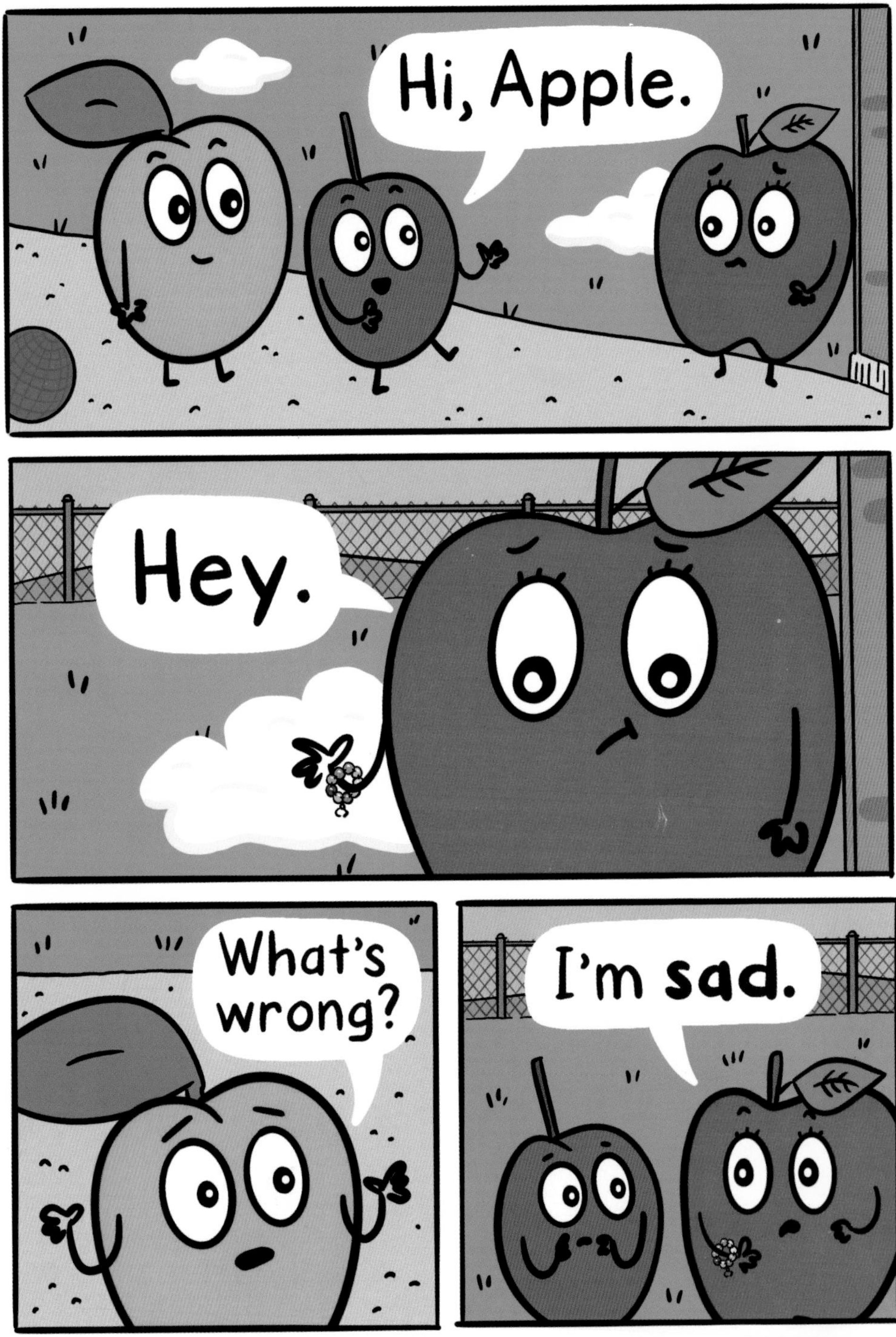
Hi, Apple.
Hey.
What's wrong?
I'm **sad**.

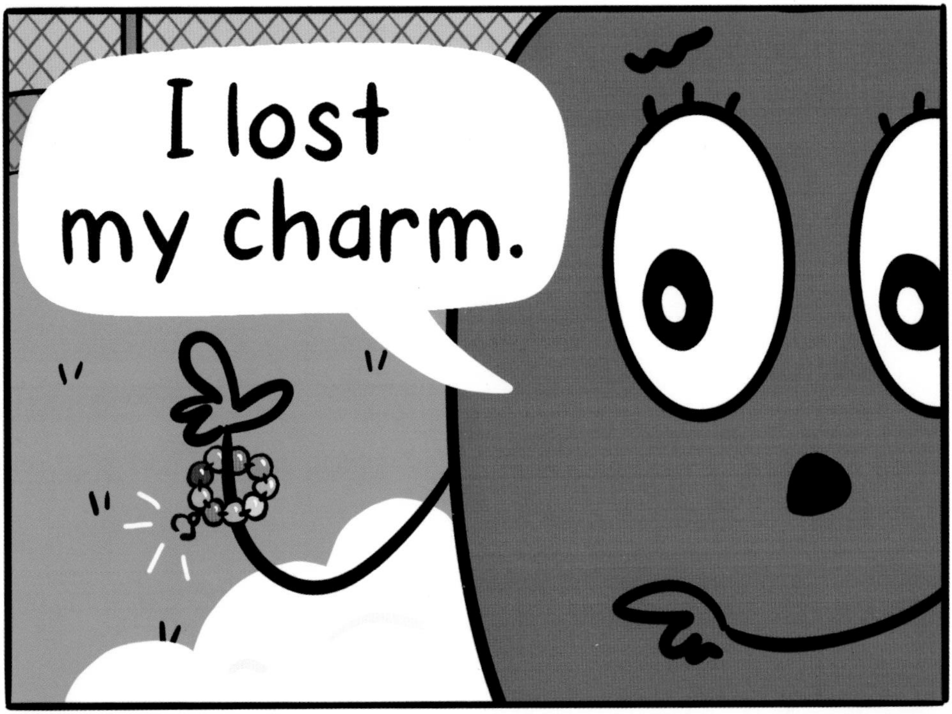
I lost my charm.

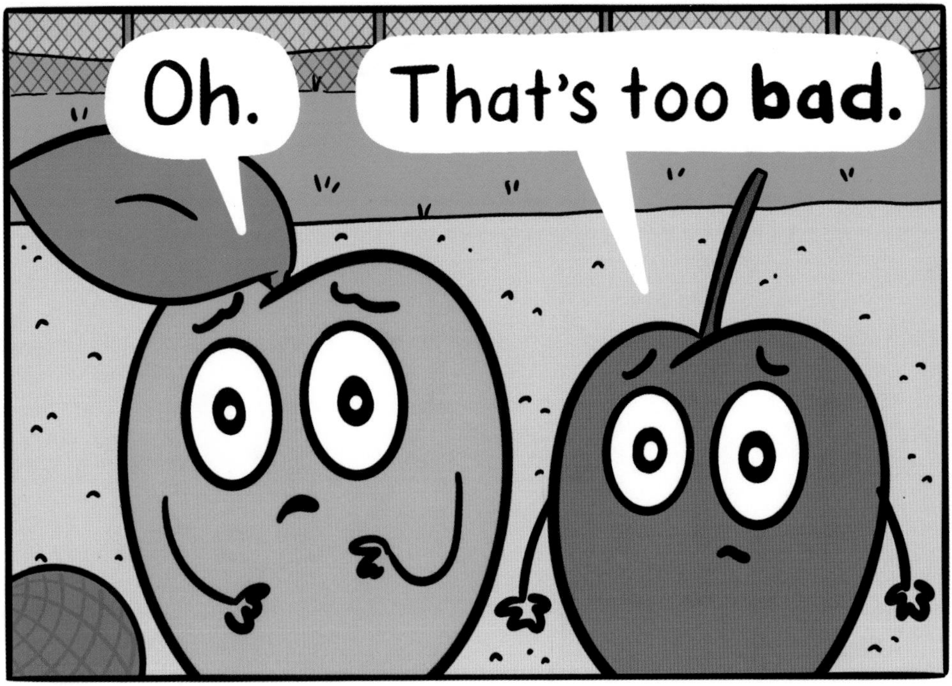
Oh.
That's too **bad.**

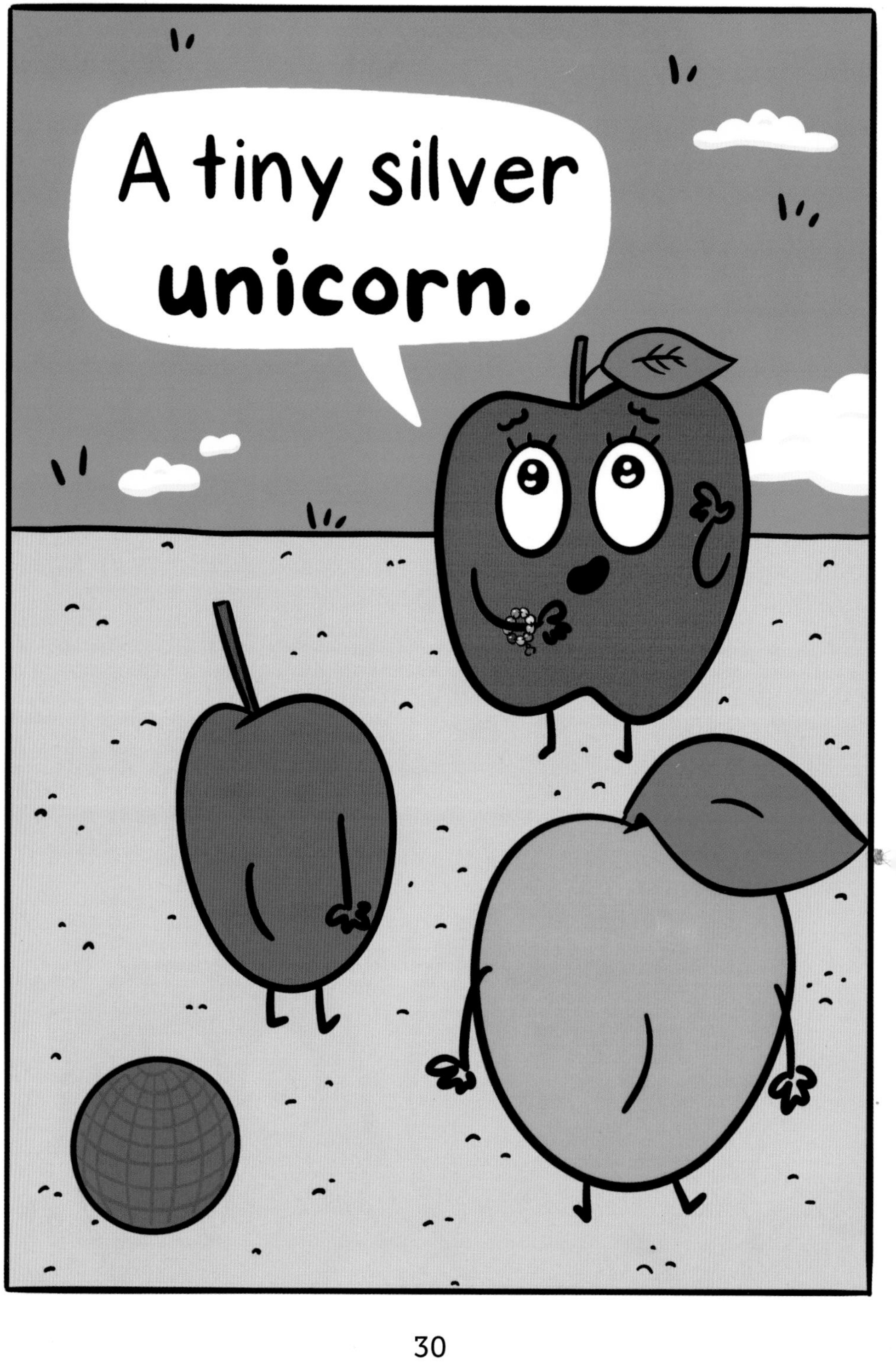
A tiny silver **unicorn.**

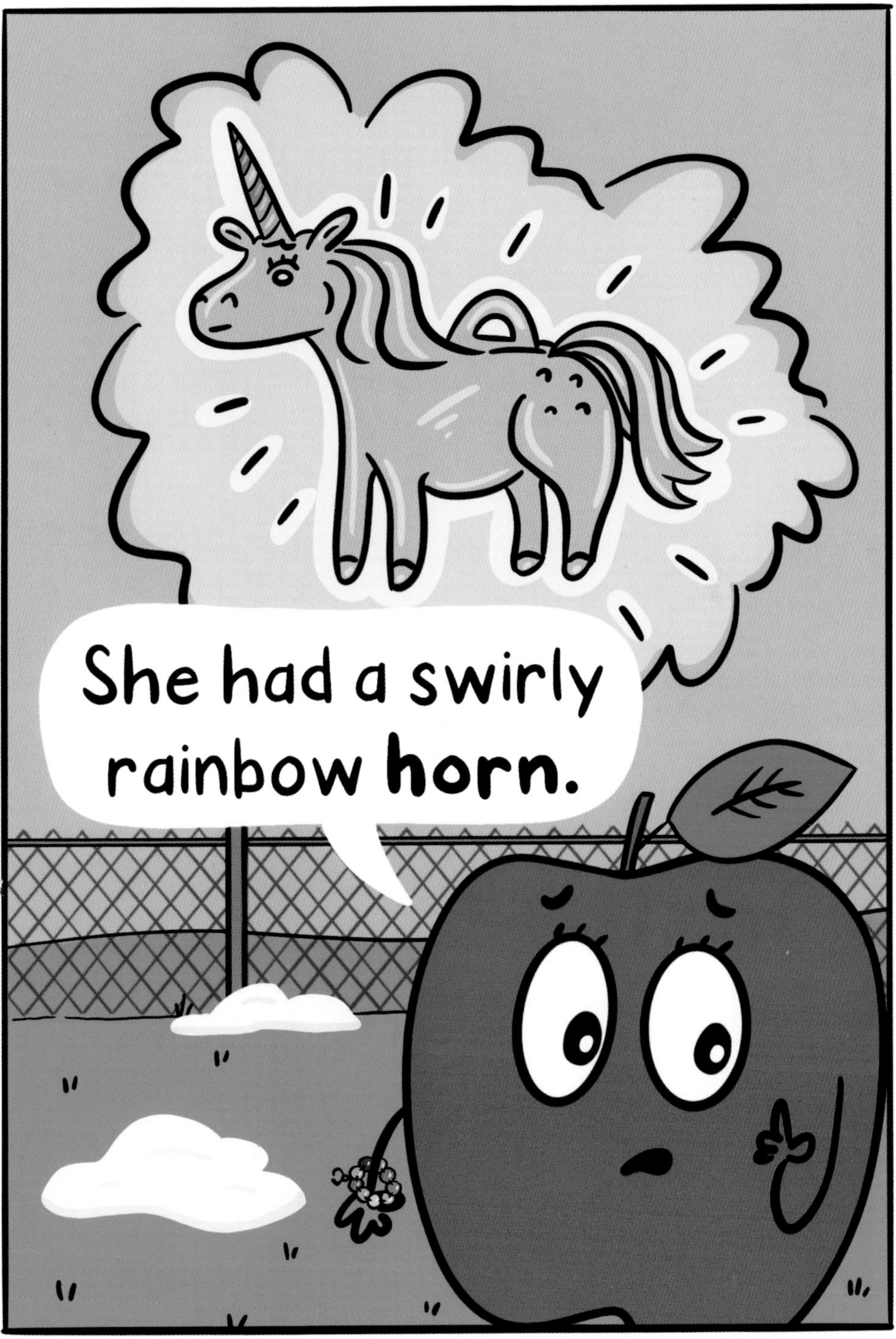
She had a swirly rainbow **horn.**

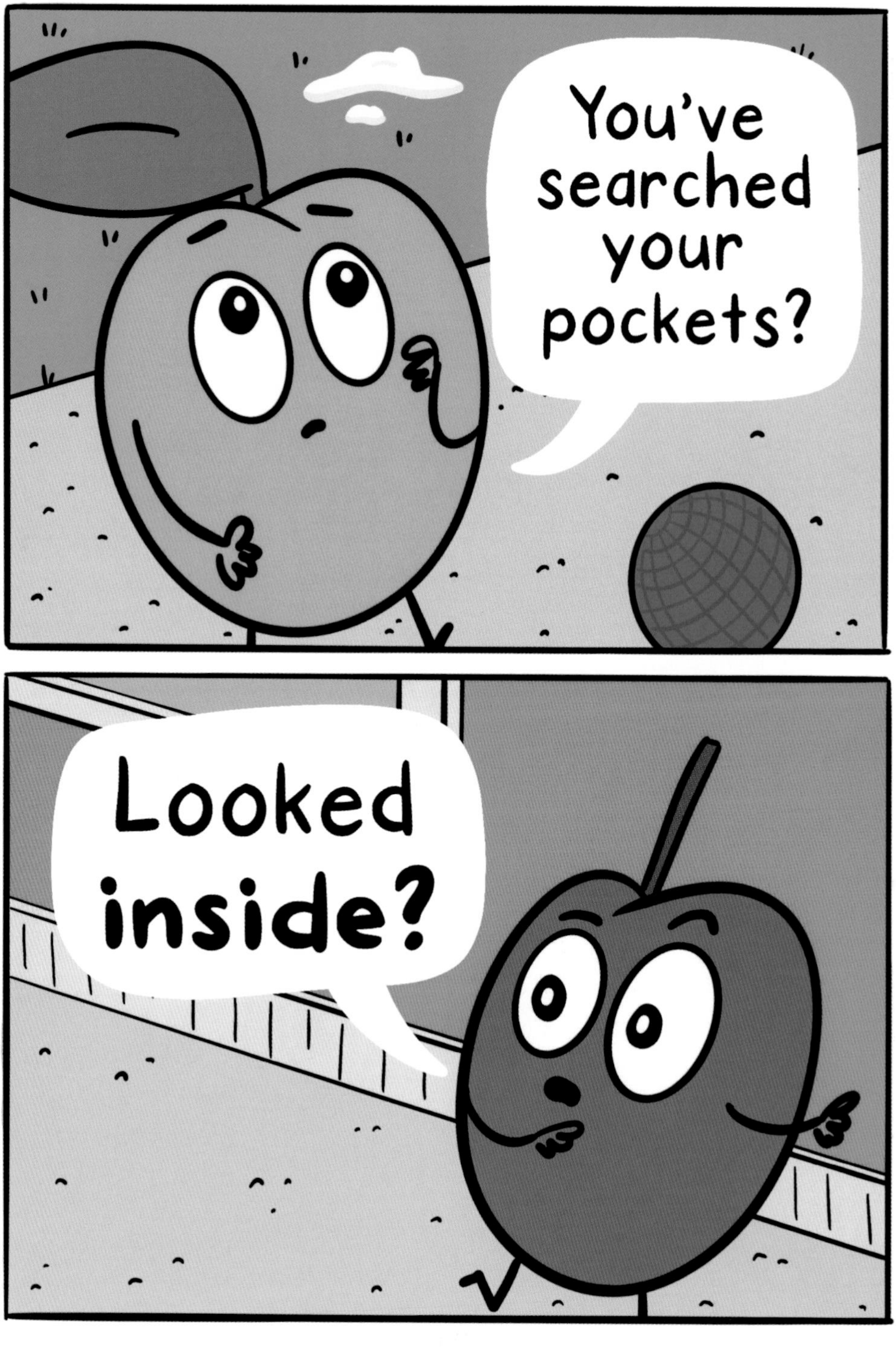
You've searched your pockets?
Looked inside?

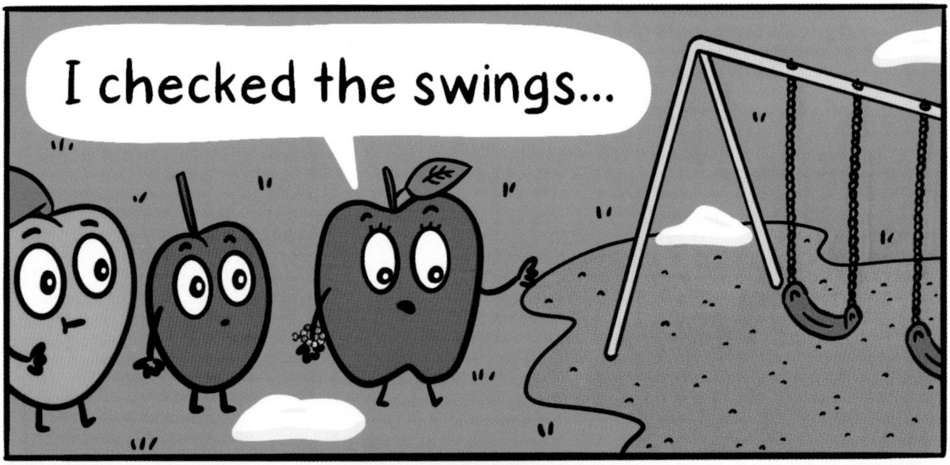
I checked the swings...
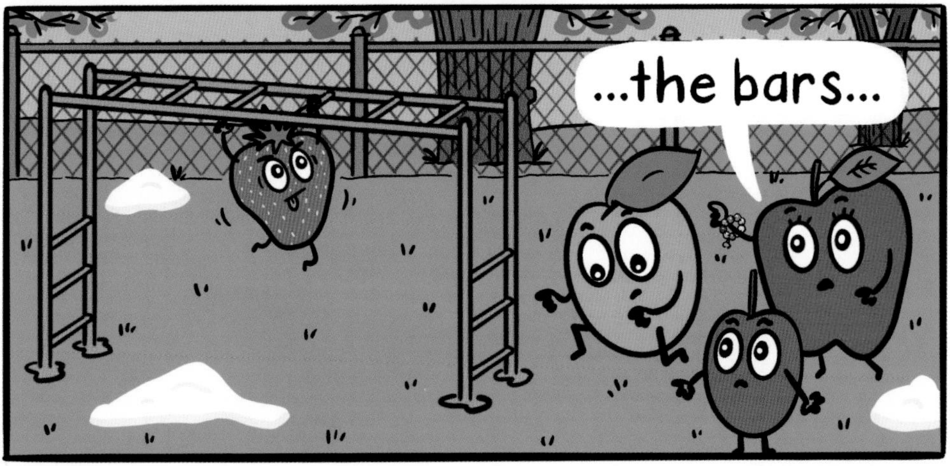
...the bars...
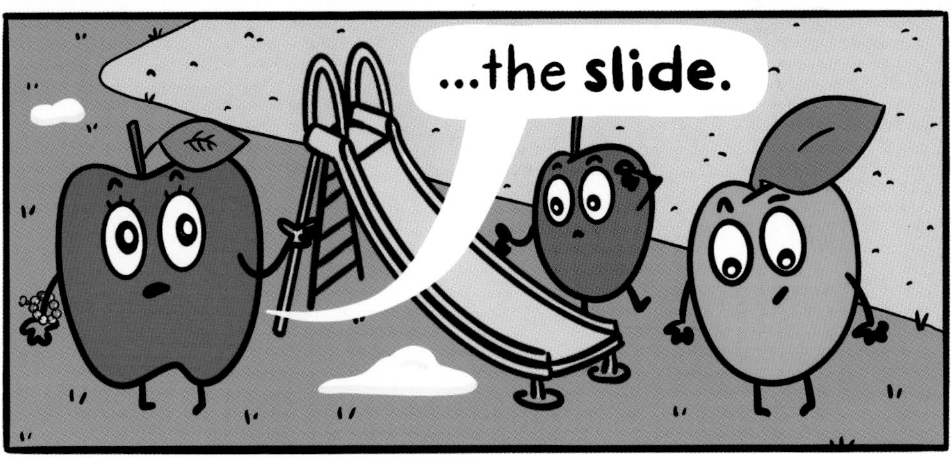
...the **slide.**

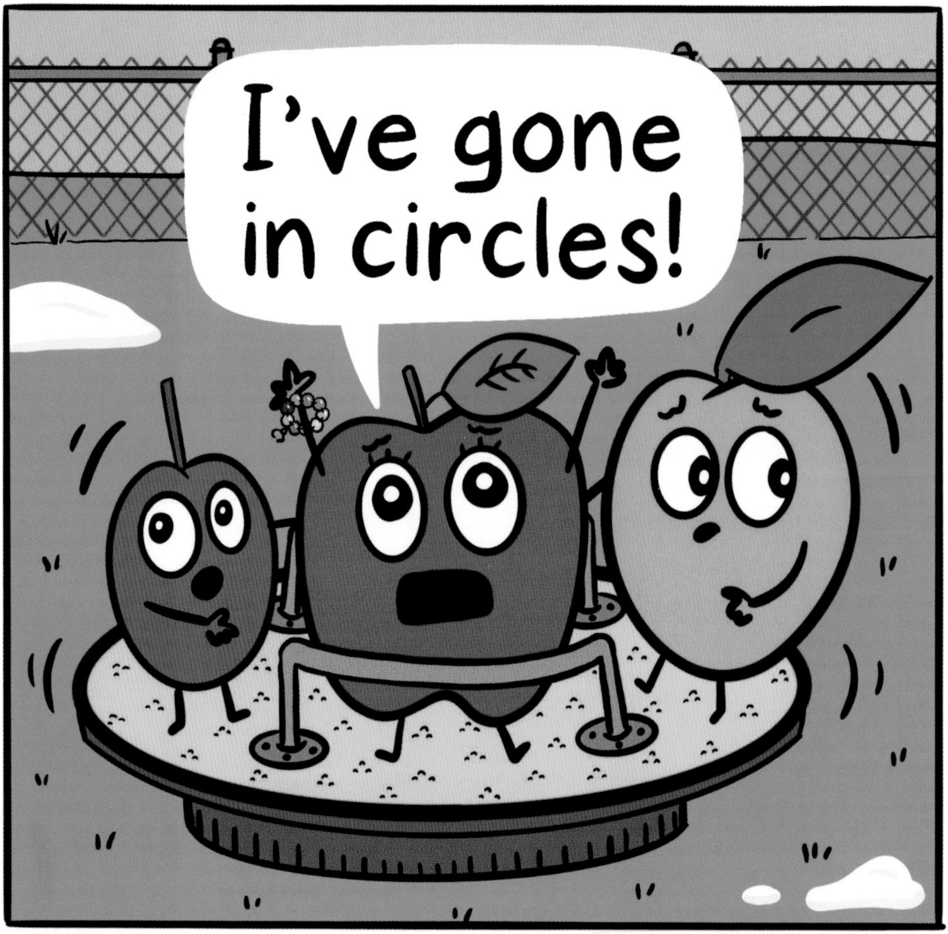
I've gone in circles!

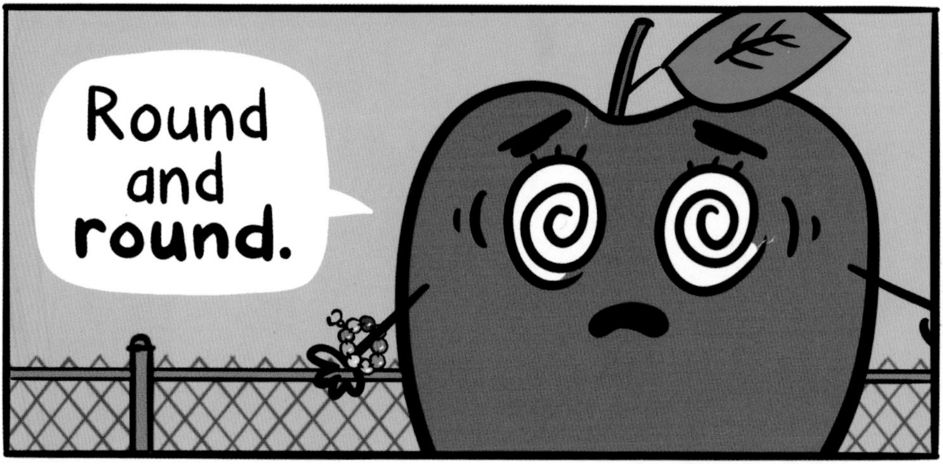
Round and **round.**

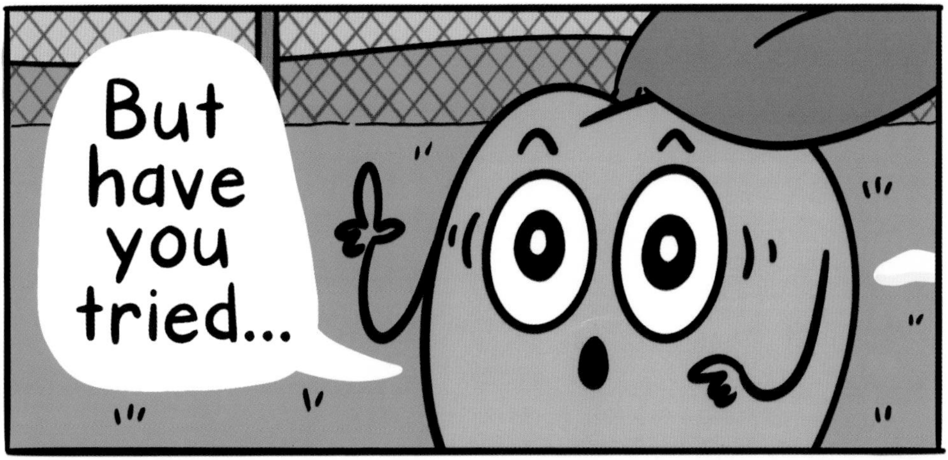
But have you tried...

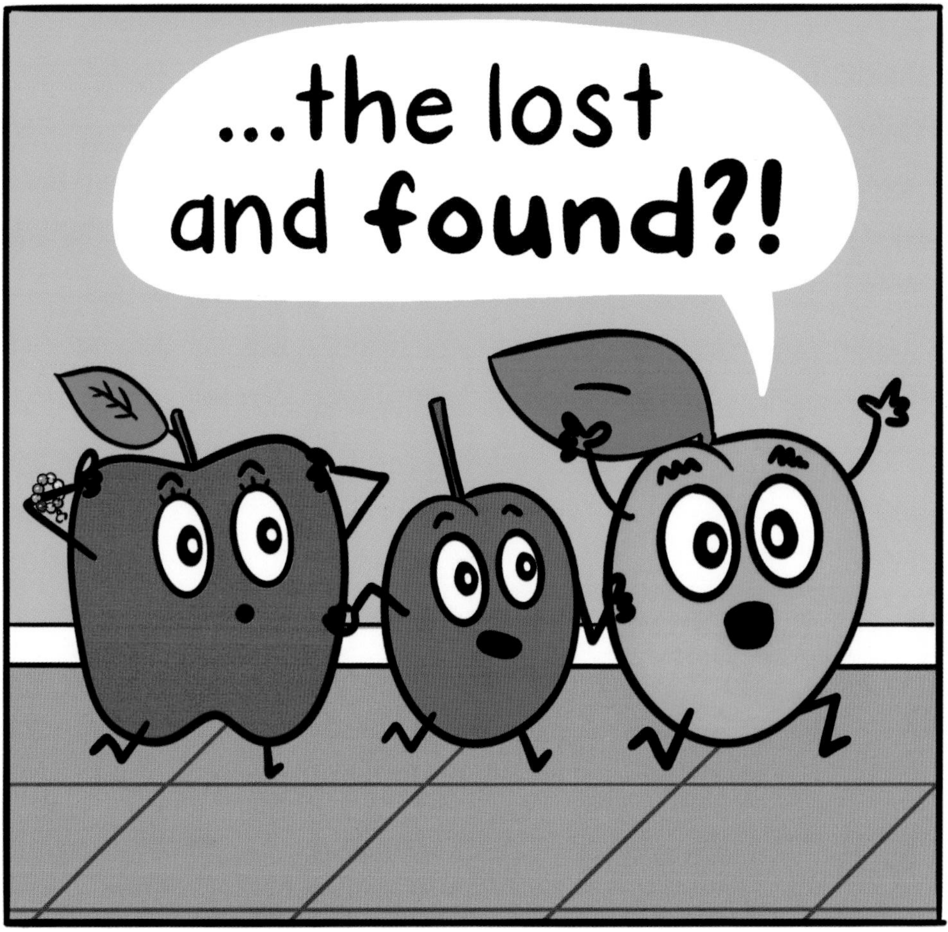
...the lost and **found**?!

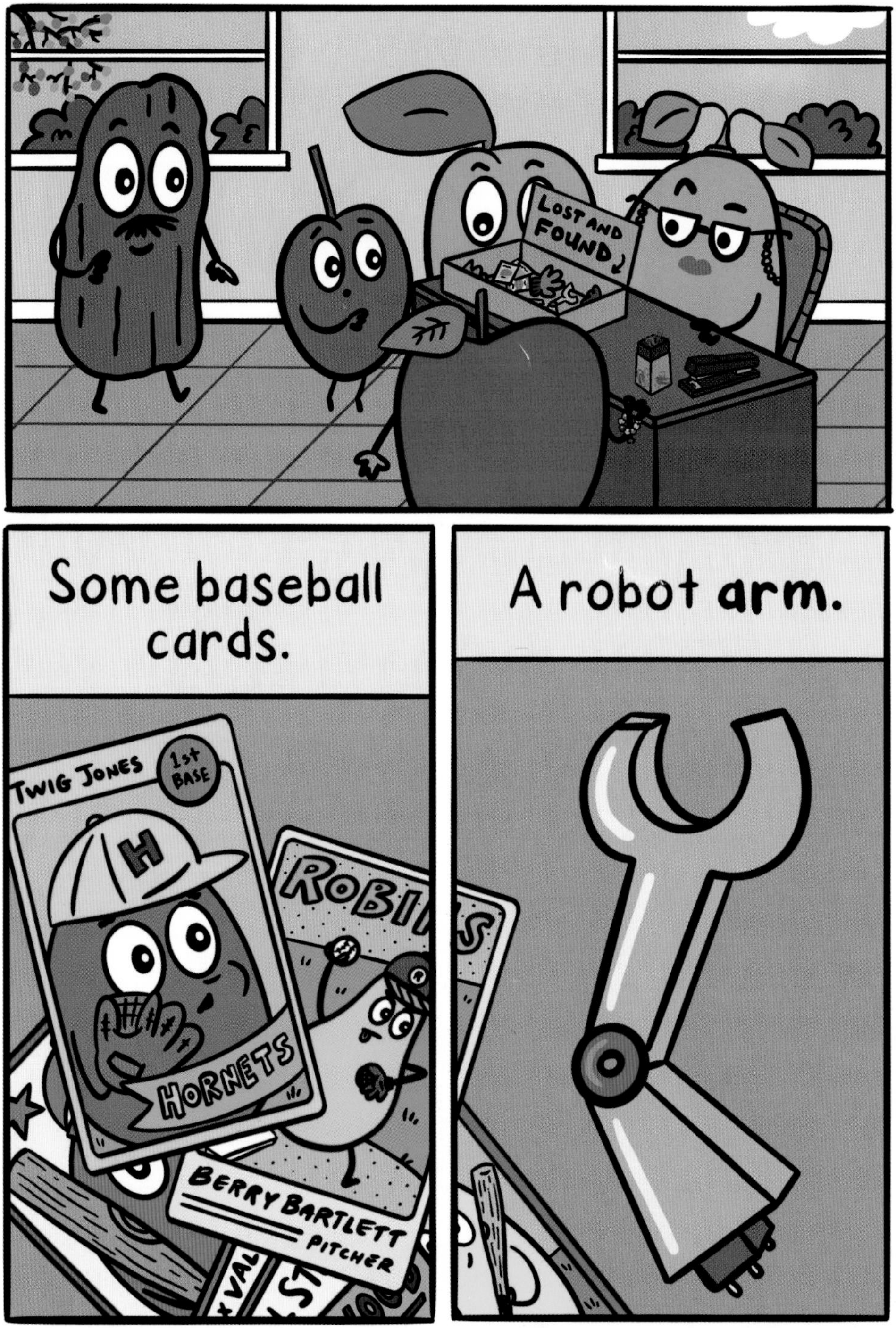
LOST AND FOUND
Some baseball cards.
TWIG JONES
1st BASE
H
HORNETS
BERRY BARTLETT
PITCHER
A robot arm.

One glove.

Two pens.

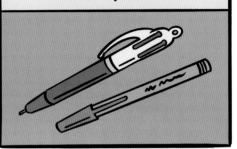

Three keys.

My **charm!**

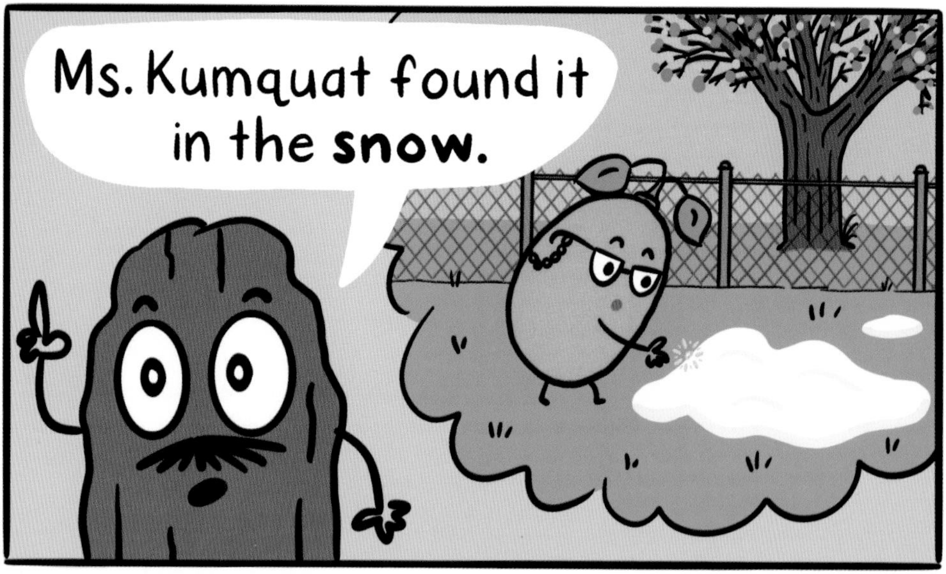
Ms. Kumquat found it in the **snow.**

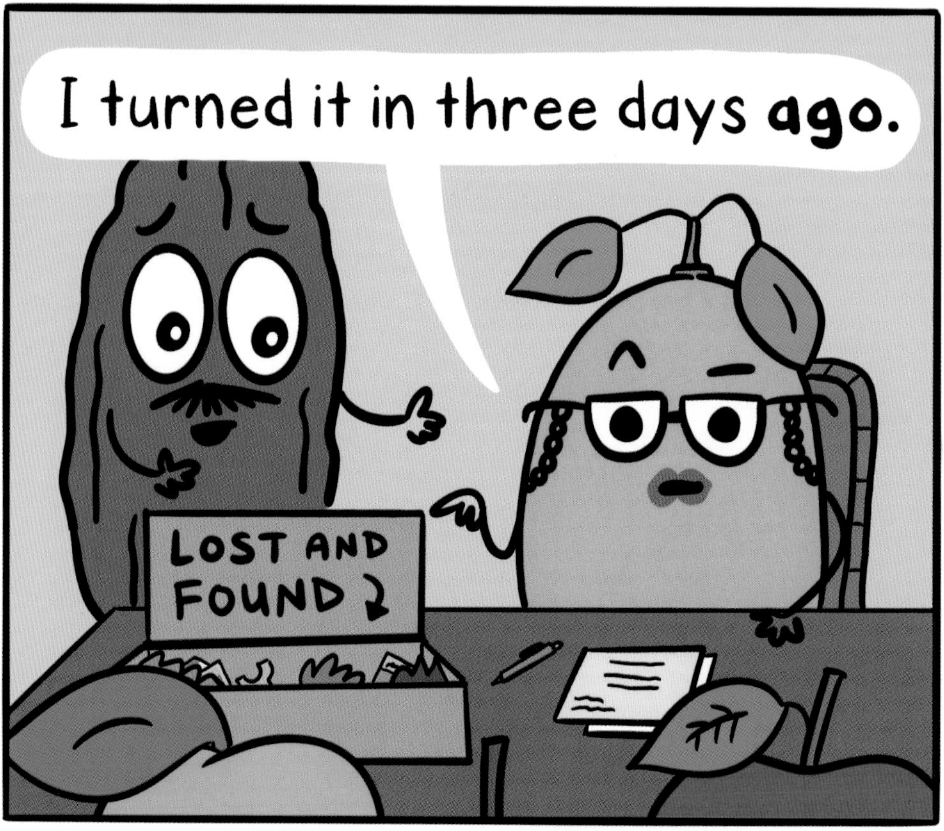
I turned it in three days **ago.**
LOST AND FOUND

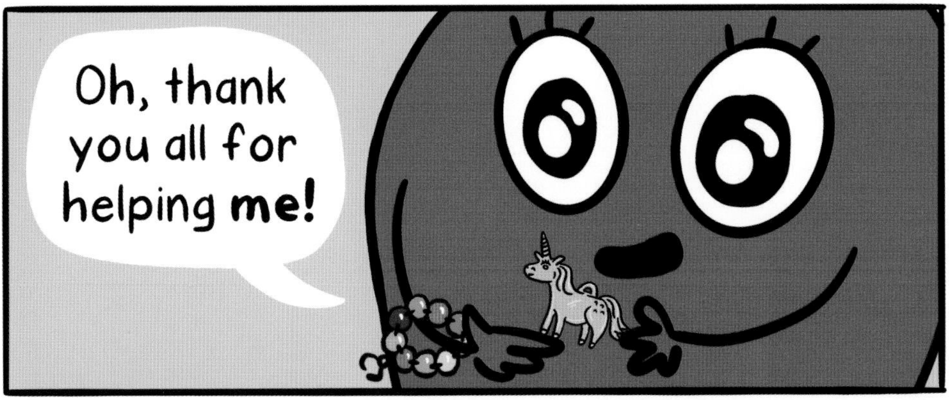
Oh, thank you all for helping me!

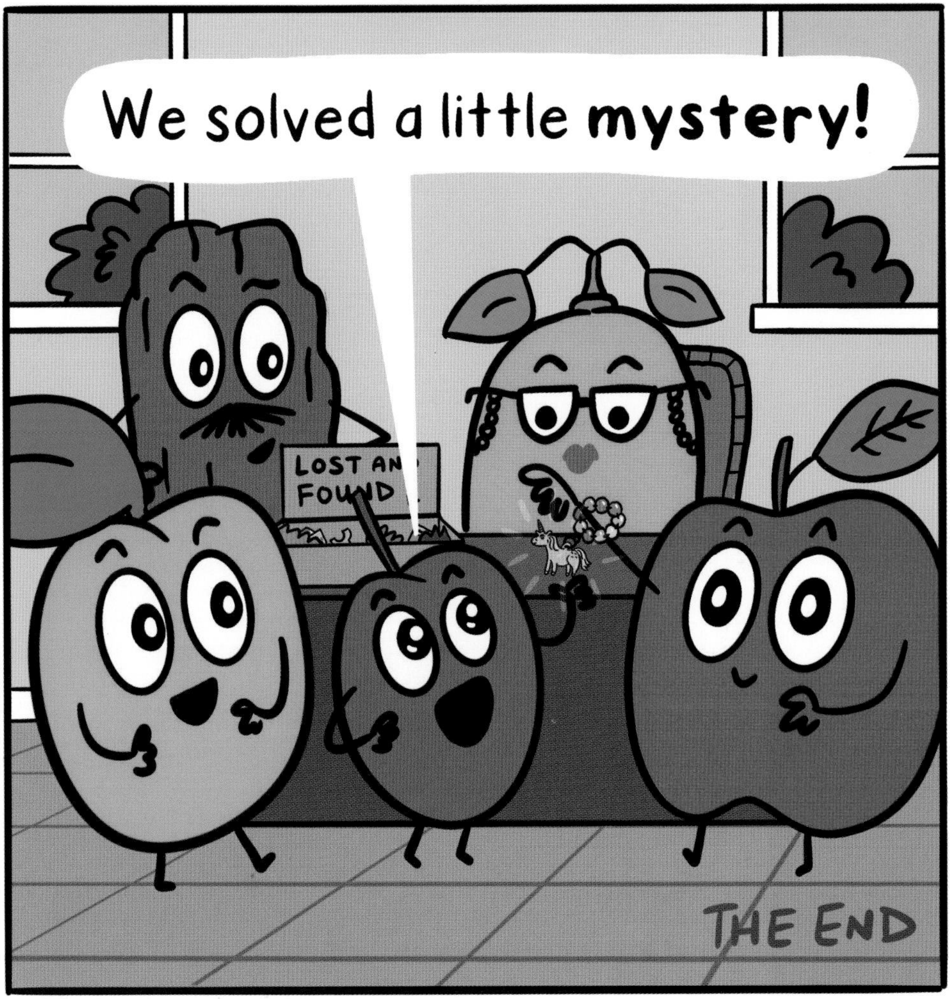
We solved a little mystery!
LOST AND FOUND
THE END

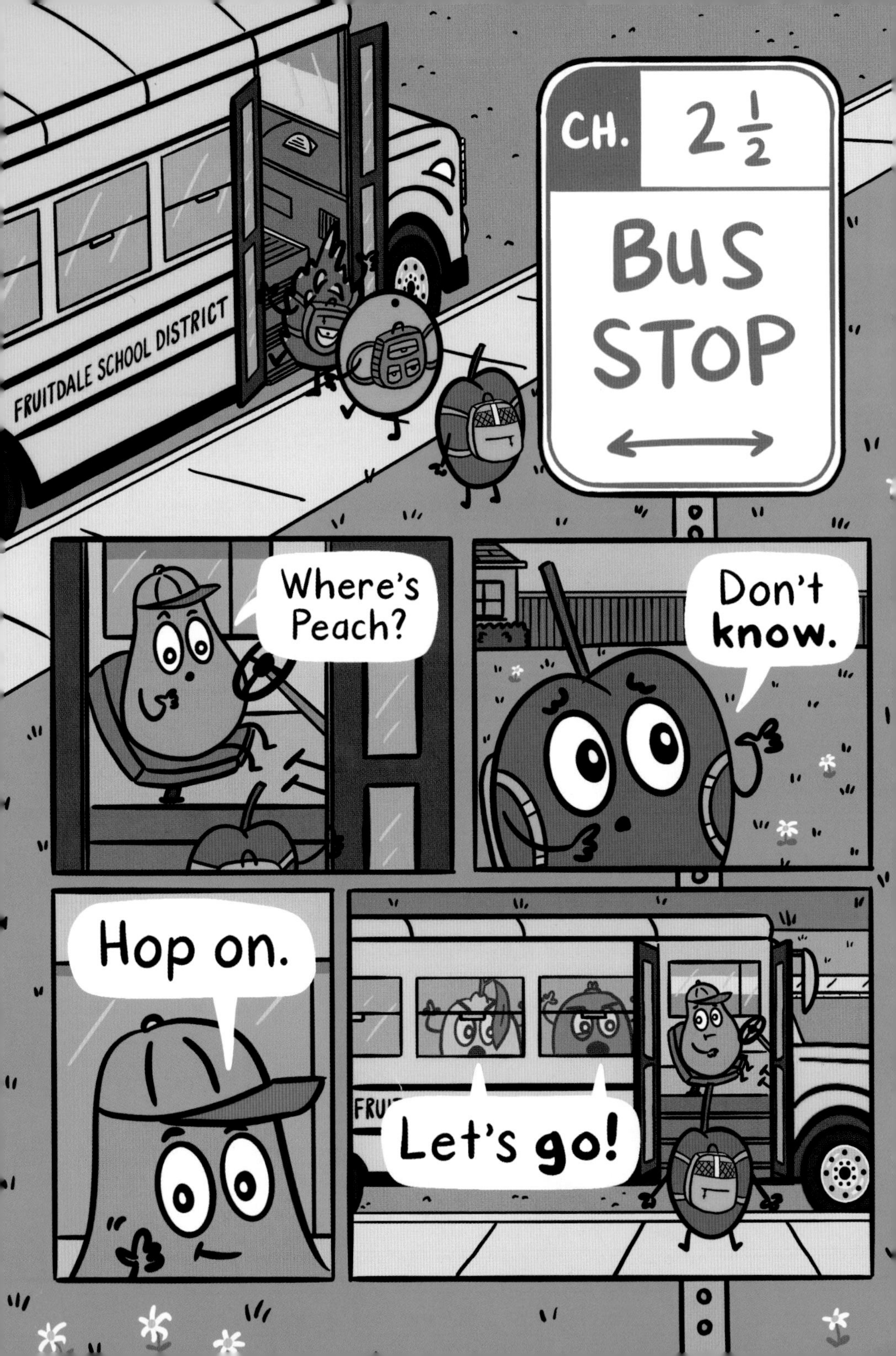
FRUITDALE SCHOOL DISTRICT
CH. 2 1/2
BUS STOP
Where's Peach?
Don't know.
Hop on.
FRUI
Let's go!

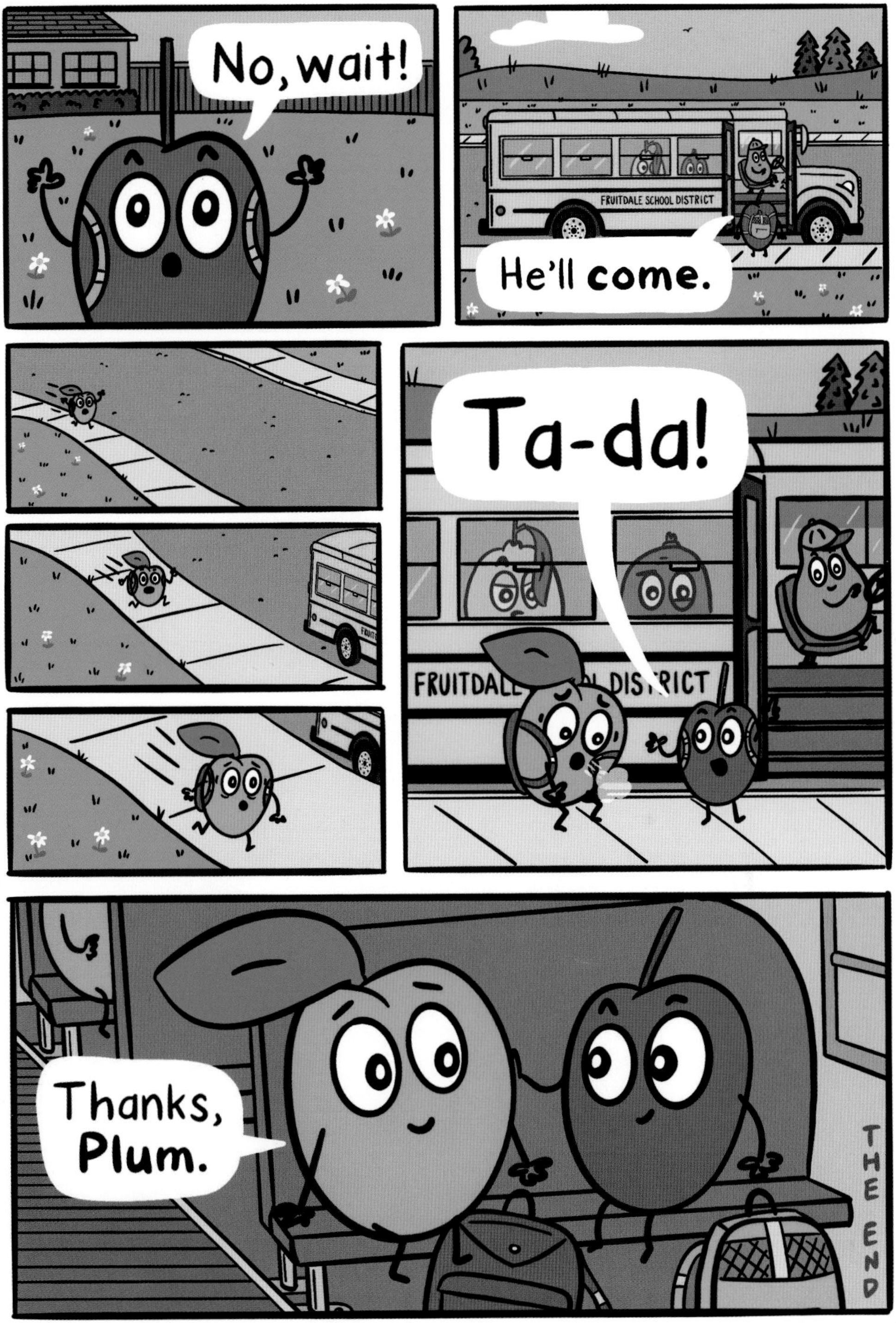
No, wait!
FRUITDALE SCHOOL DISTRICT
He'll **come.**
Ta-da!
FRUITDALE DISTRICT
Thanks, **Plum.**
THE END

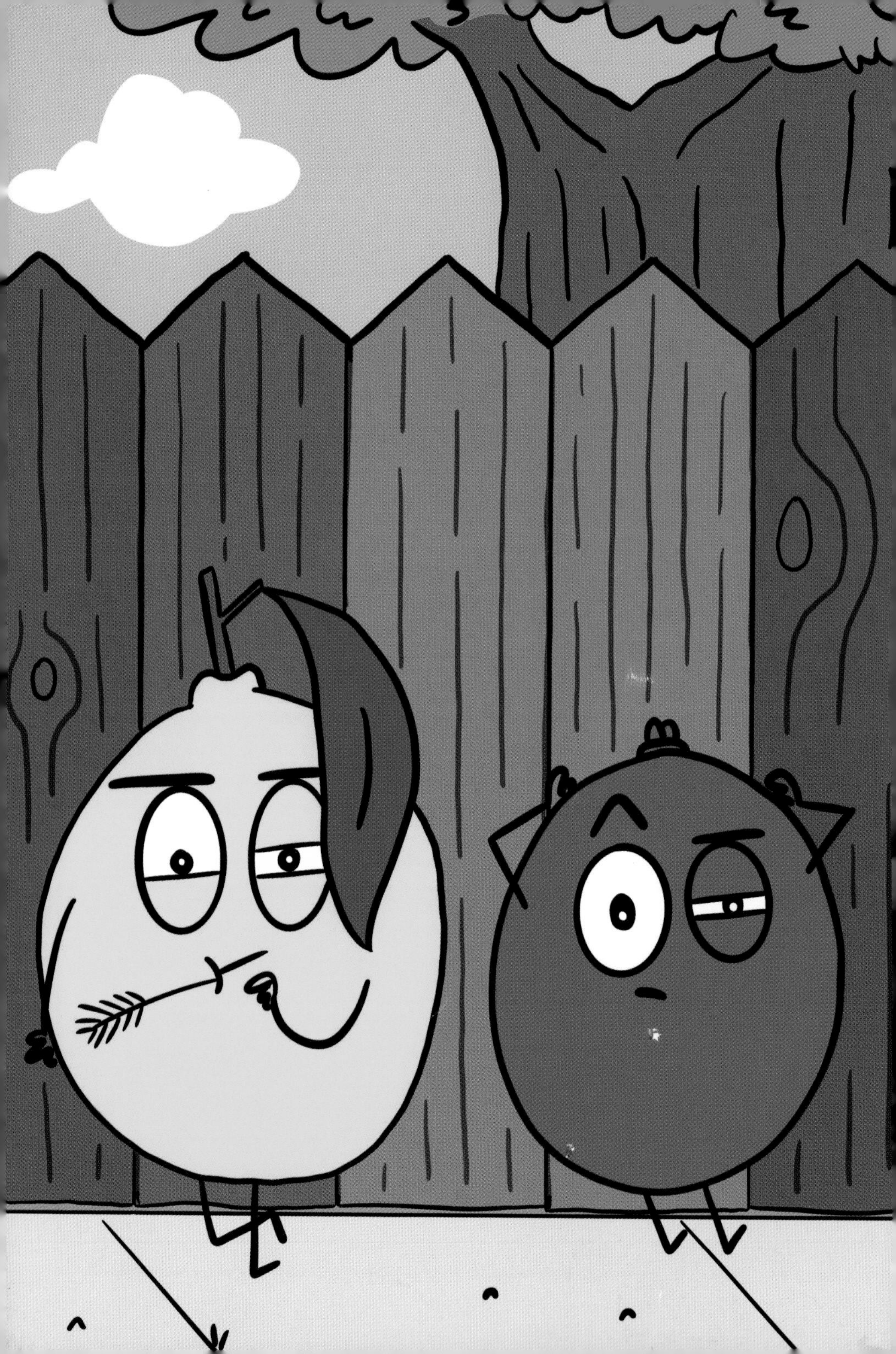

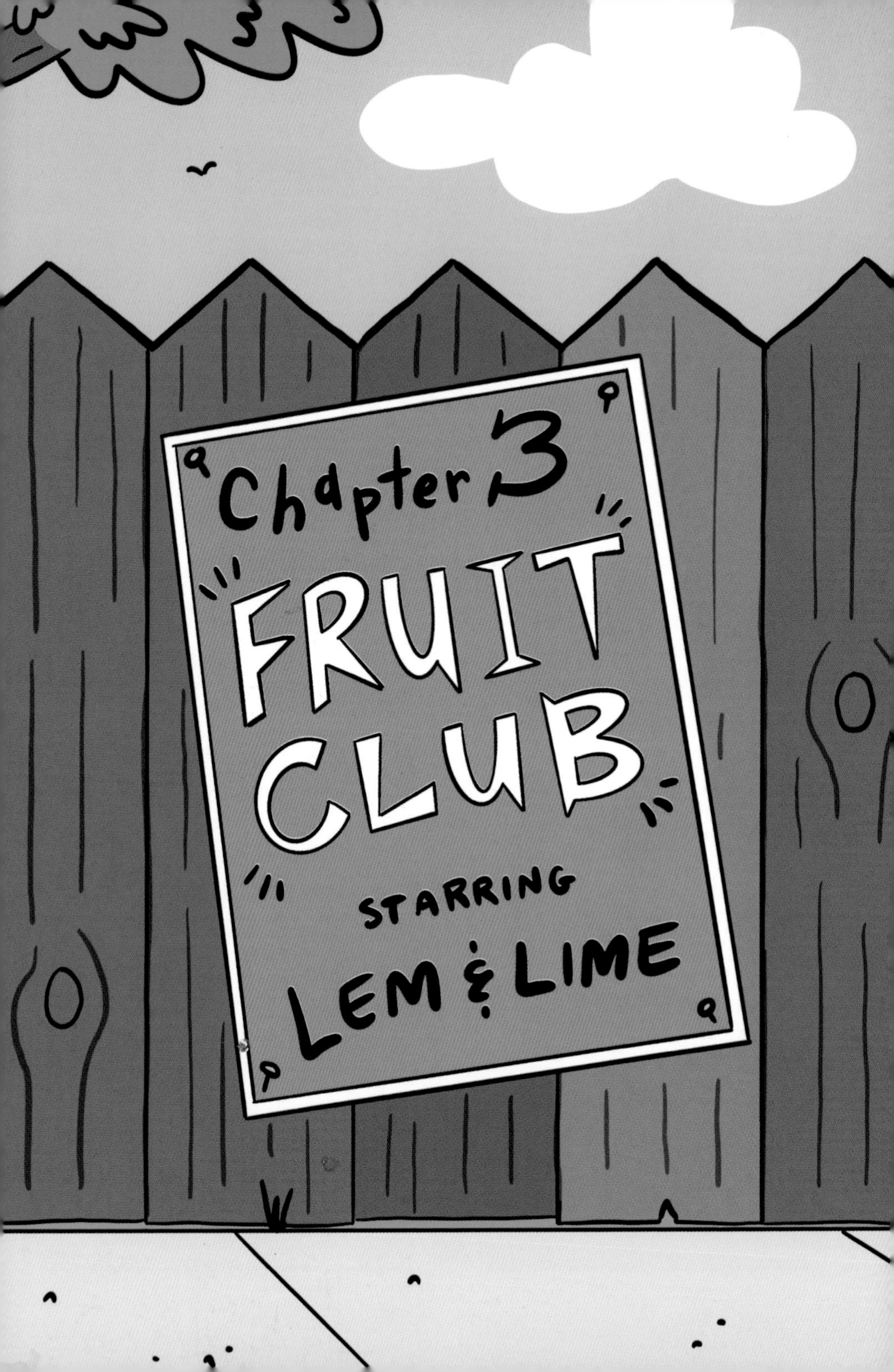
Chapter 3
FRUIT CLUB
STARRING
LEM & LIME

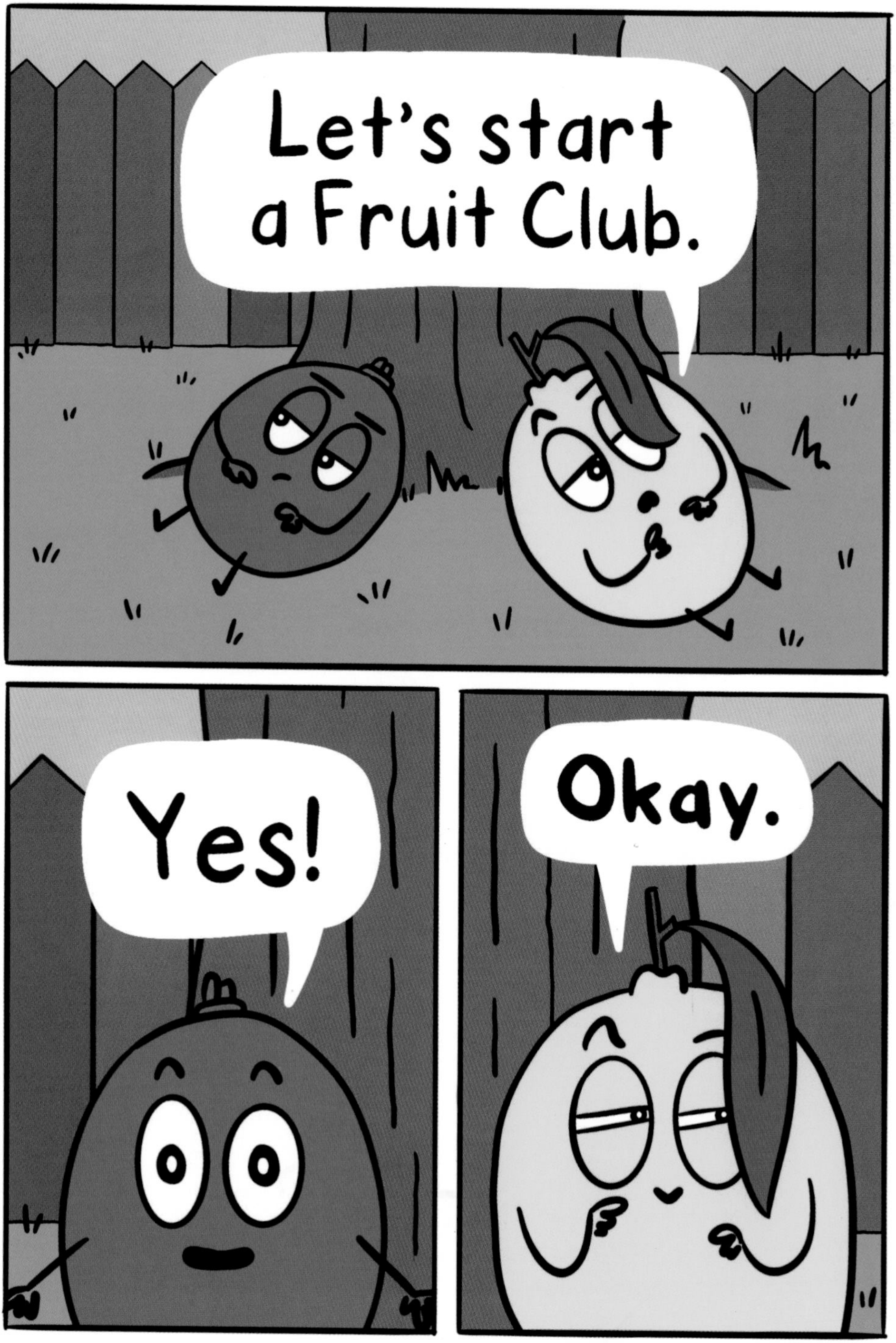
Let's start a Fruit Club.
Yes!
Okay.

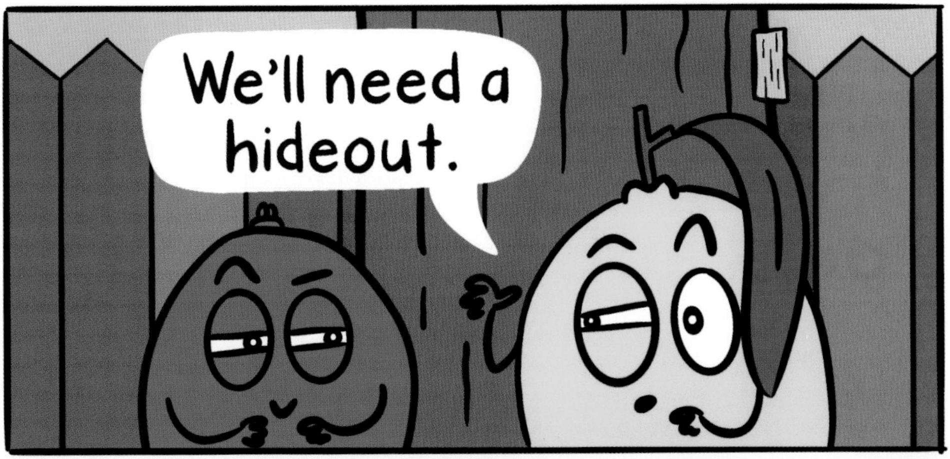
We'll need a hideout.

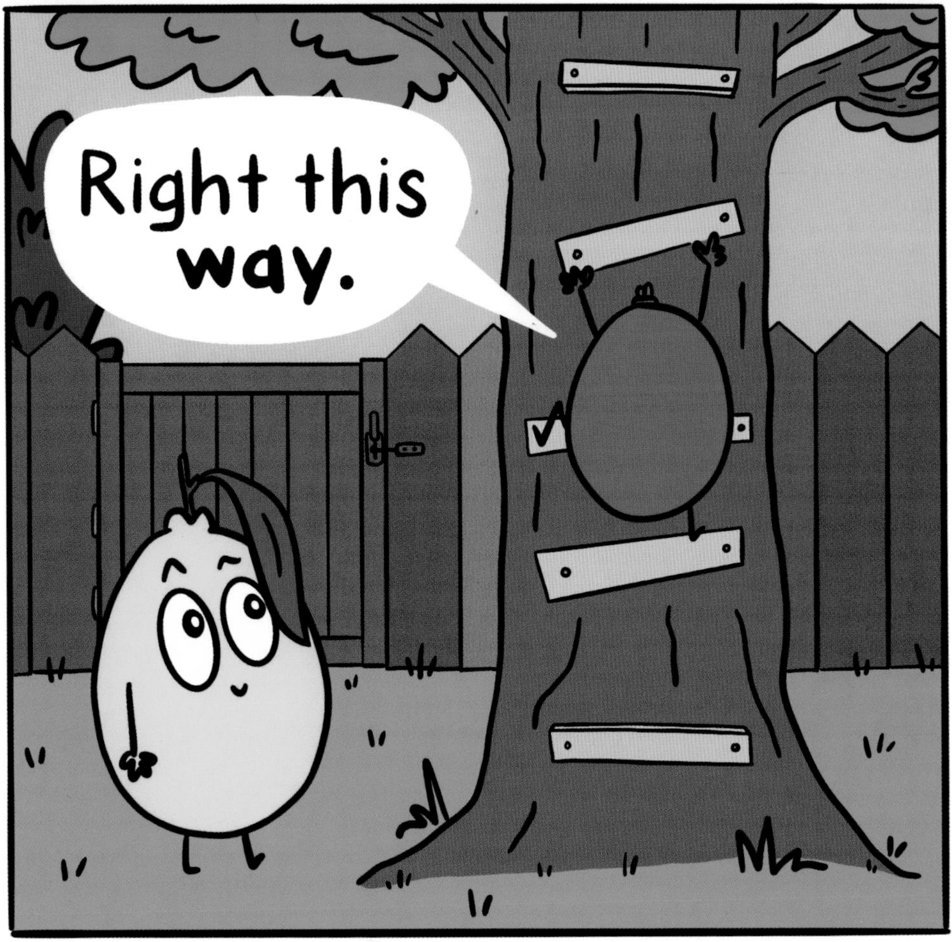
Right this **way.**

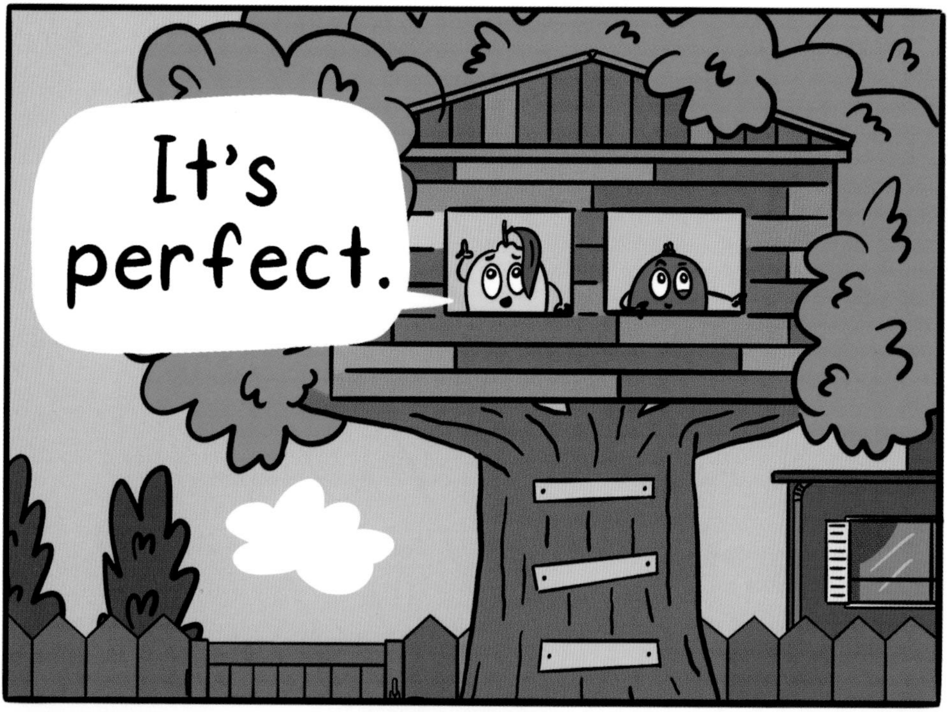
It's perfect.
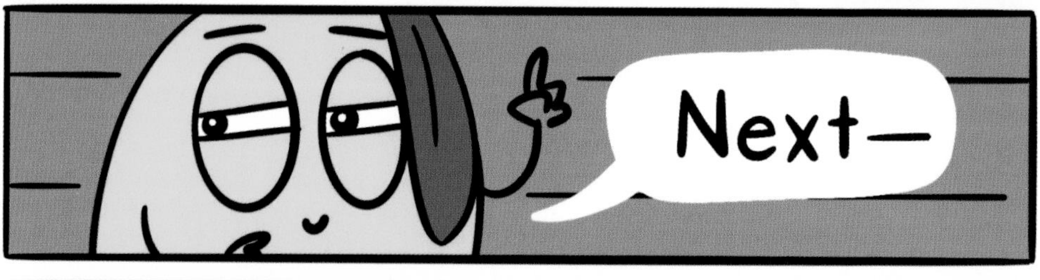
Next—
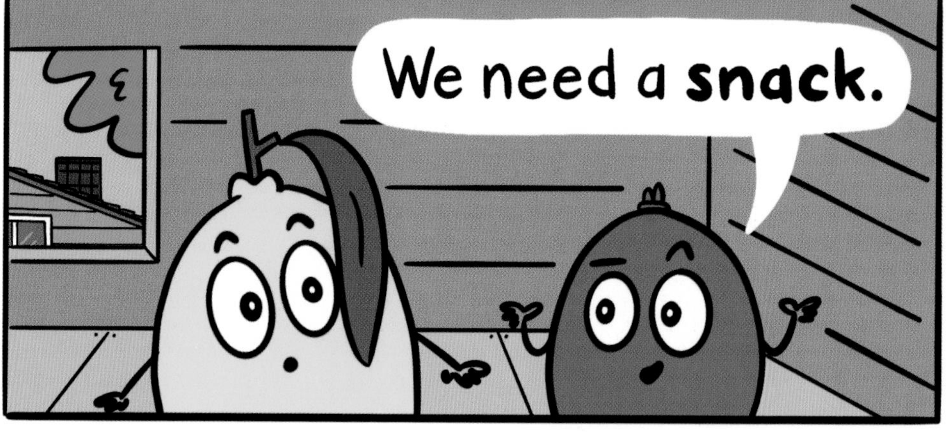
We need a **snack.**

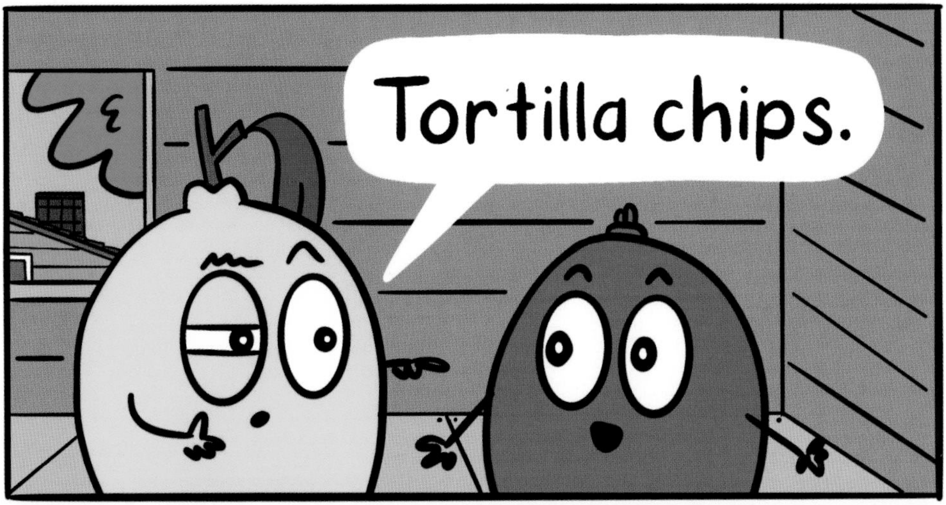
Tortilla chips.

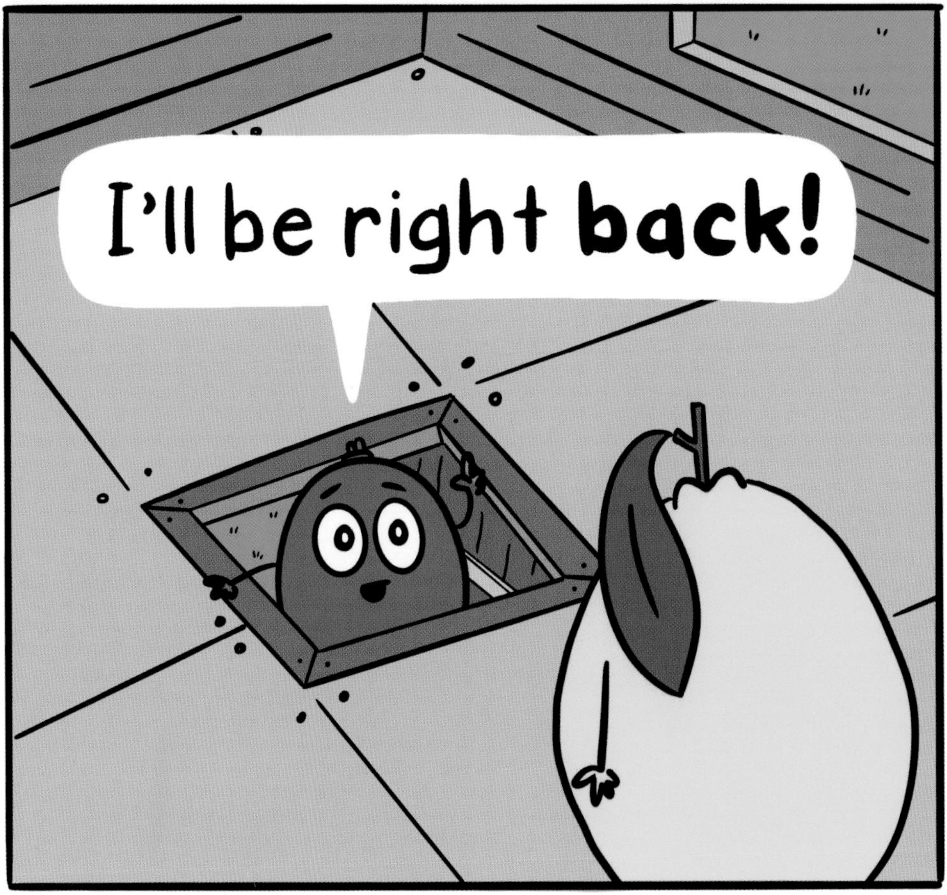
I'll be right **back!**

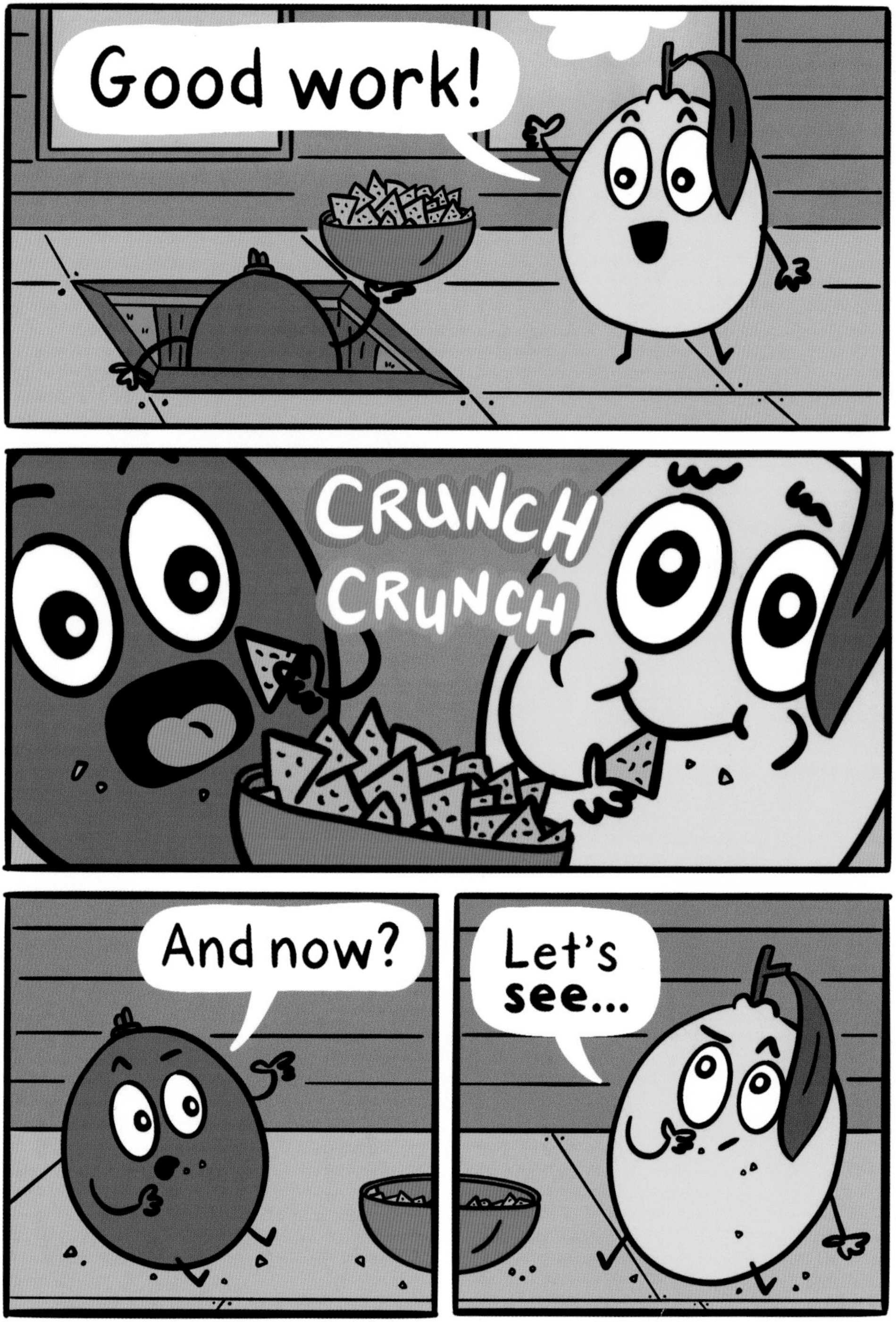

Good work!
CRUNCH
CRUNCH
And now?
Let's see...

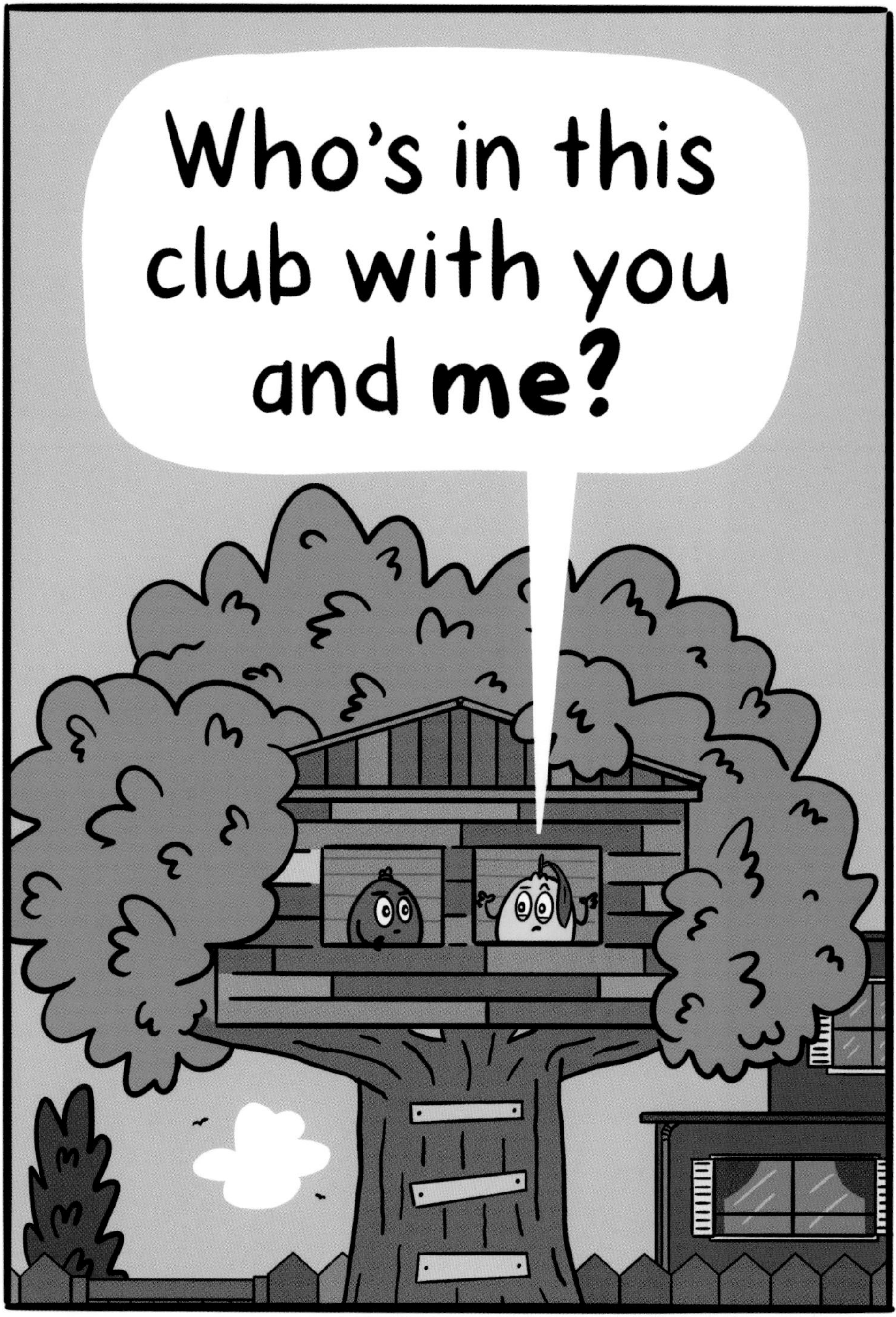
Who's in this club with you and **me**?

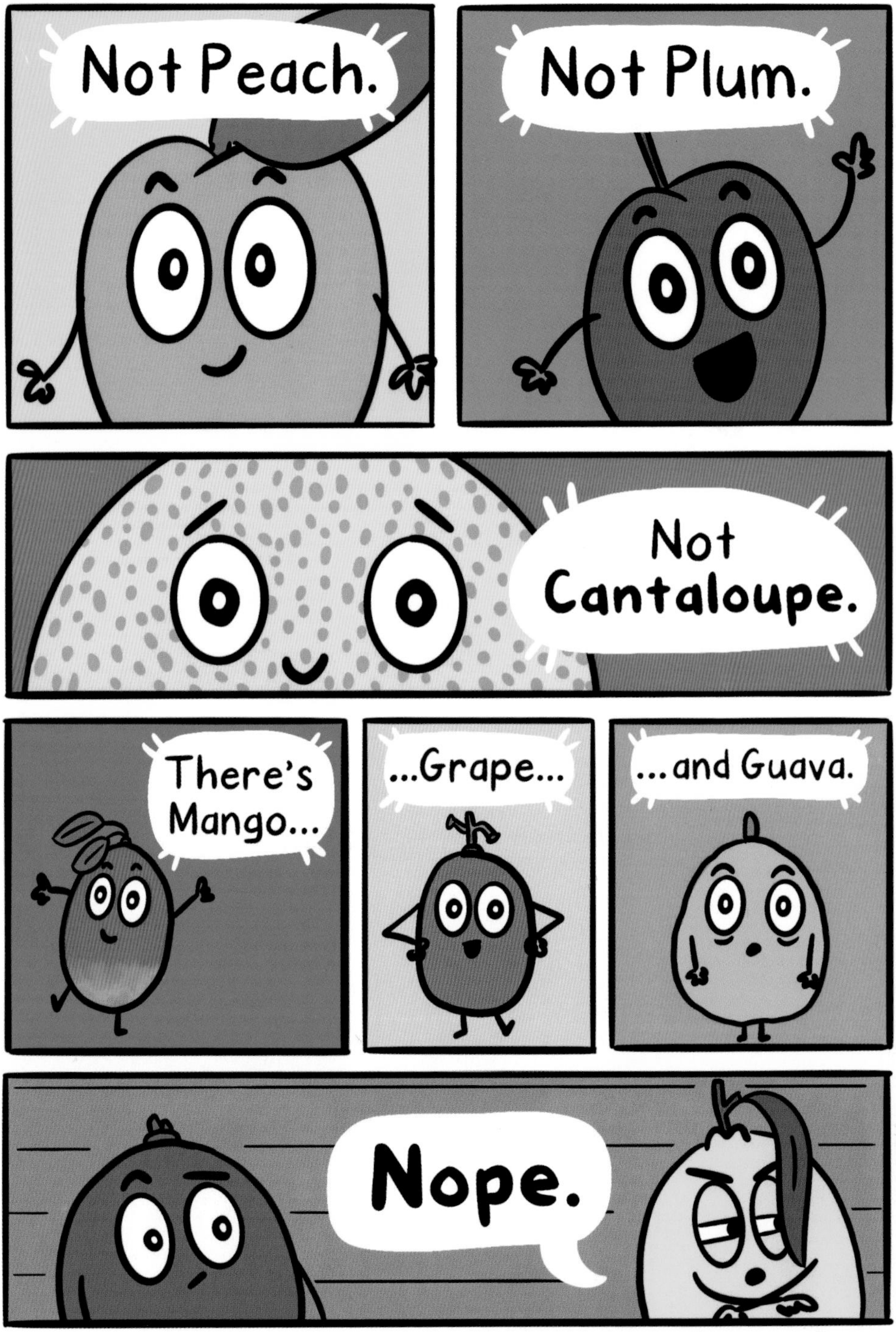
Not Peach.
Not Plum.
Not Cantaloupe.
There's Mango...
...Grape...
...and Guava.
Nope.

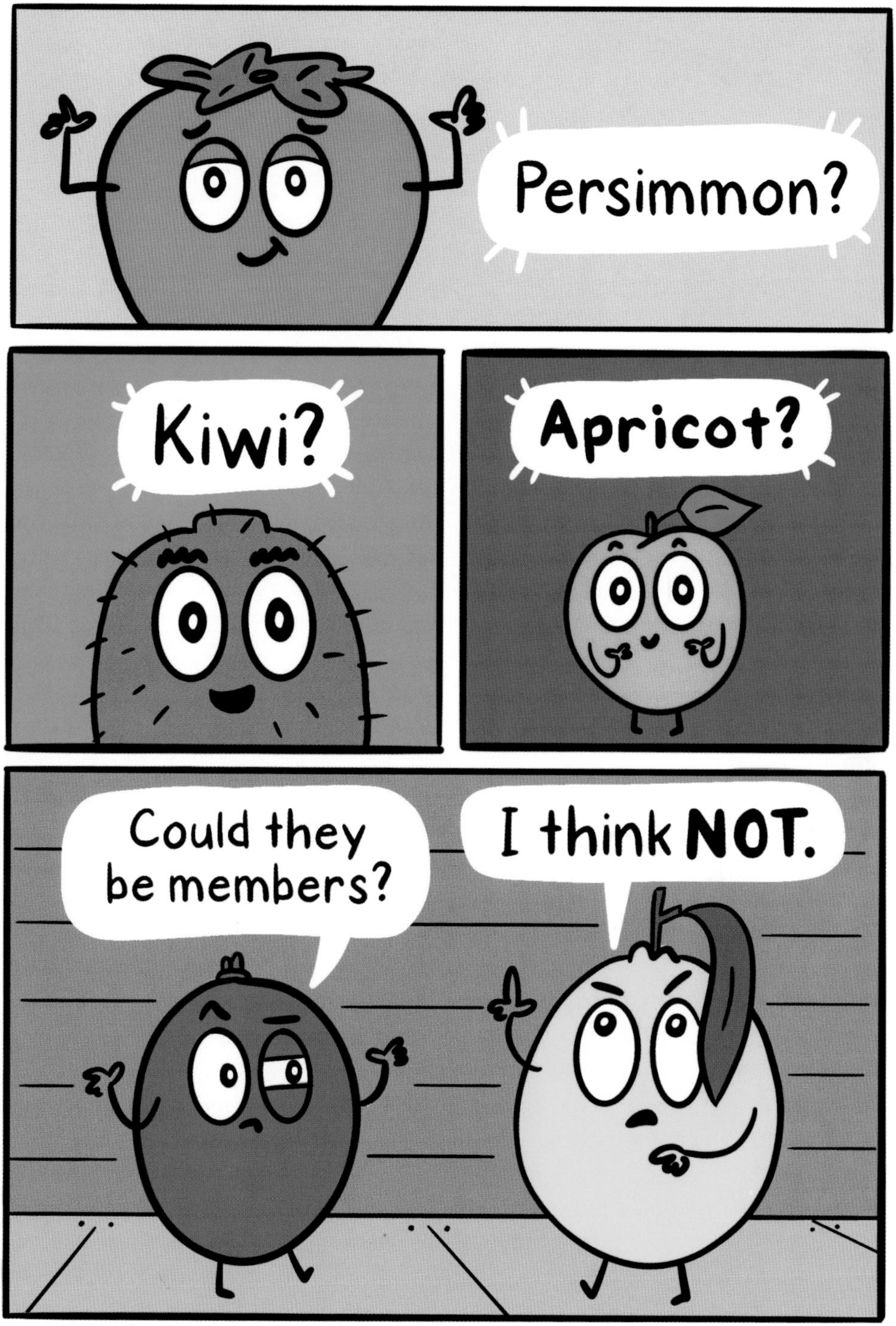
Persimmon?
Kiwi?
Apricot?
Could they be members?
I think NOT.

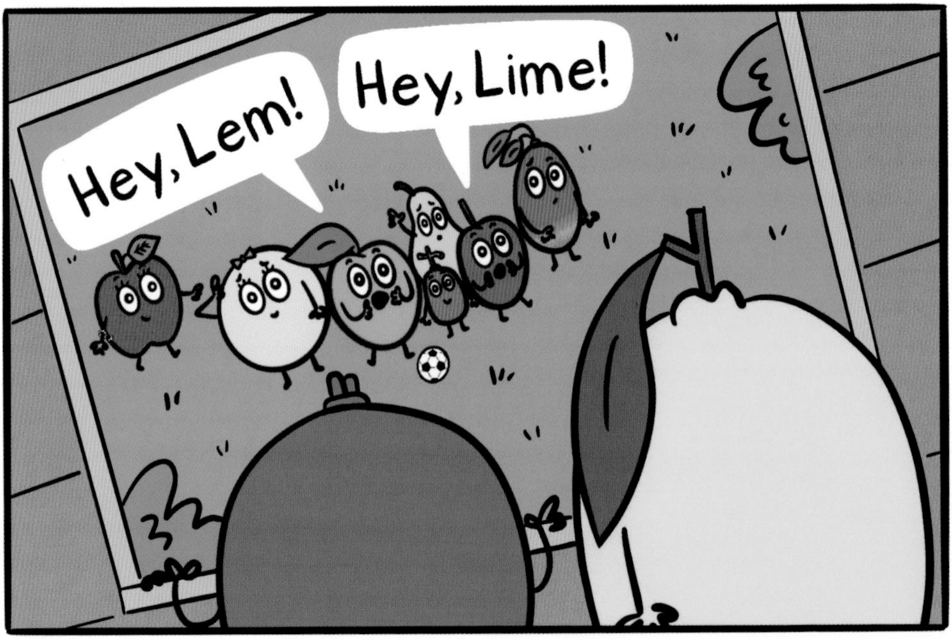
Hey, Lem!
Hey, Lime!

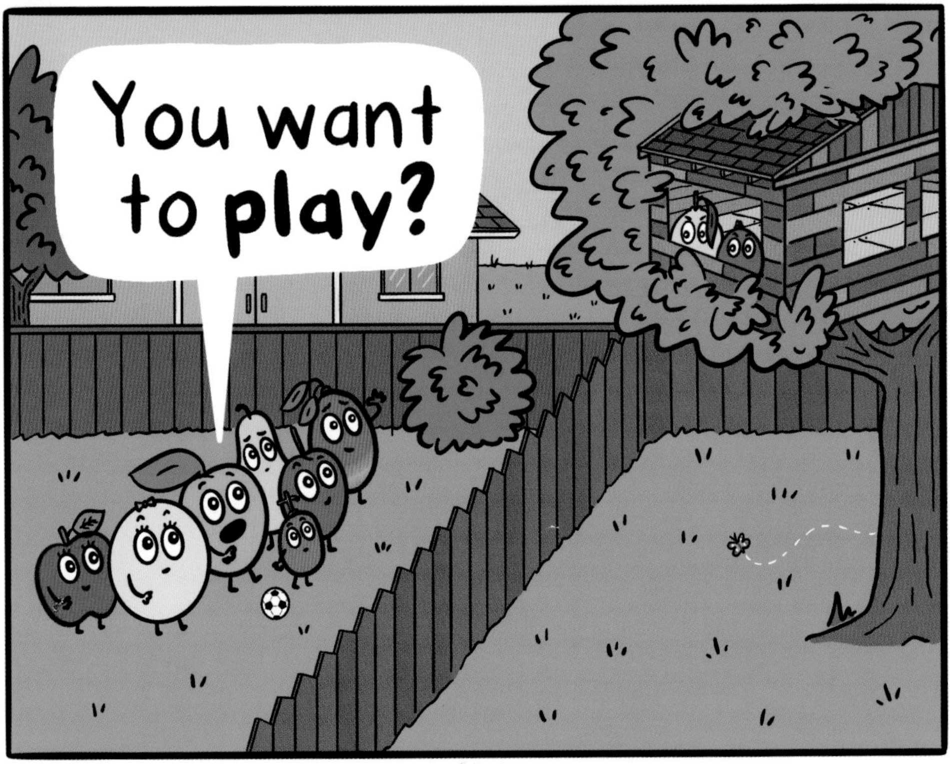
You want to **play**?

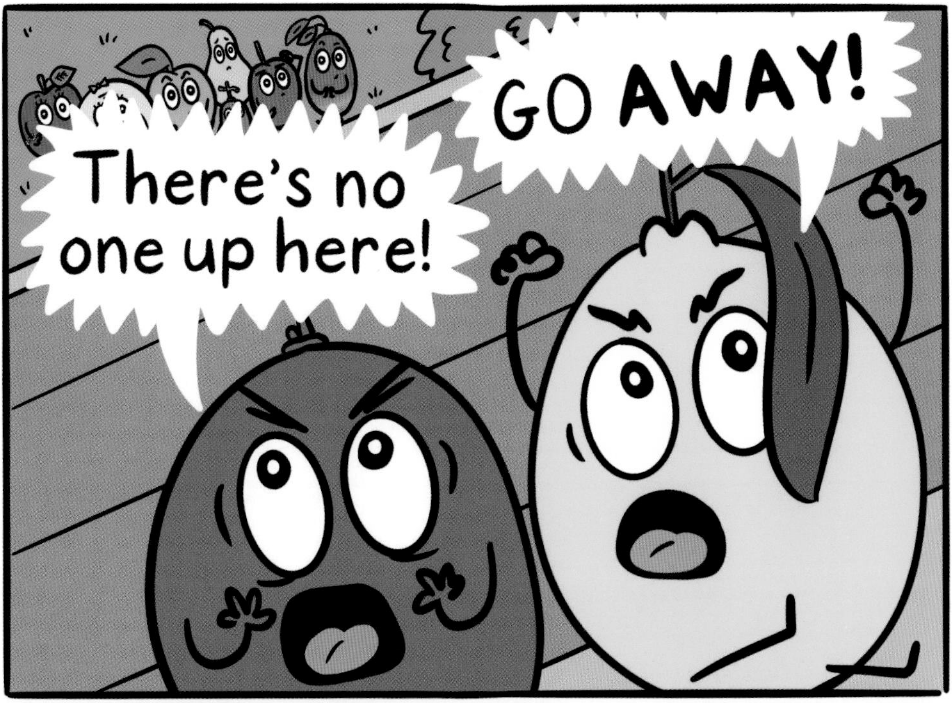
There's no one up here!
GO AWAY!

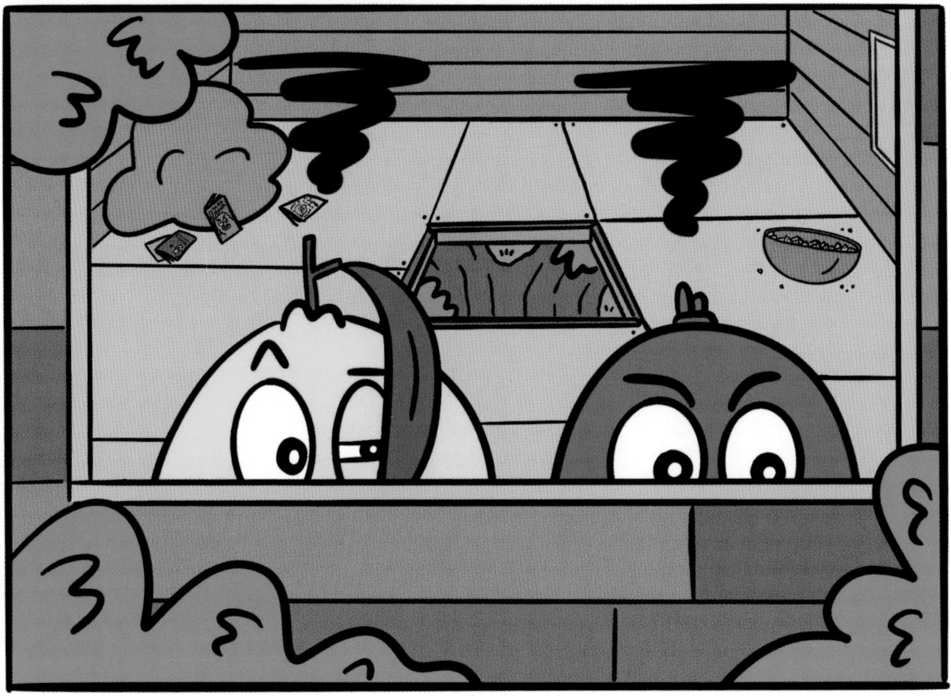

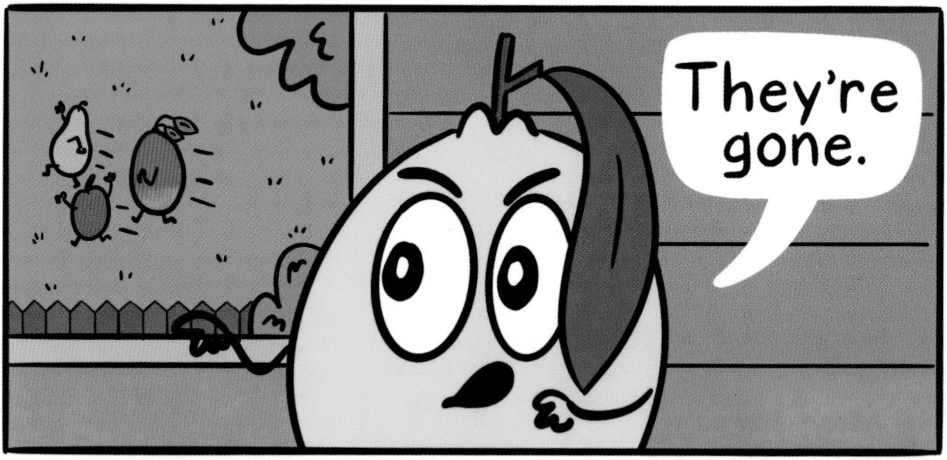
They're gone.

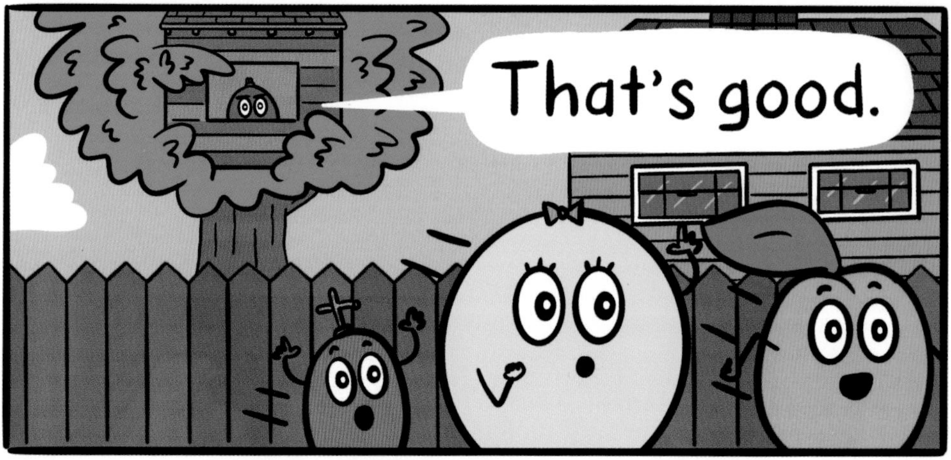
That's good.

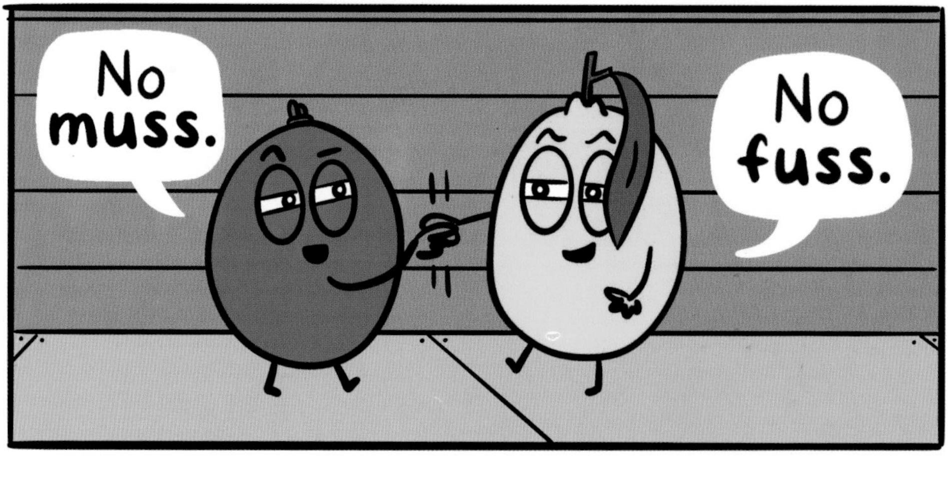
No muss.
No fuss.

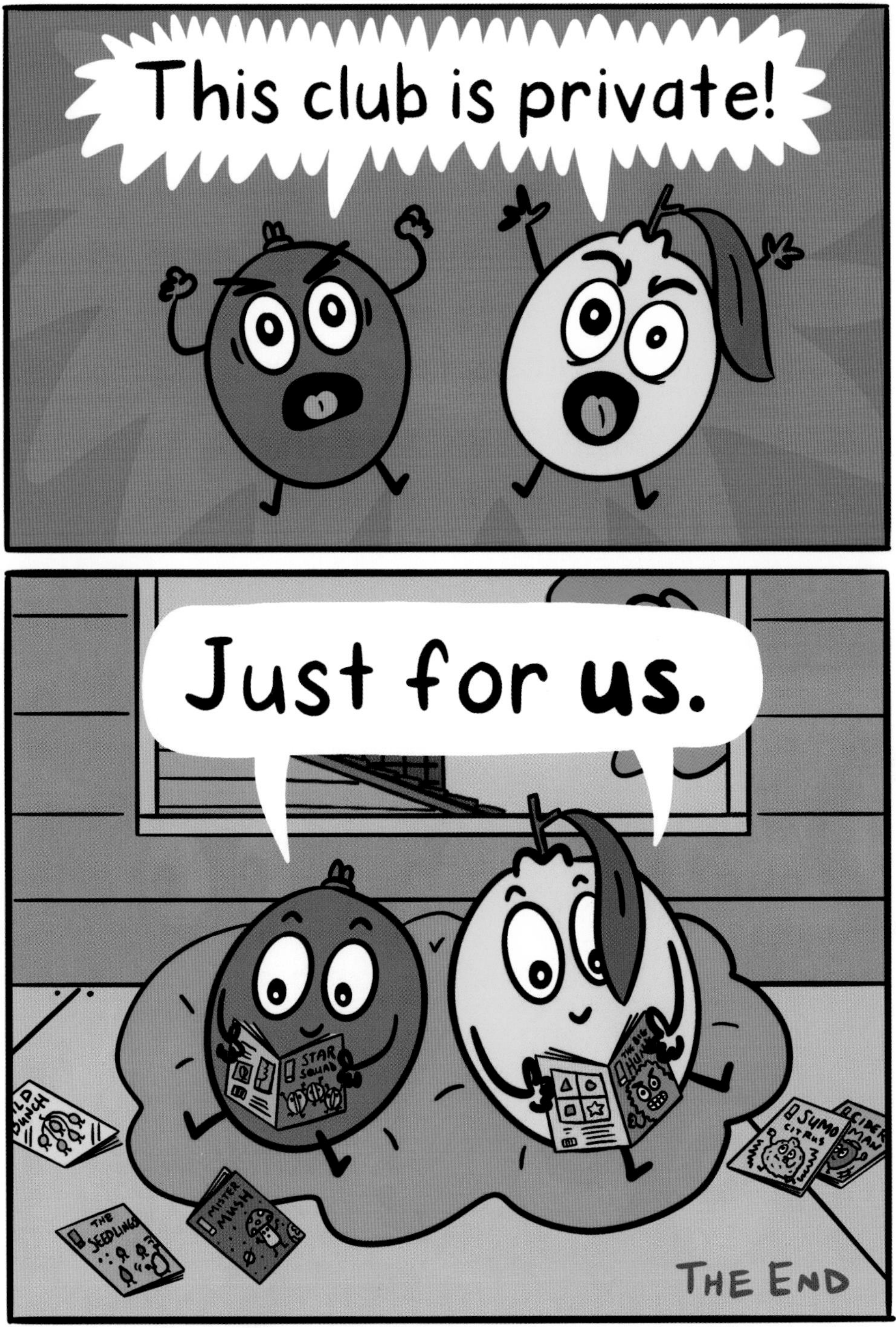
This club is private!
Just for **us**.
STAR SQUAD
SUMO CITRUS
MISTER MUSH
THE SEEDLINGS
THE END

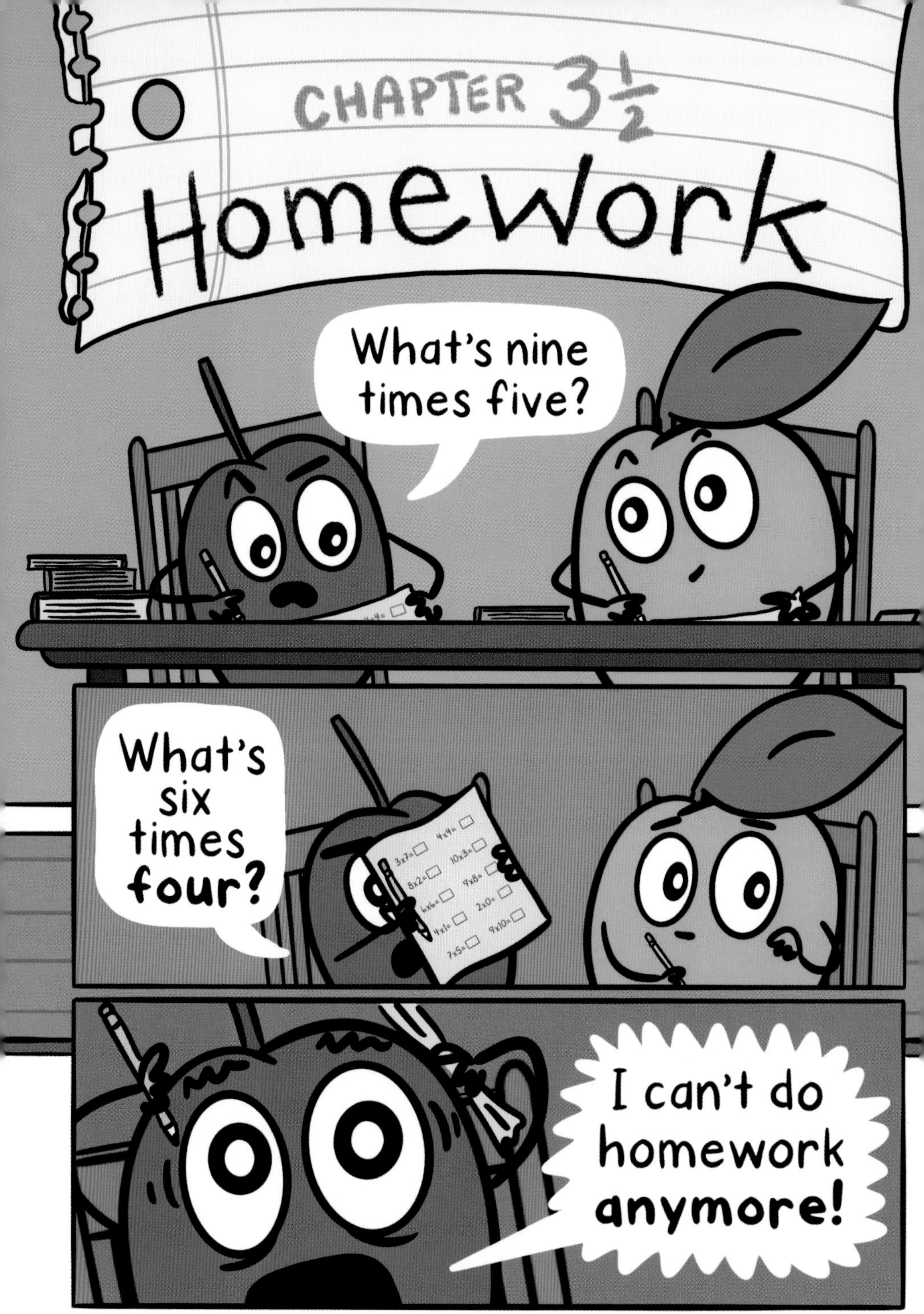
CHAPTER 3½
Homework
What's nine times five?
What's six times four?
3x7= 4x4=
8x2= 10x3=
6x6= 9x8=
4x1= 2x0=
7x5= 9x10=
I can't do homework anymore!

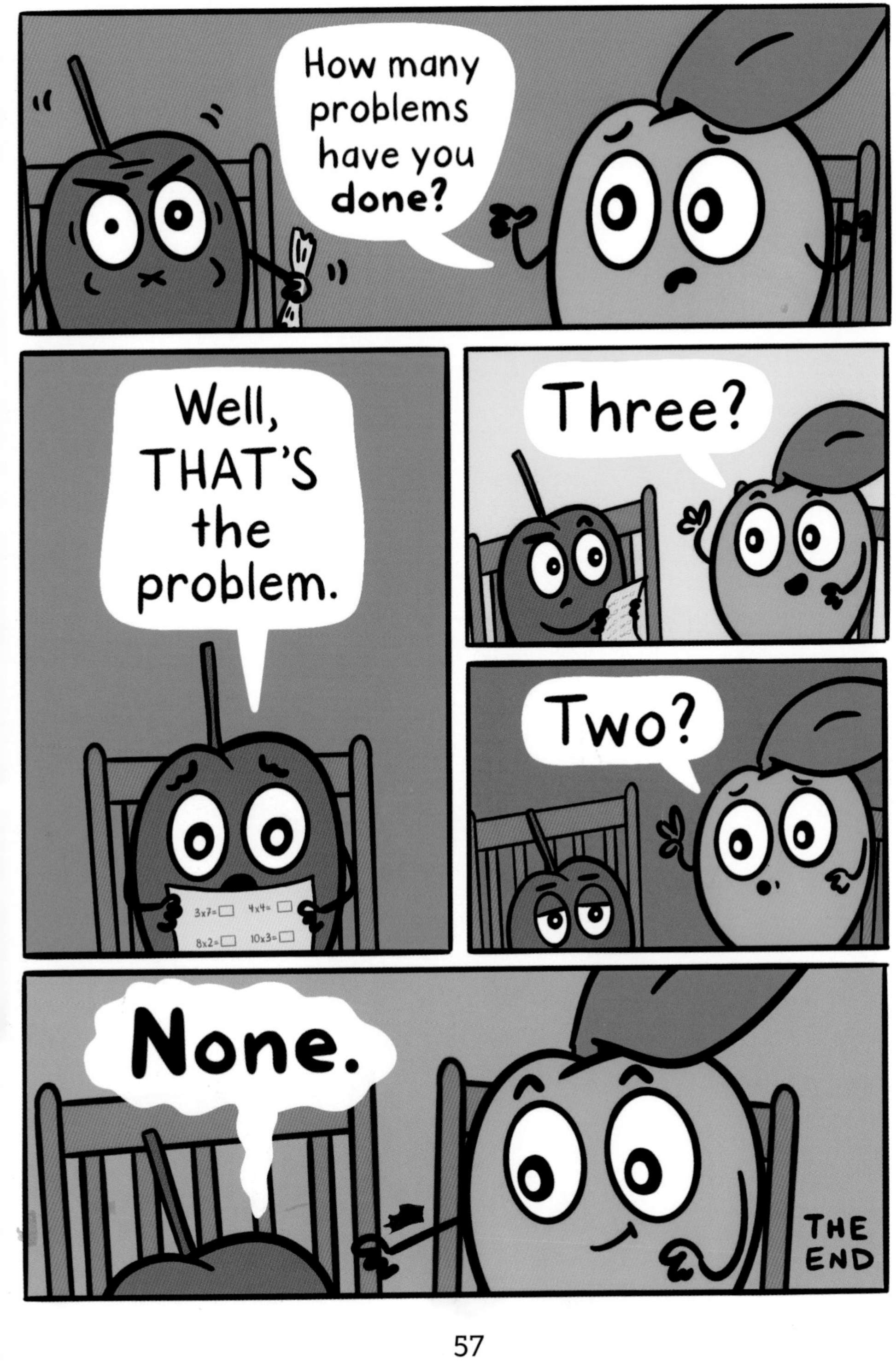
How many problems have you **done?**
Well, THAT'S the problem.
3x7= 4x4= 8x2= 10x3=
Three?
Two?
None.
THE END

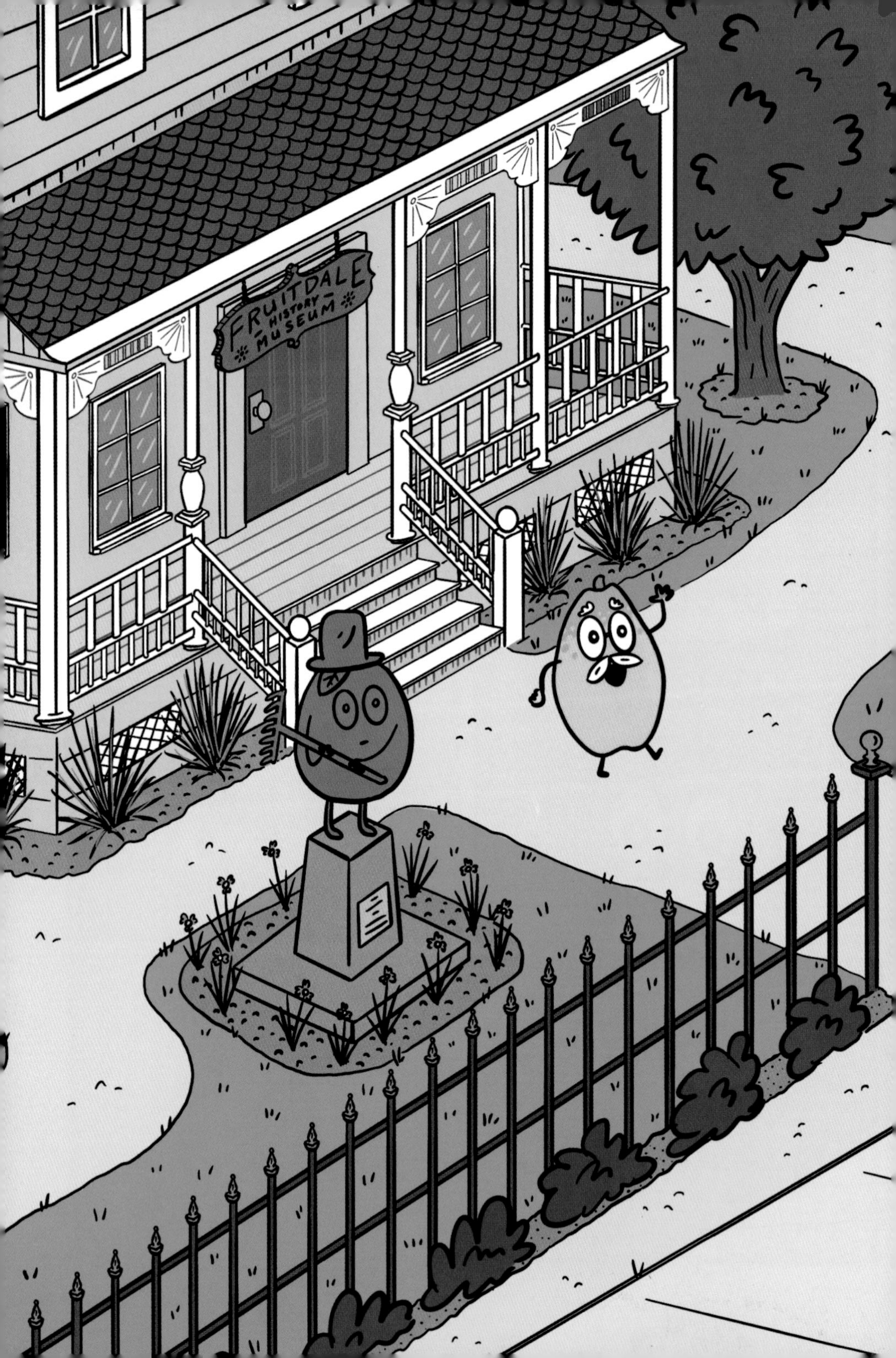
FRUITDALE
HISTORY
MUSEUM

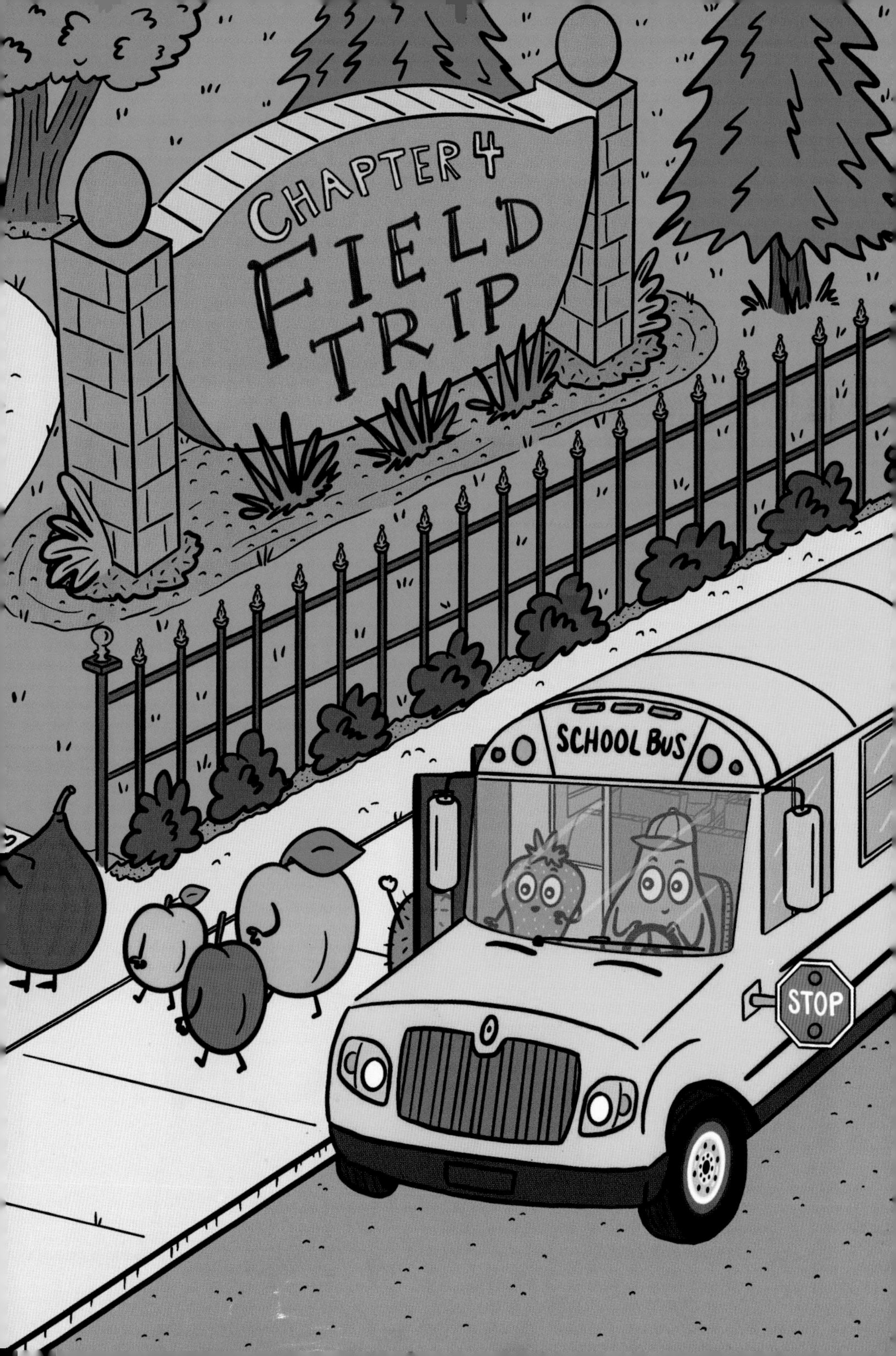
CHAPTER 4
FIELD TRIP
SCHOOL BUS
STOP

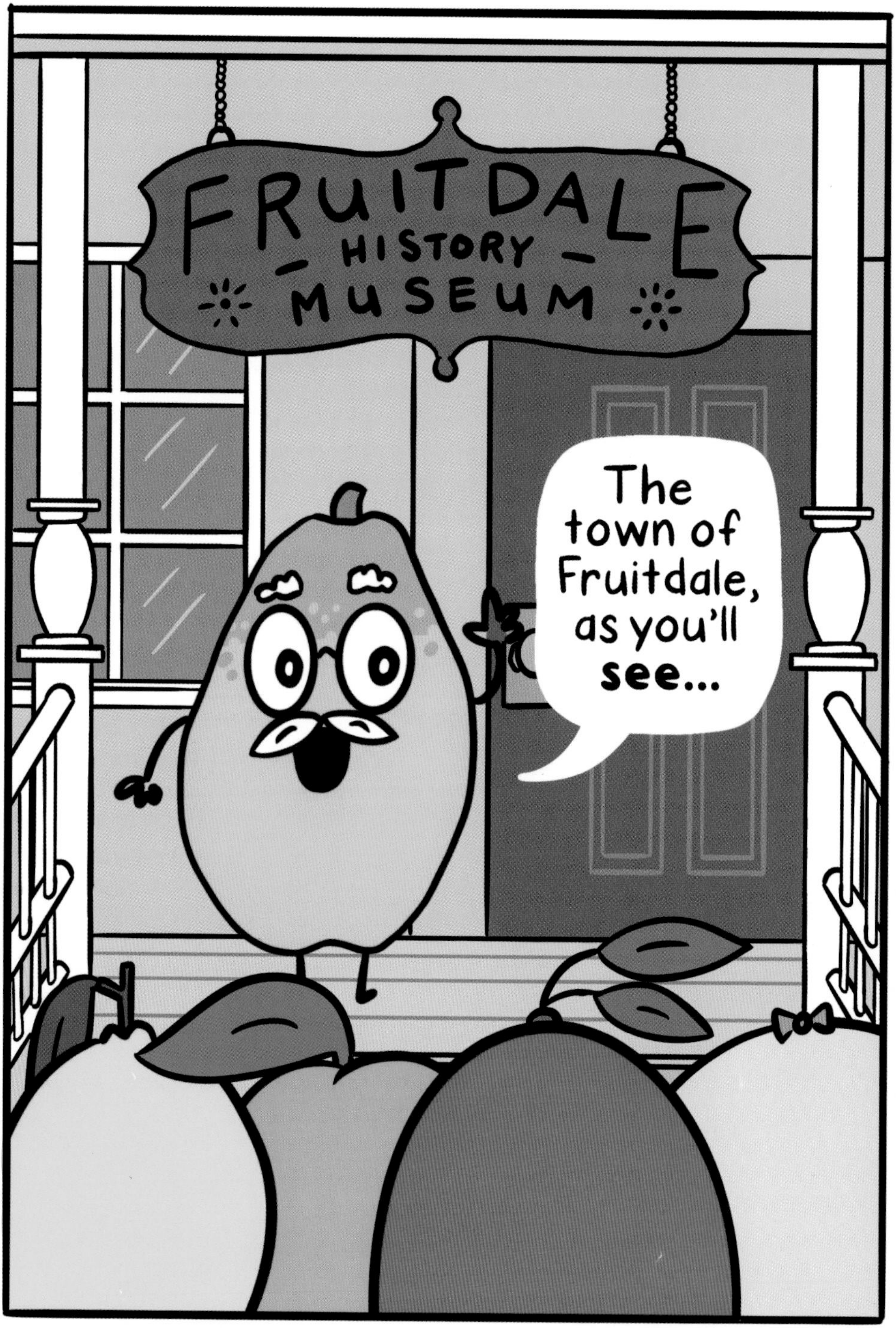
FRUITDALE
HISTORY
MUSEUM
The town of Fruitdale, as you'll **see...**

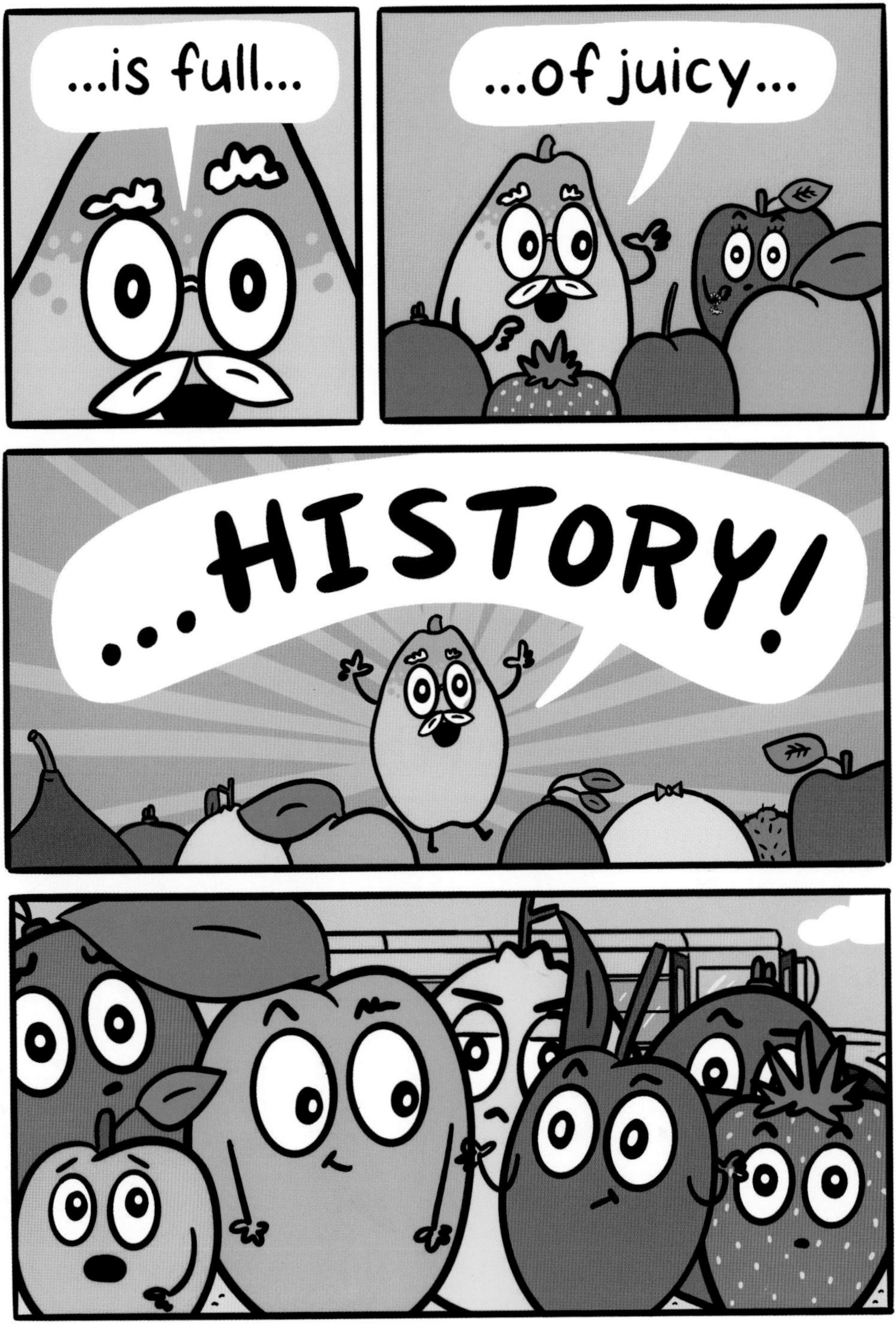
...is full...
...of juicy...
...HISTORY!

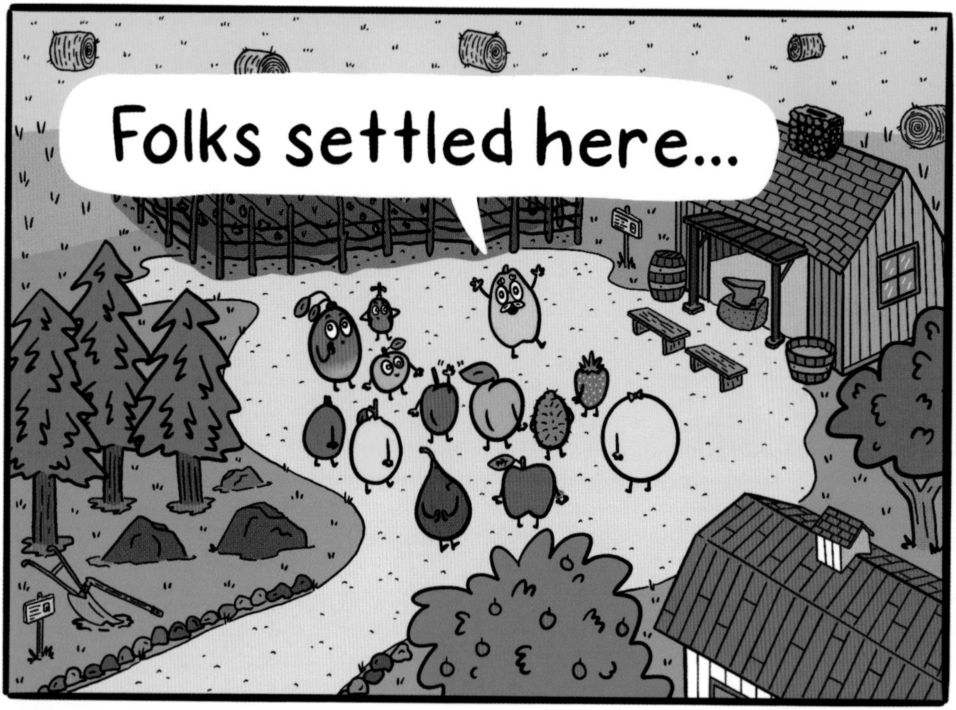
Folks settled here...

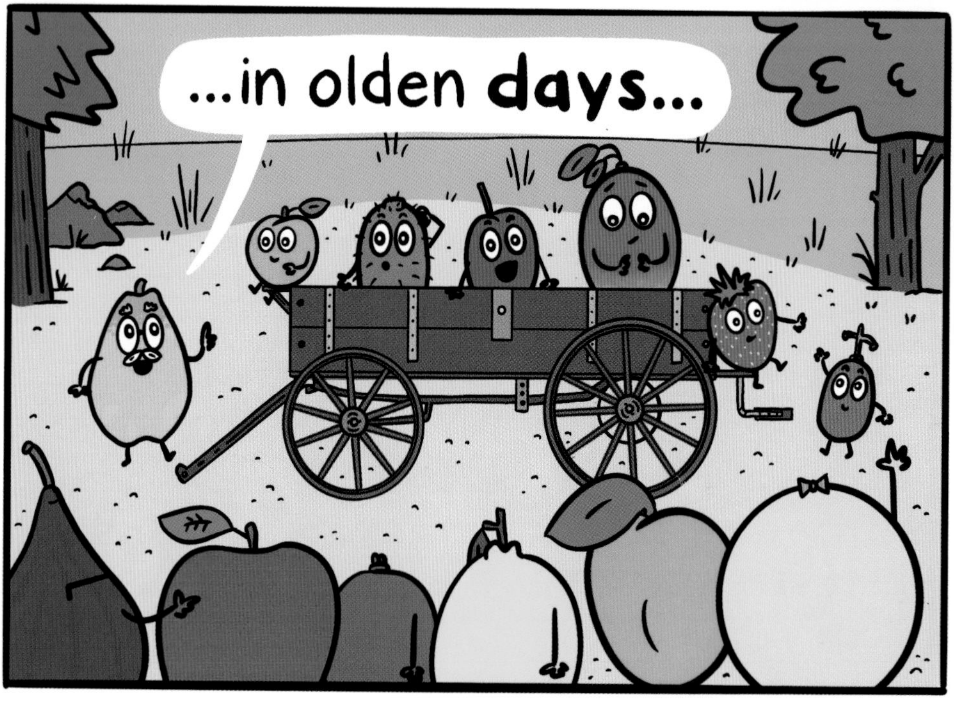
...in olden days...

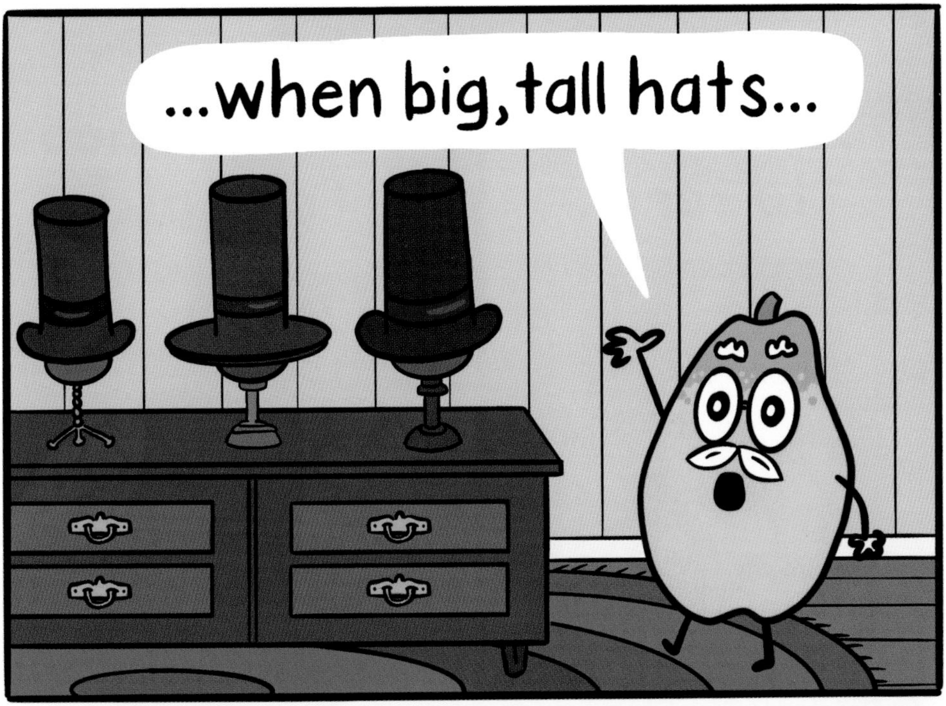
...when big, tall hats...

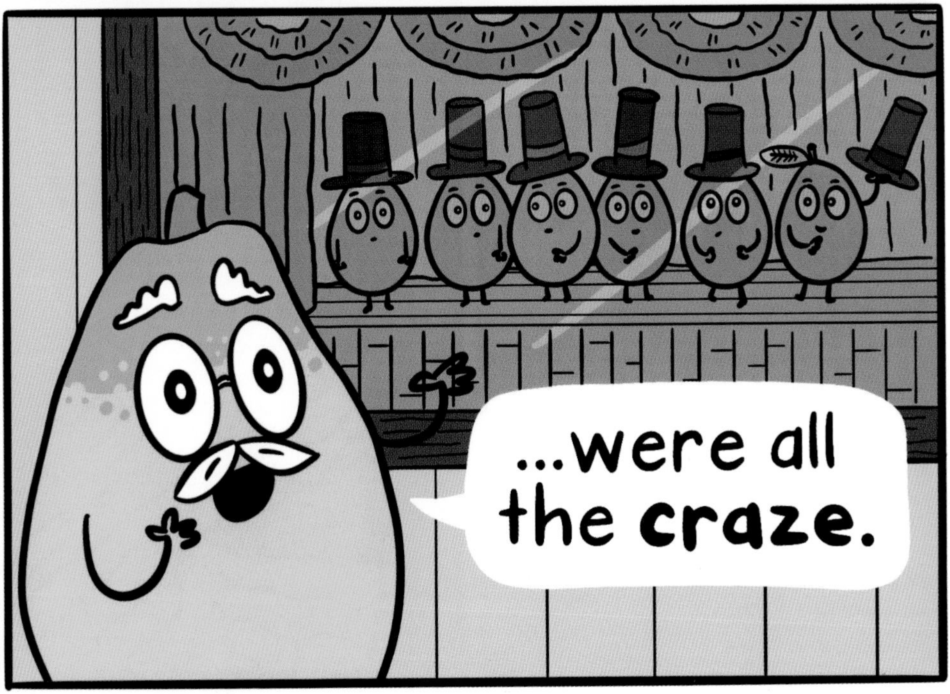
...were all the **craze.**

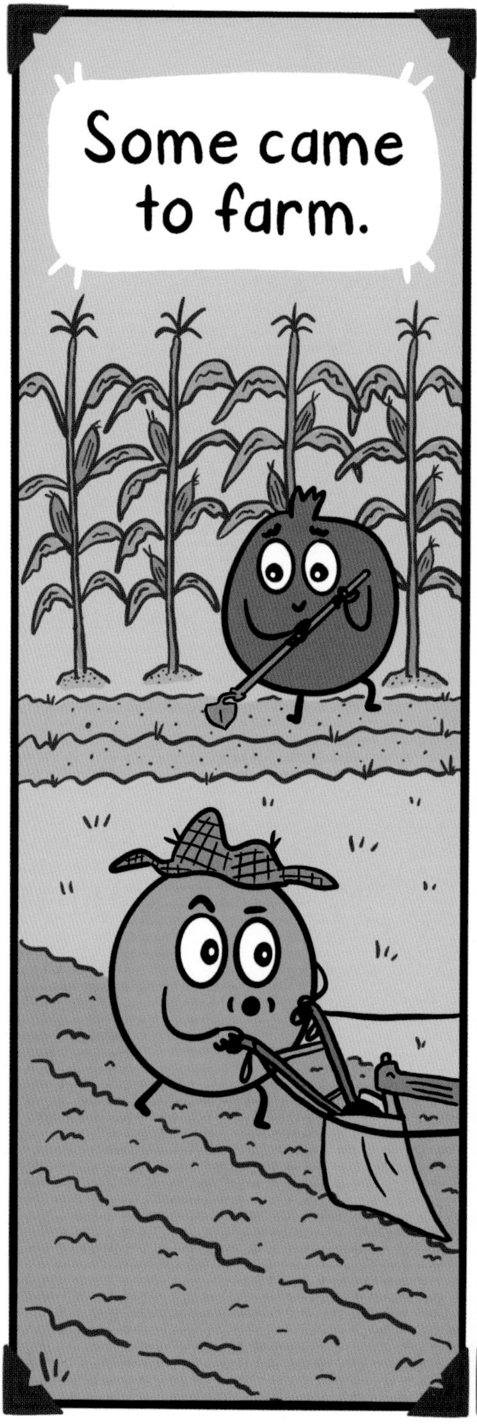
Some came to farm.

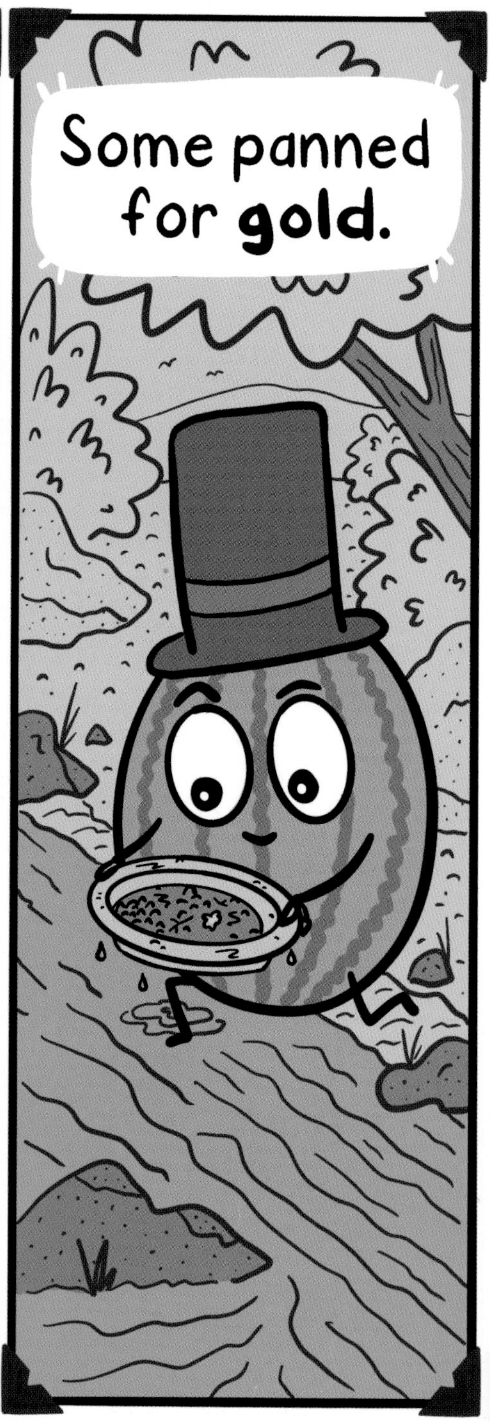
Some panned for **gold**.

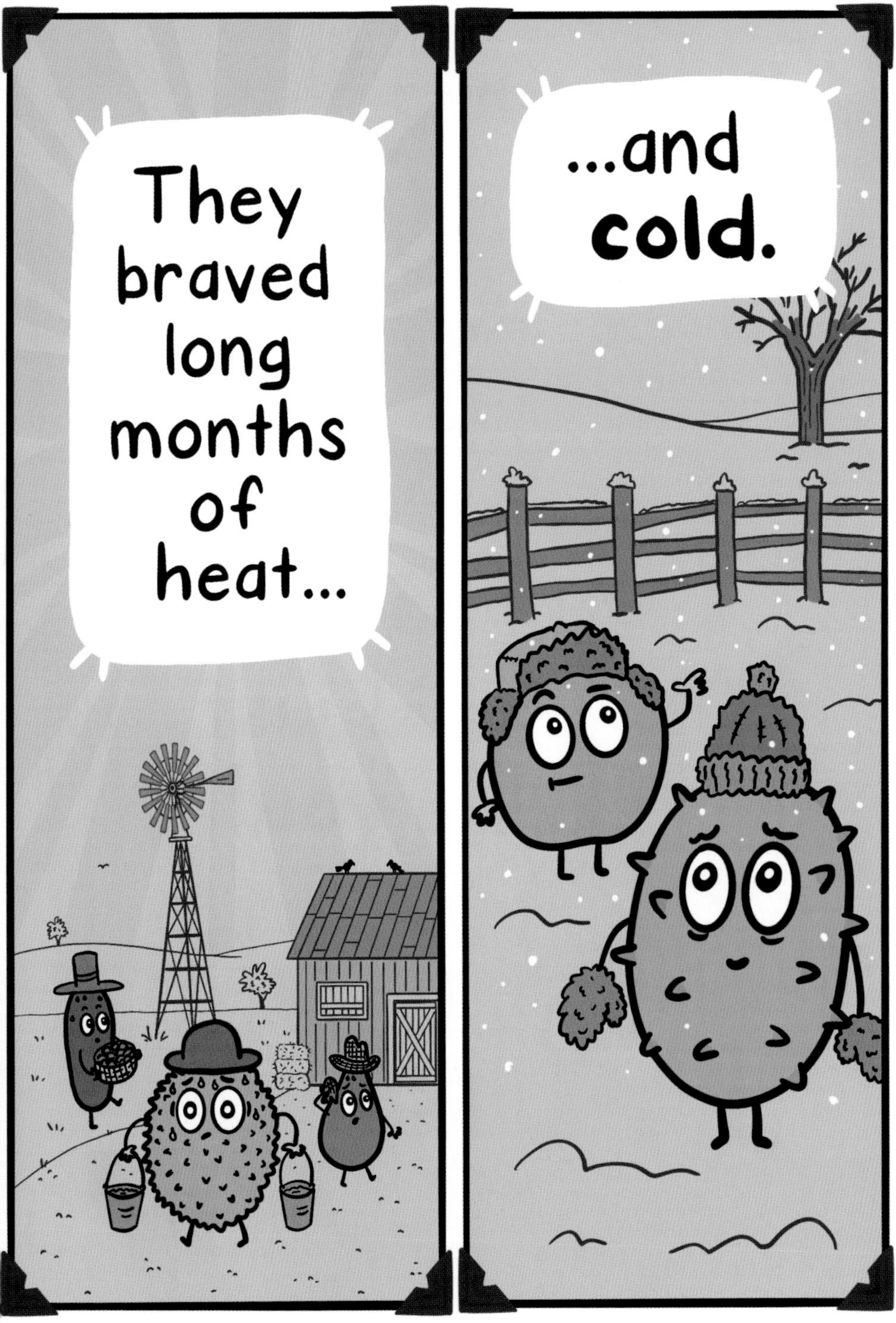
They braved long months of heat...
...and cold.

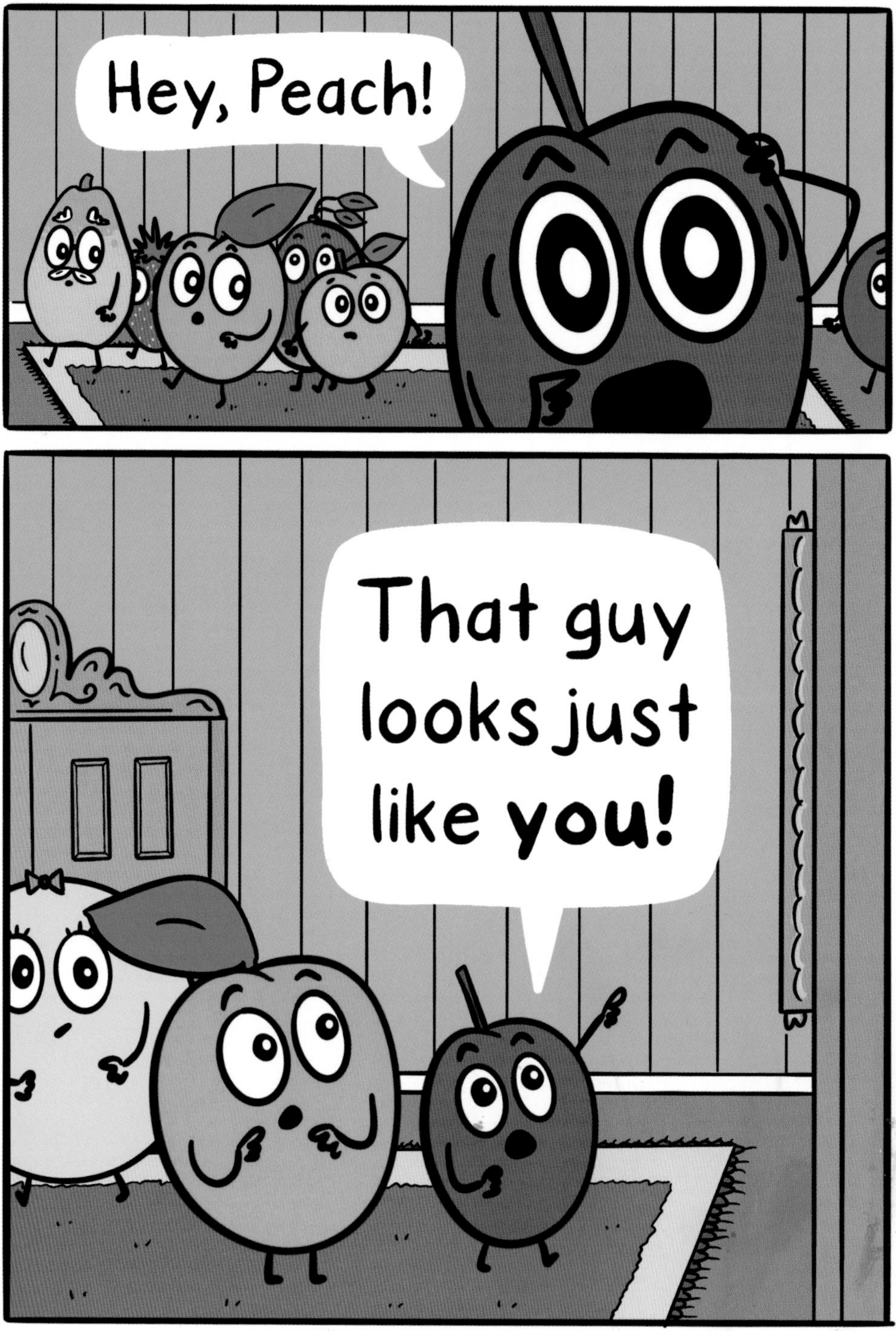
Hey, Peach!
That guy looks just like **you**!

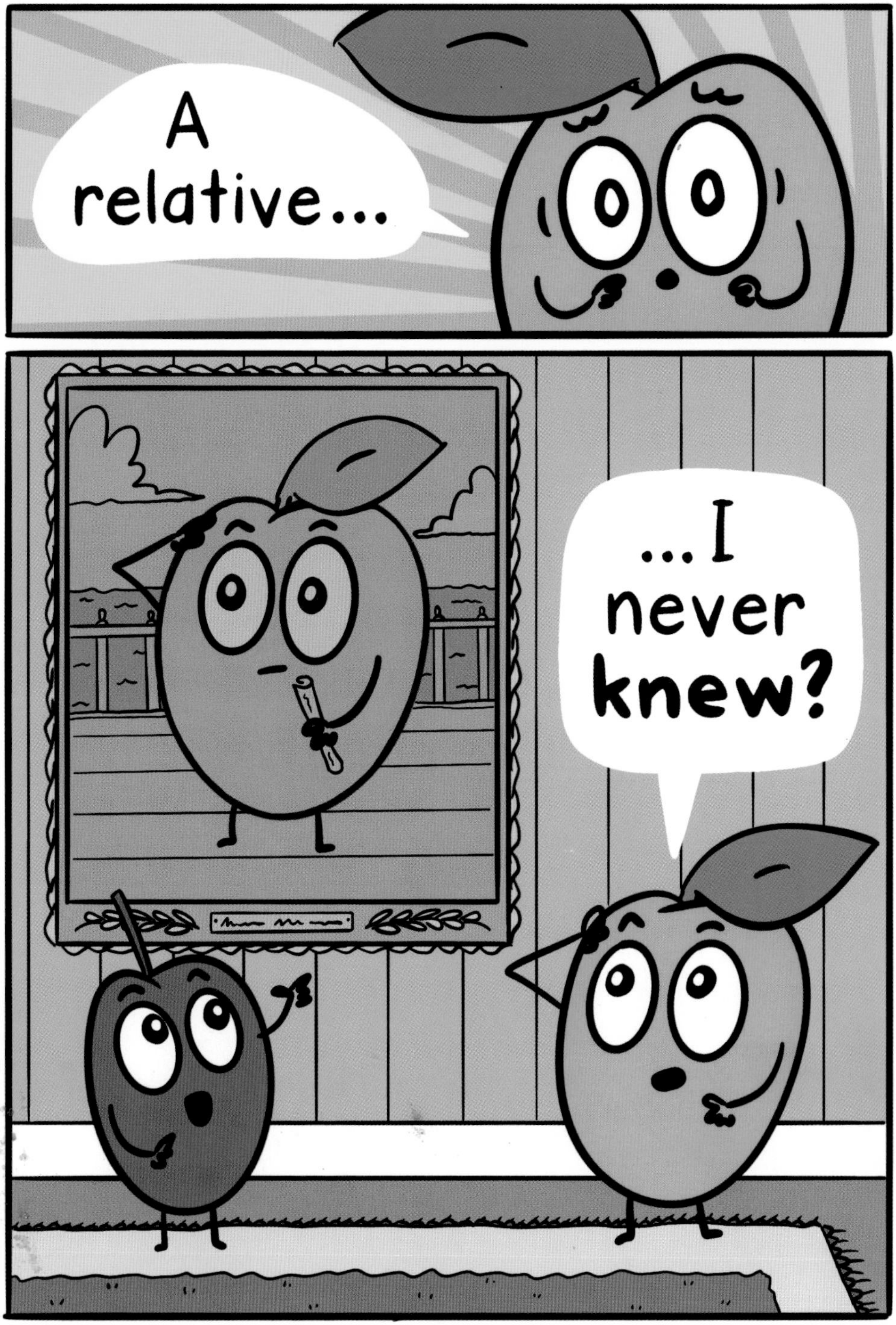
A relative...
...I never knew?

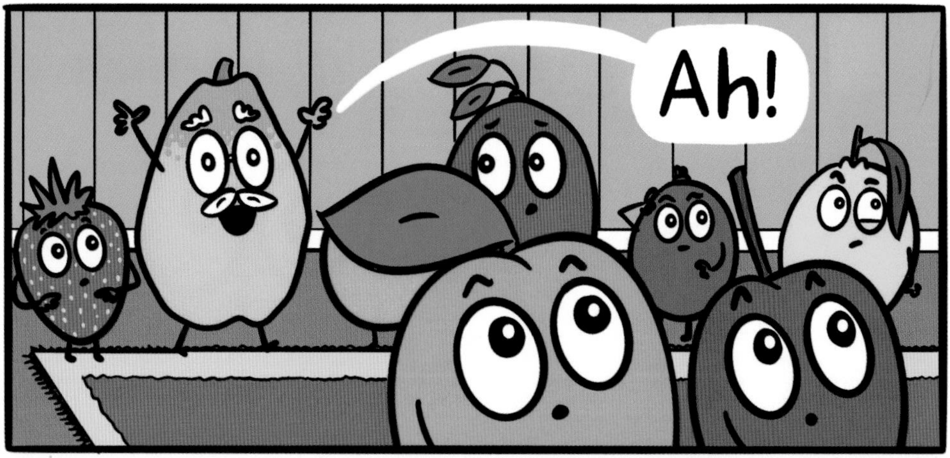
Ah!

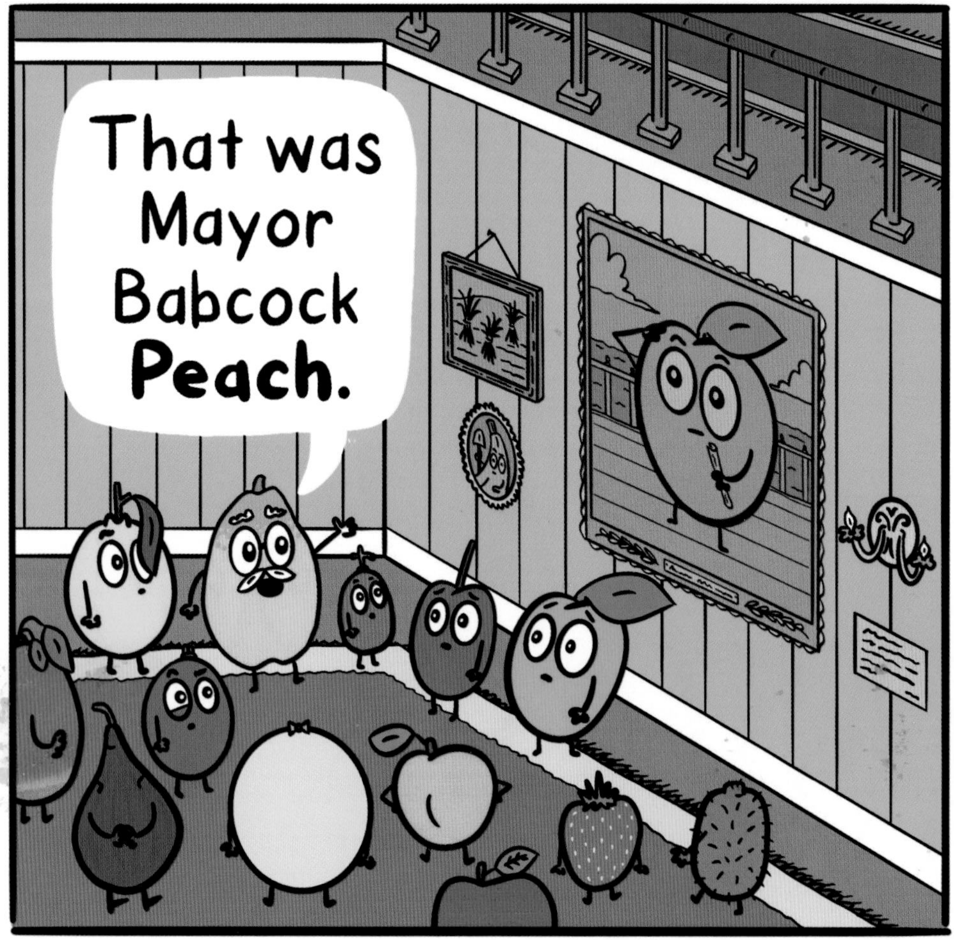
That was Mayor Babcock **Peach**.

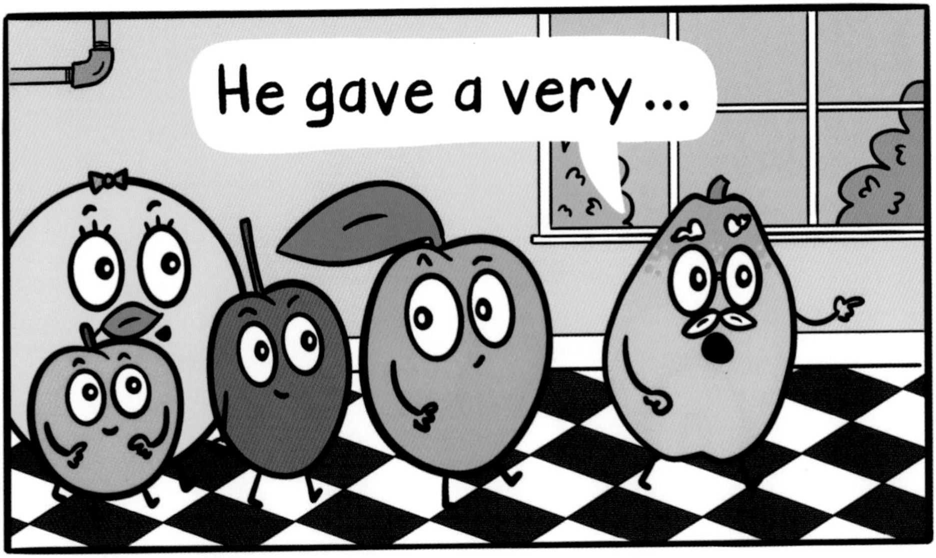
He gave a very...

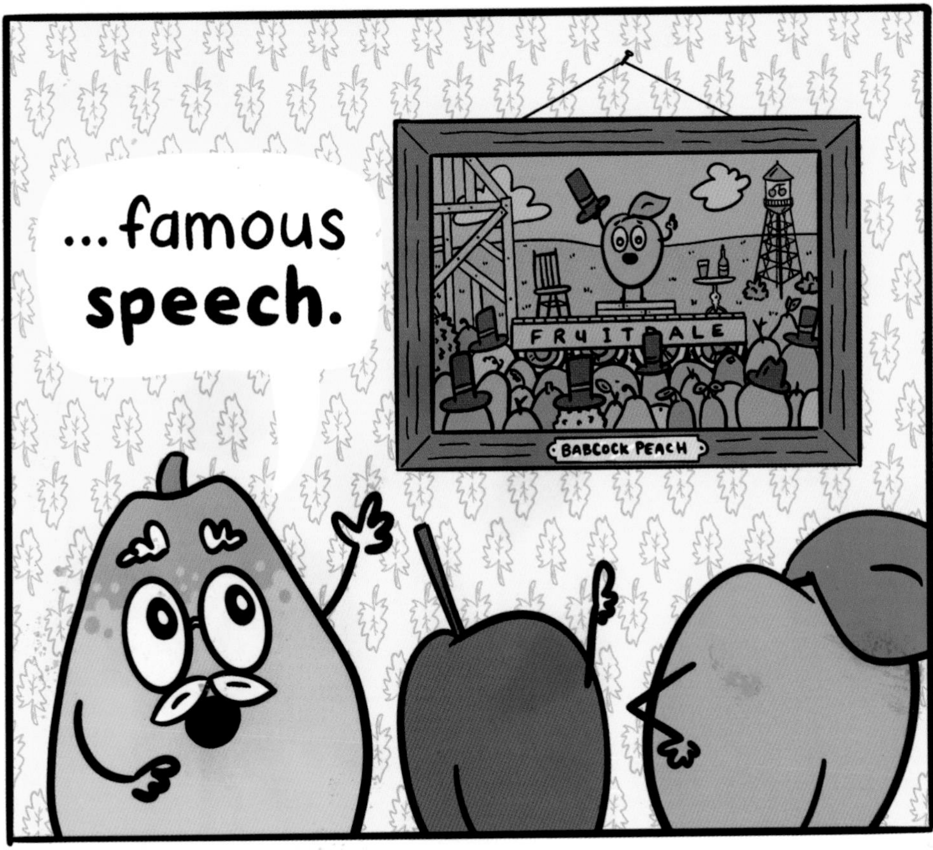
...famous speech.
FRUIT ALE
BABCOCK PEACH

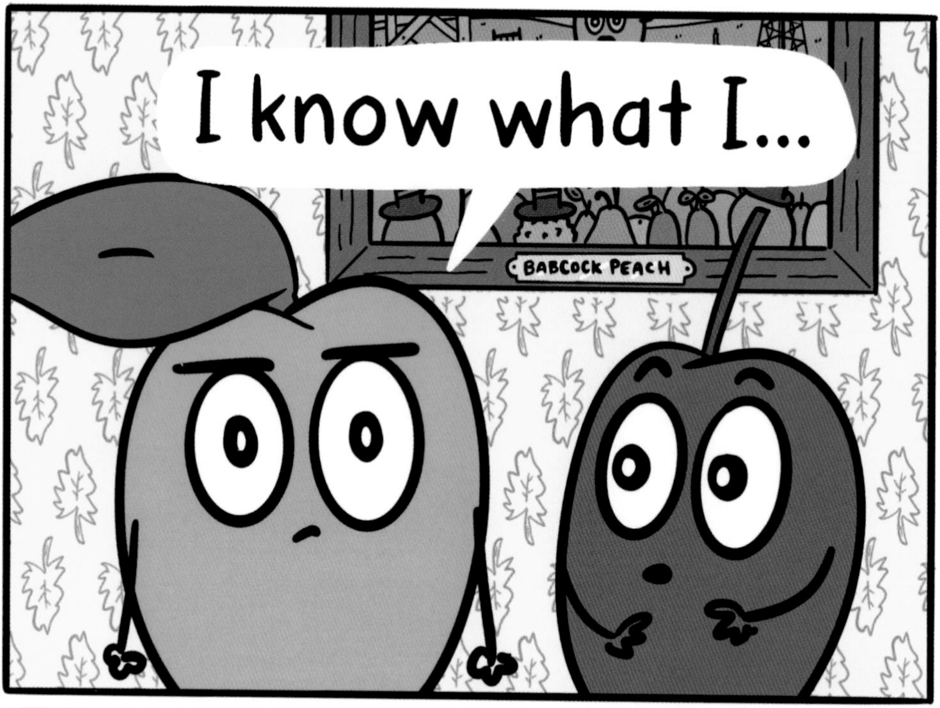
I know what I...
BABCOCK PEACH

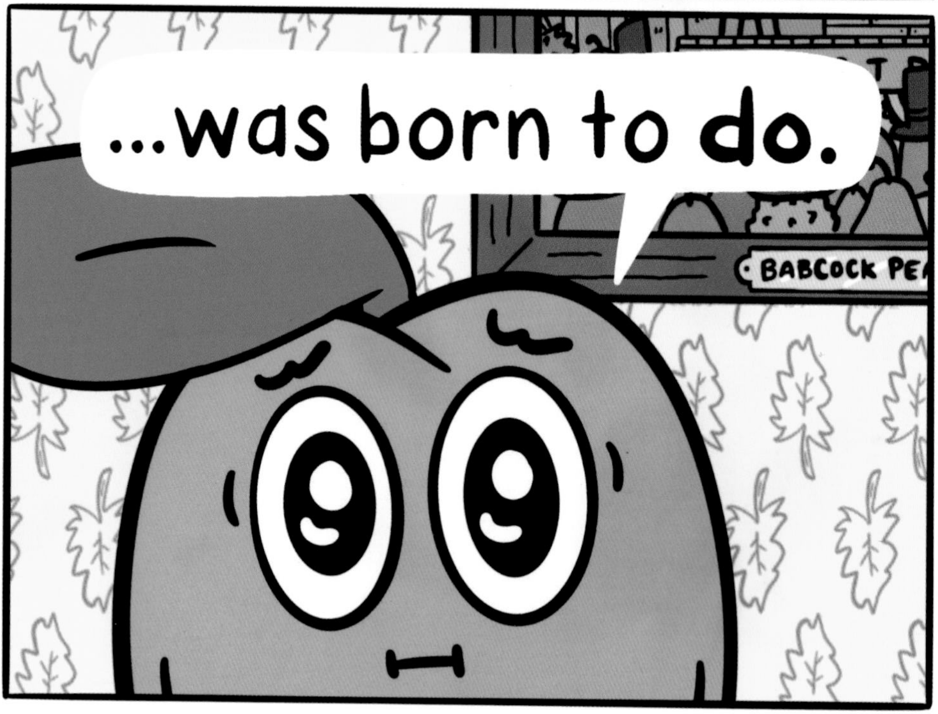
...was born to do.

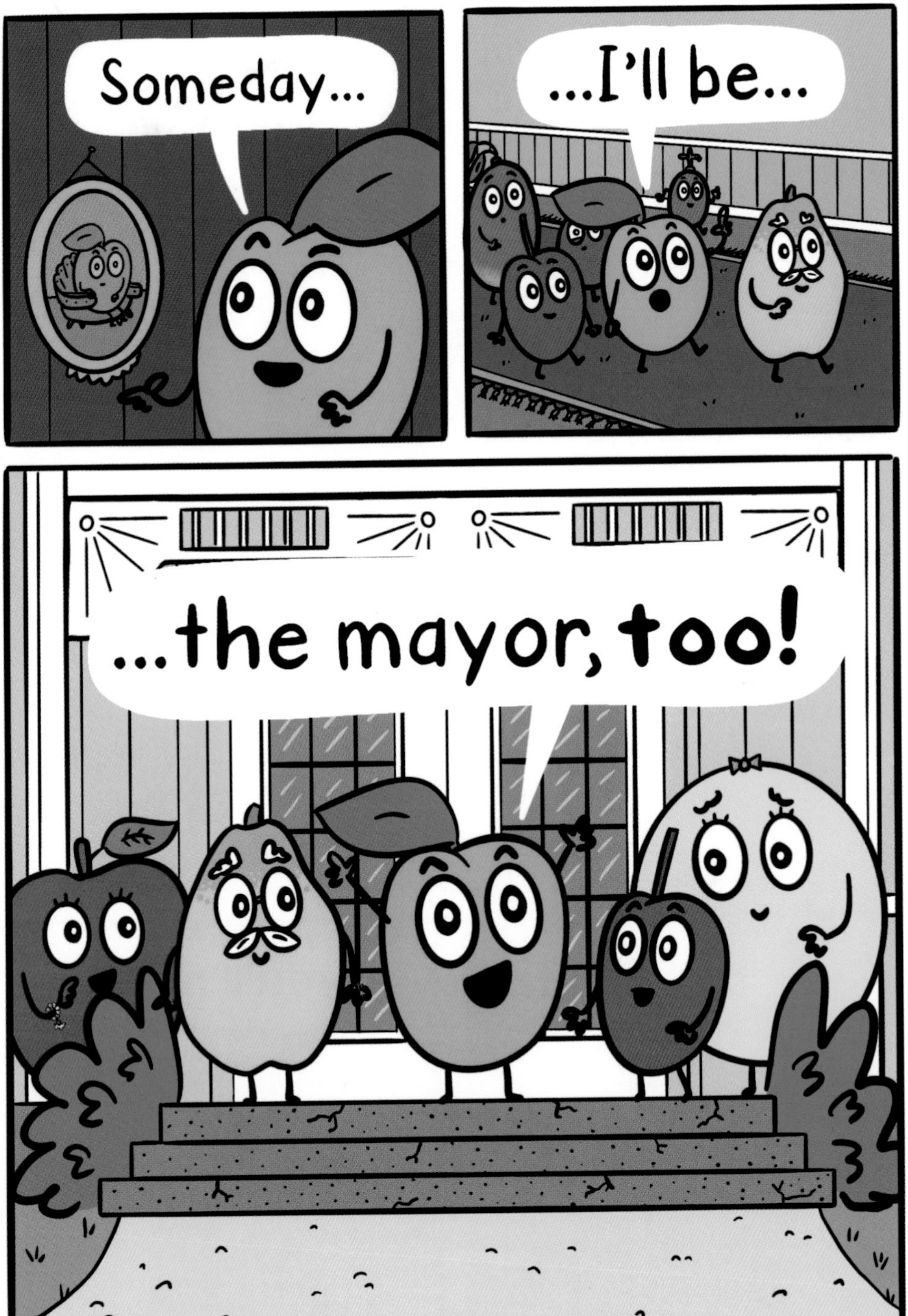
Someday...
...I'll be...
...the mayor, too!

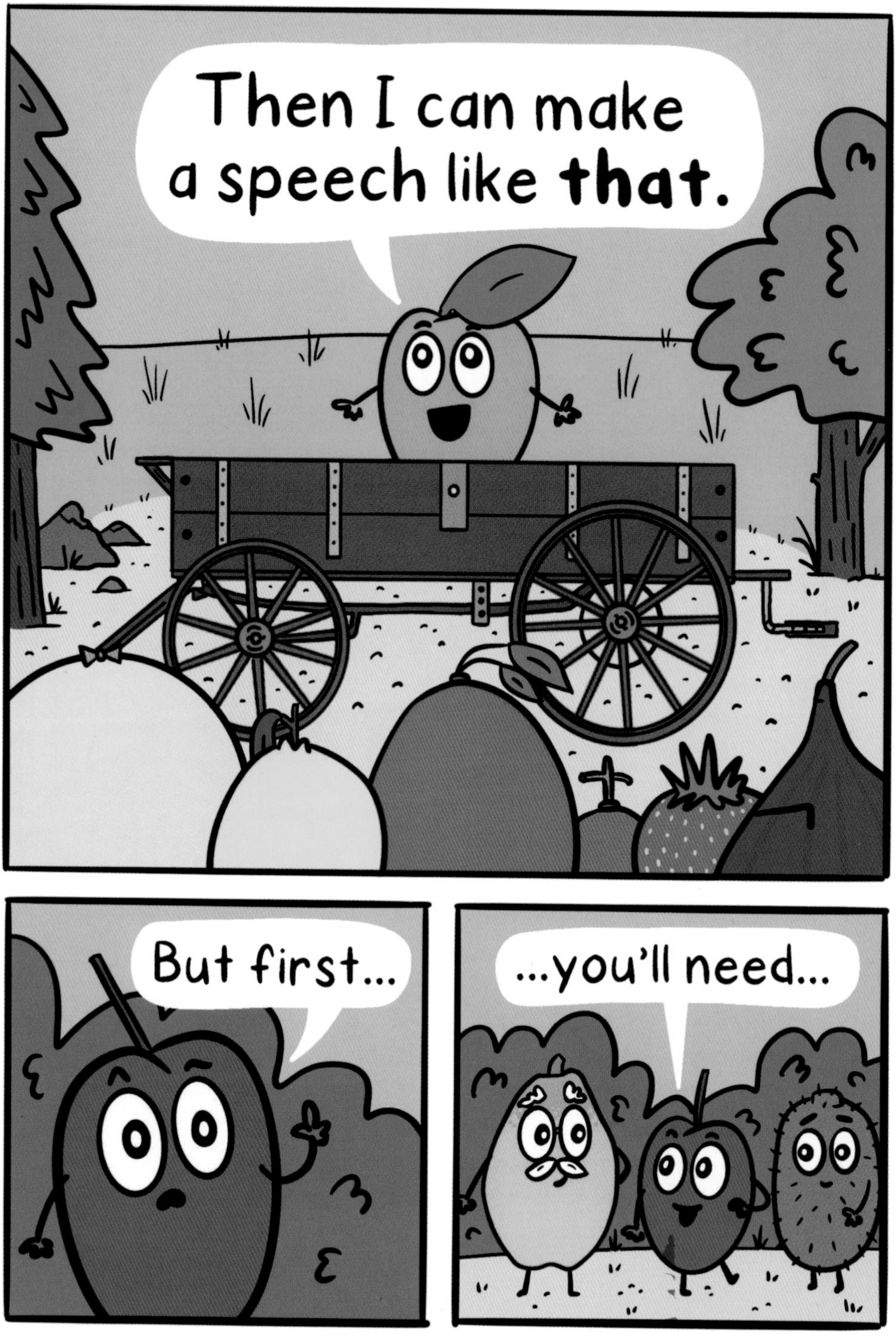
Then I can make a speech like **that.**
But first...
...you'll need...

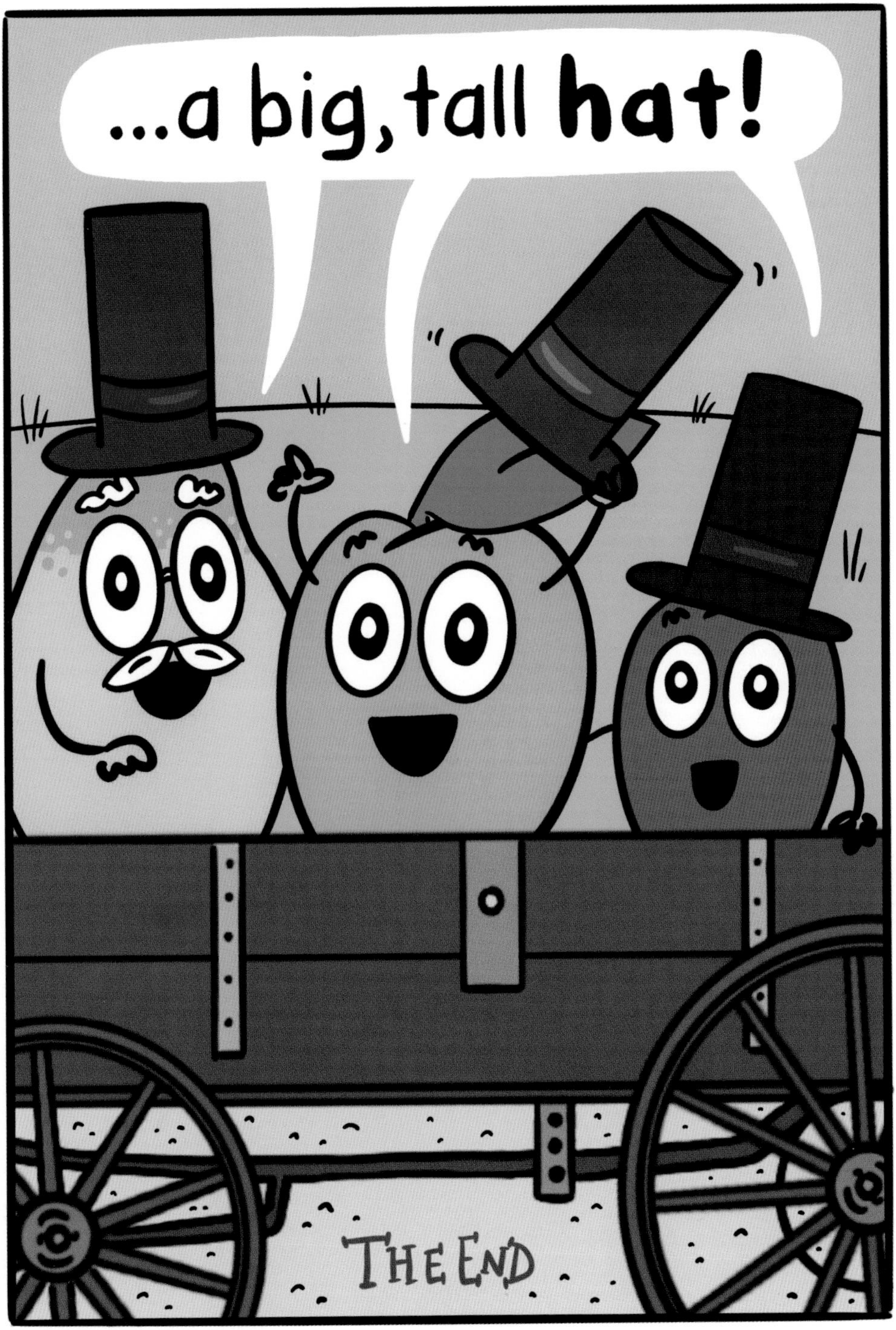
...a big, tall **hat!**
THE END

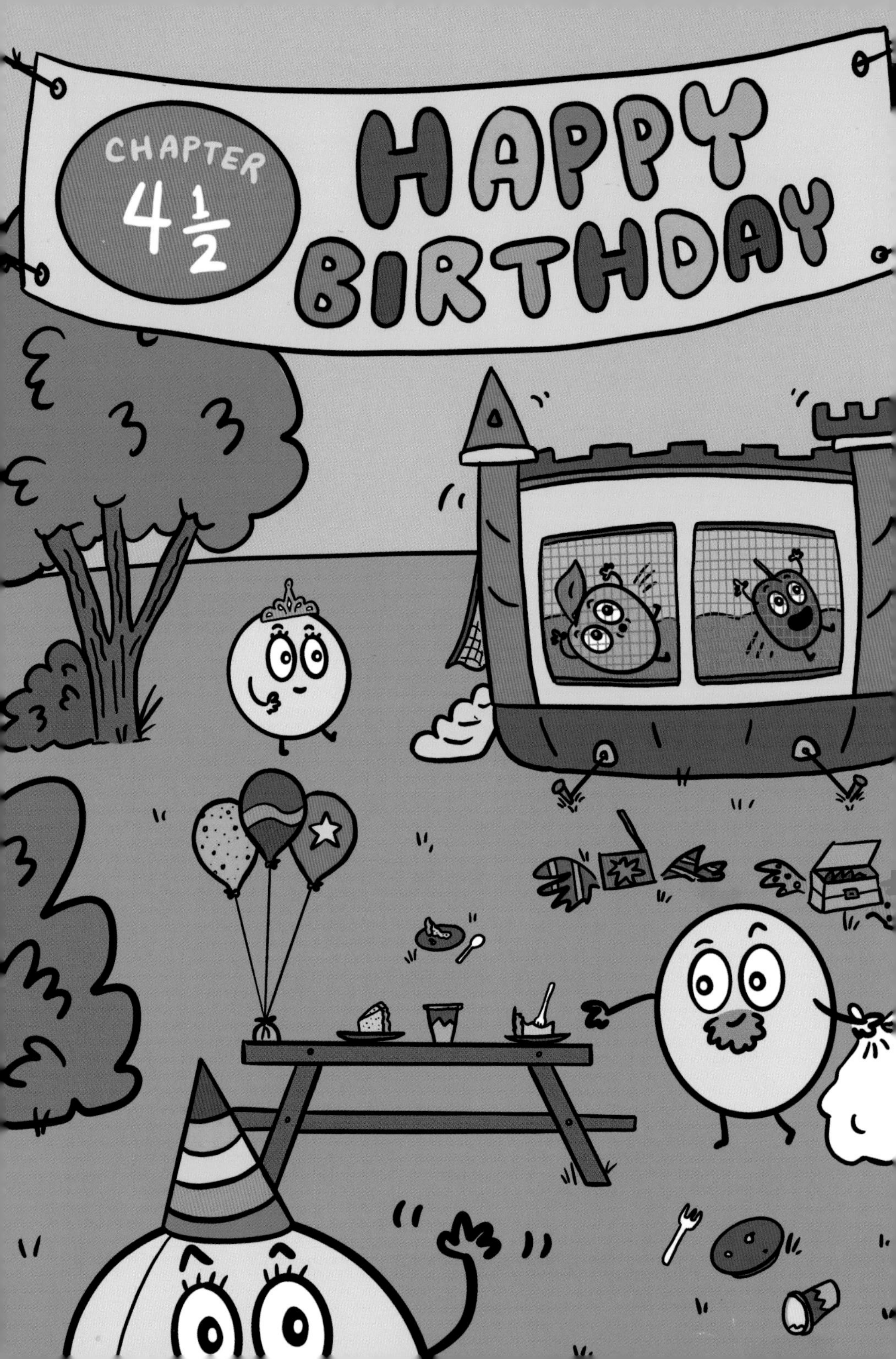
CHAPTER
4 1/2
HAPPY BIRTHDAY

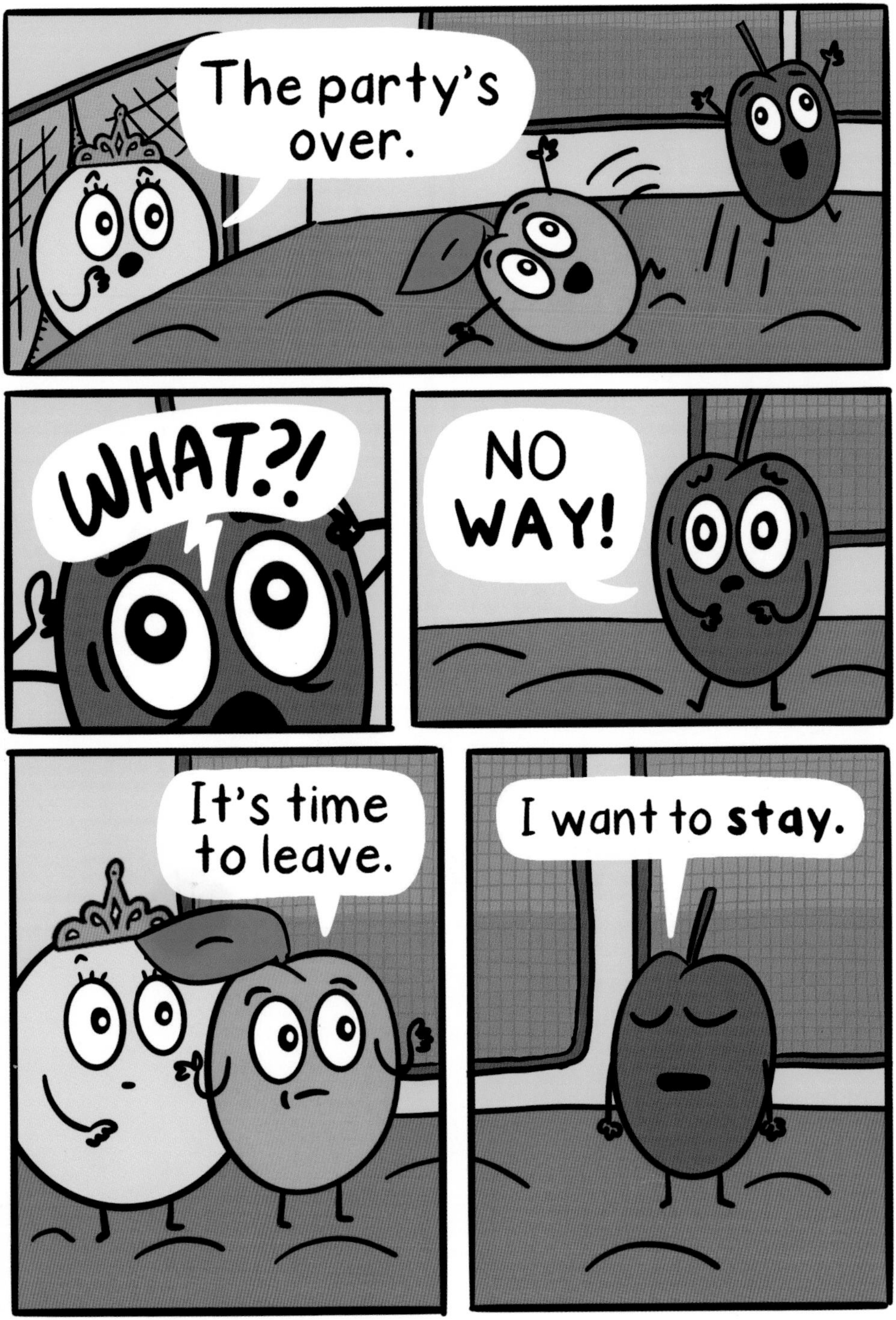
The party's over.
WHAT?!
NO WAY!
It's time to leave.
I want to **stay**.

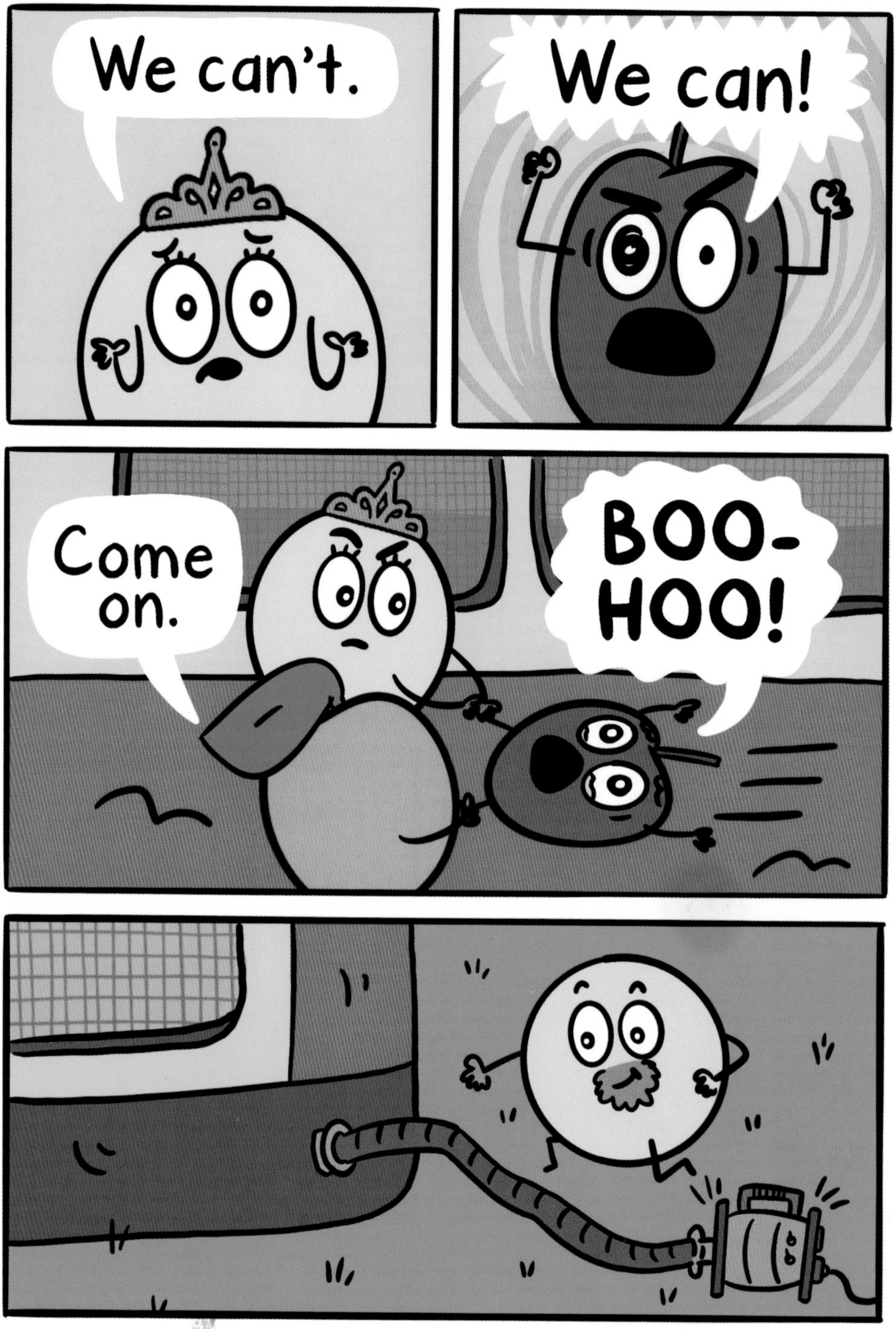
We can't.
We can!
Come on.
BOO-HOO!

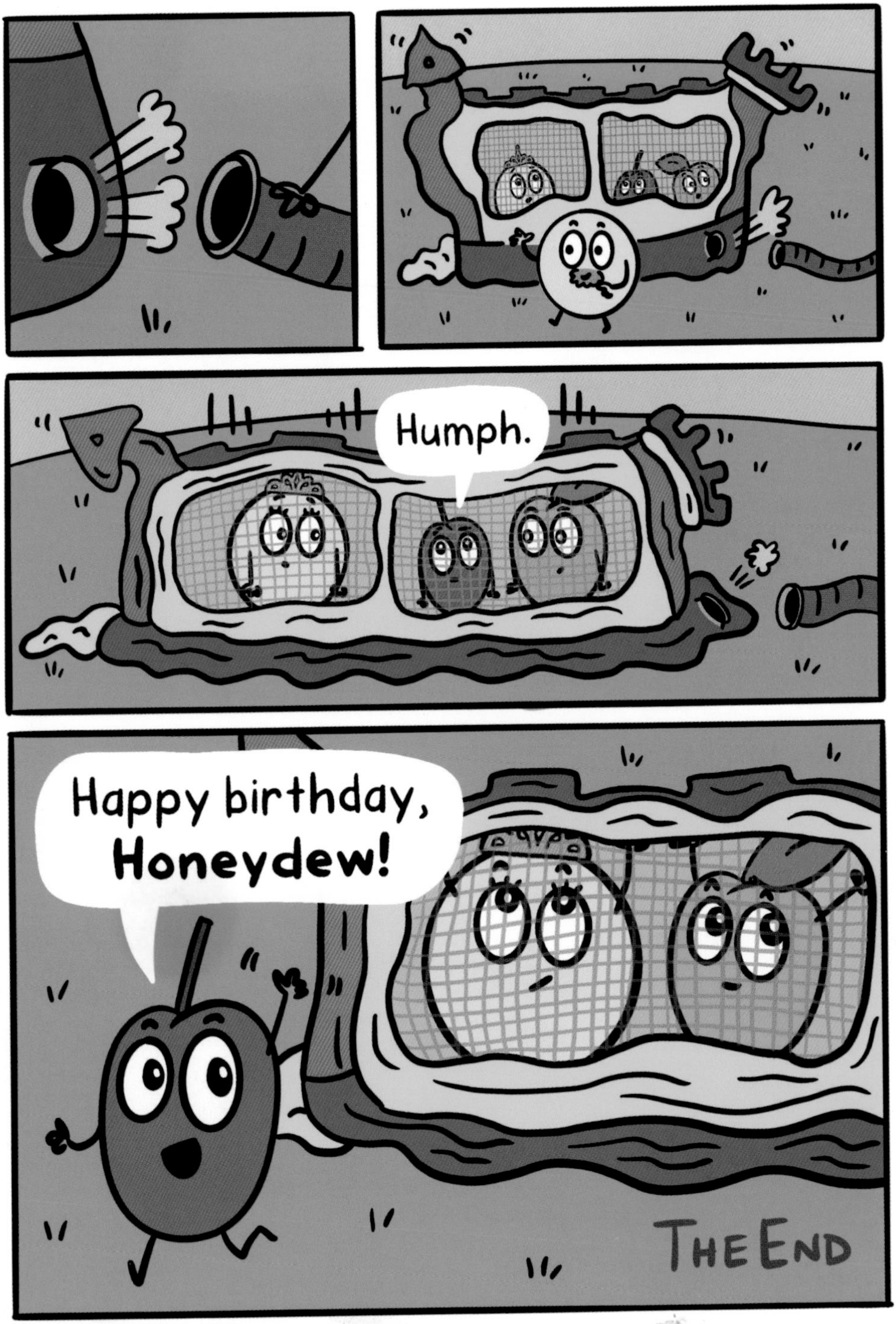
Humph.
Happy birthday, **Honeydew!**
THE END

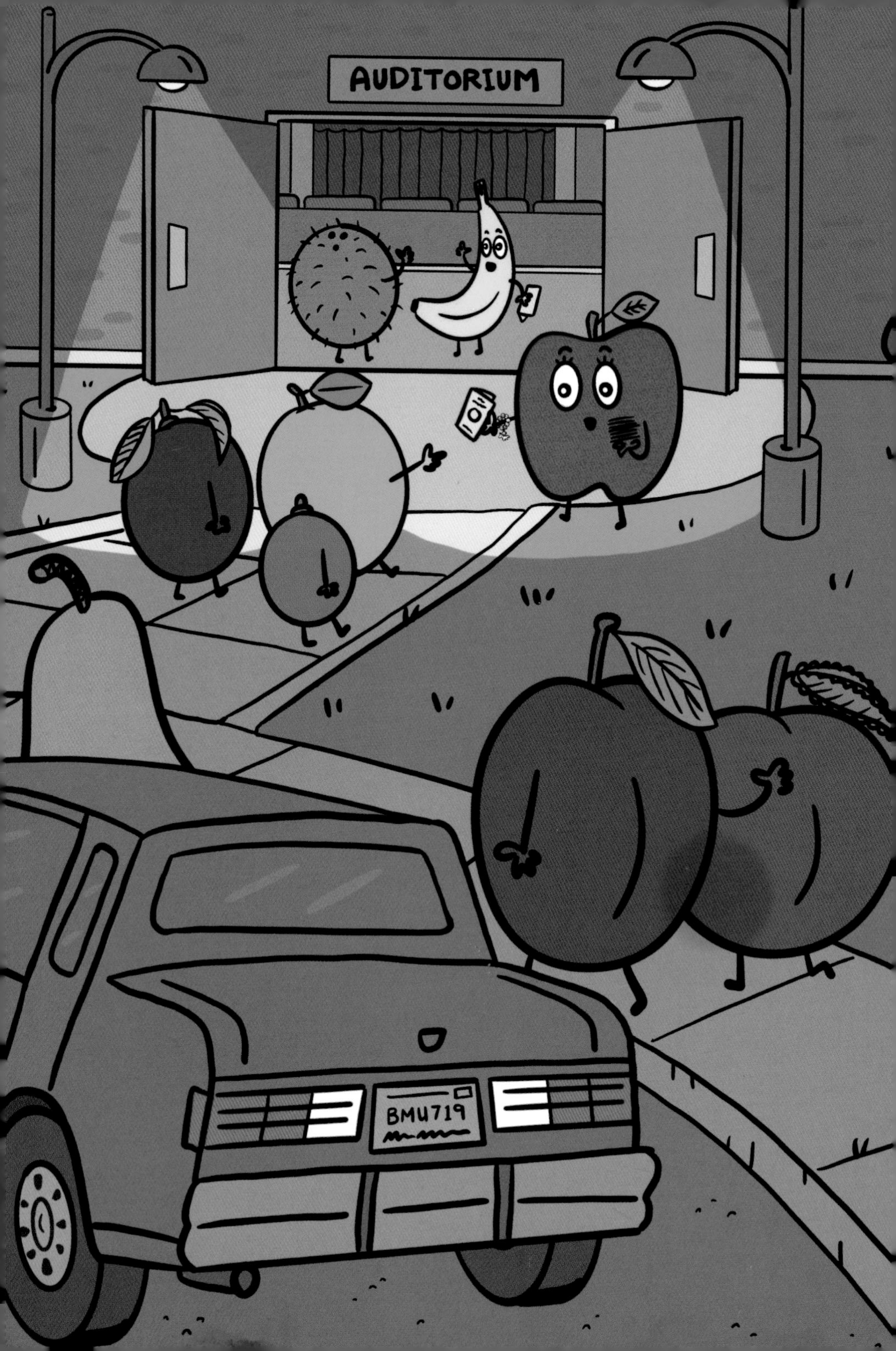
AUDITORIUM
BMU719

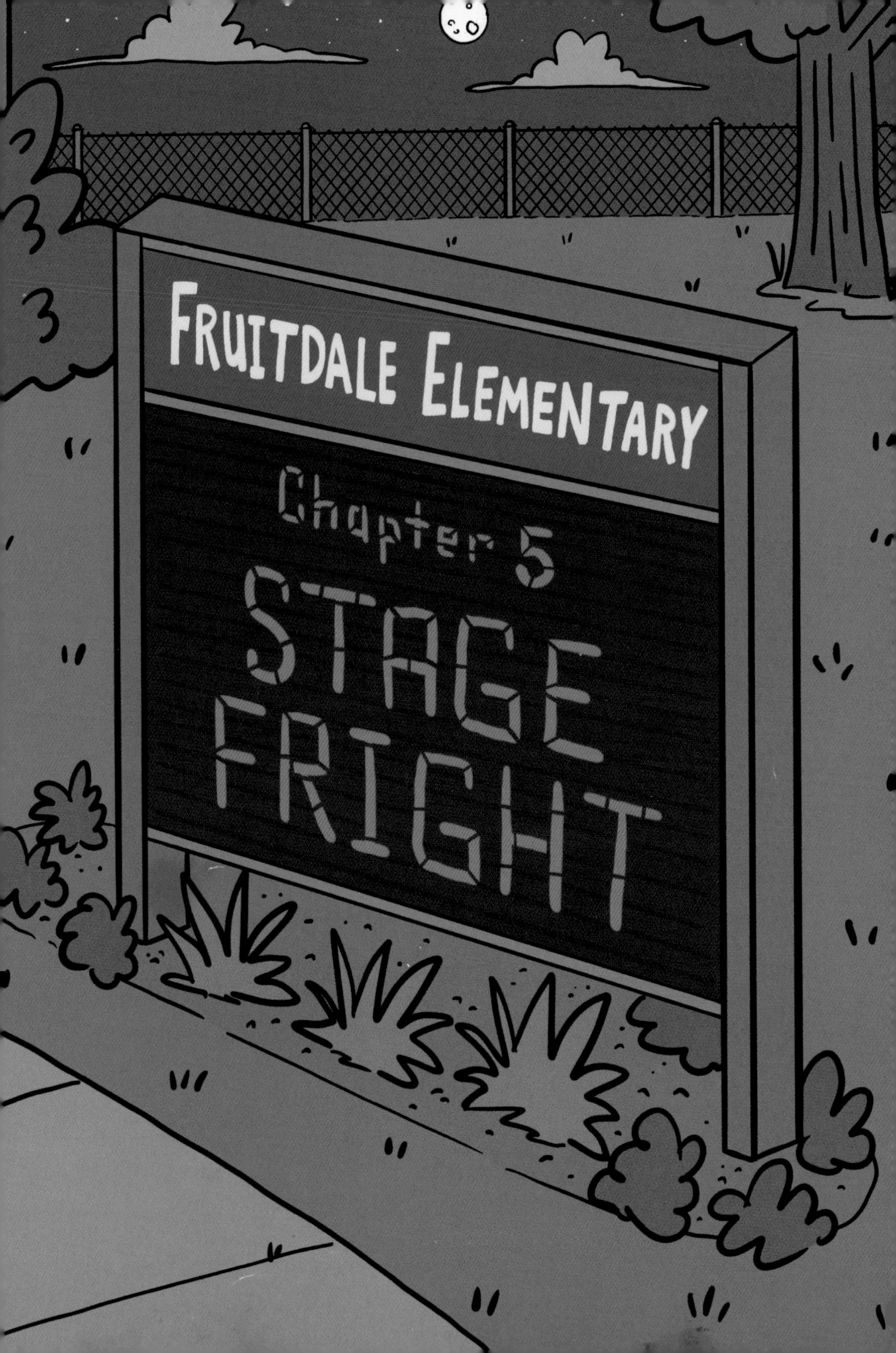
FRUITDALE ELEMENTARY
Chapter 5
STAGE FRIGHT

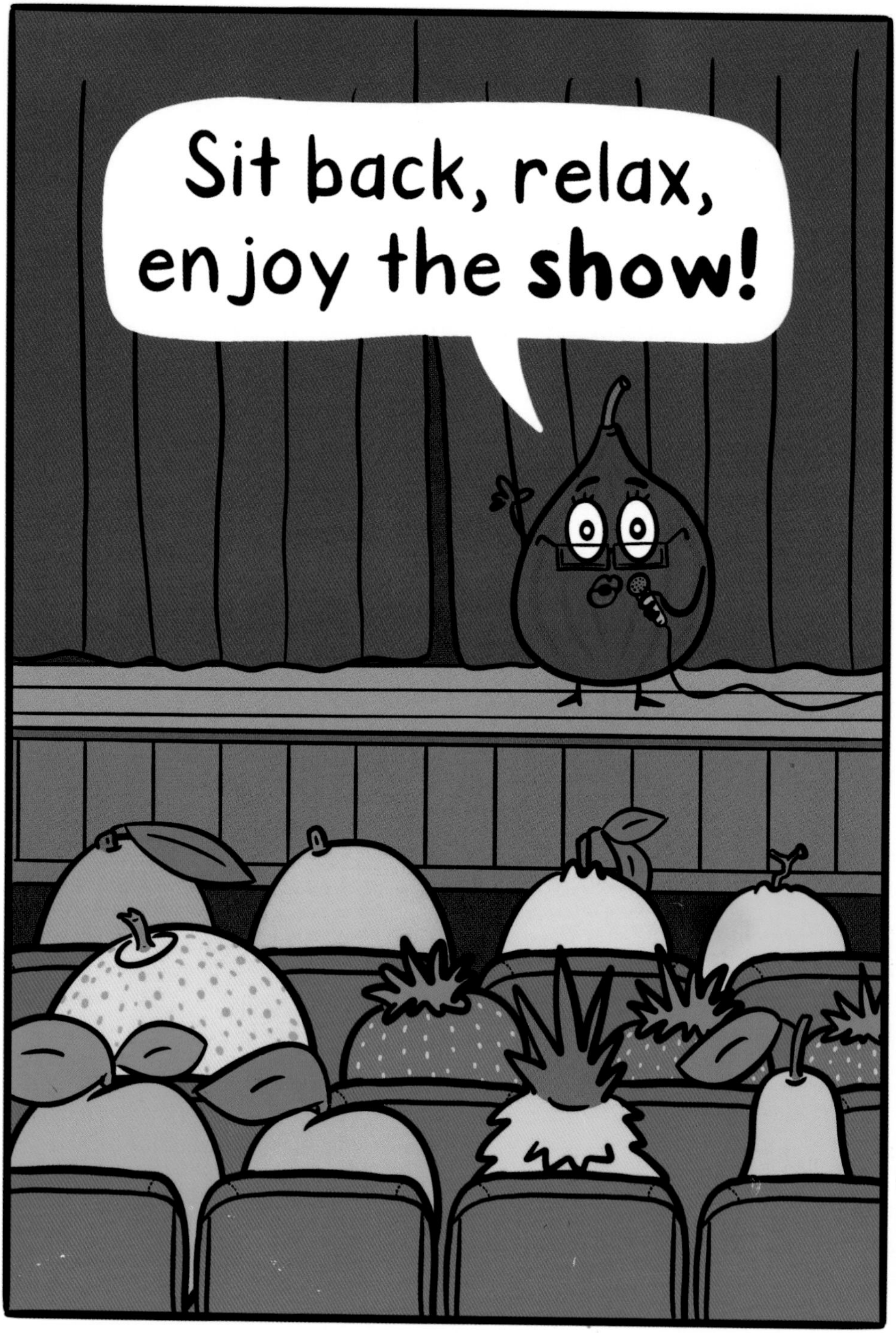
Sit back, relax, enjoy the **show!**

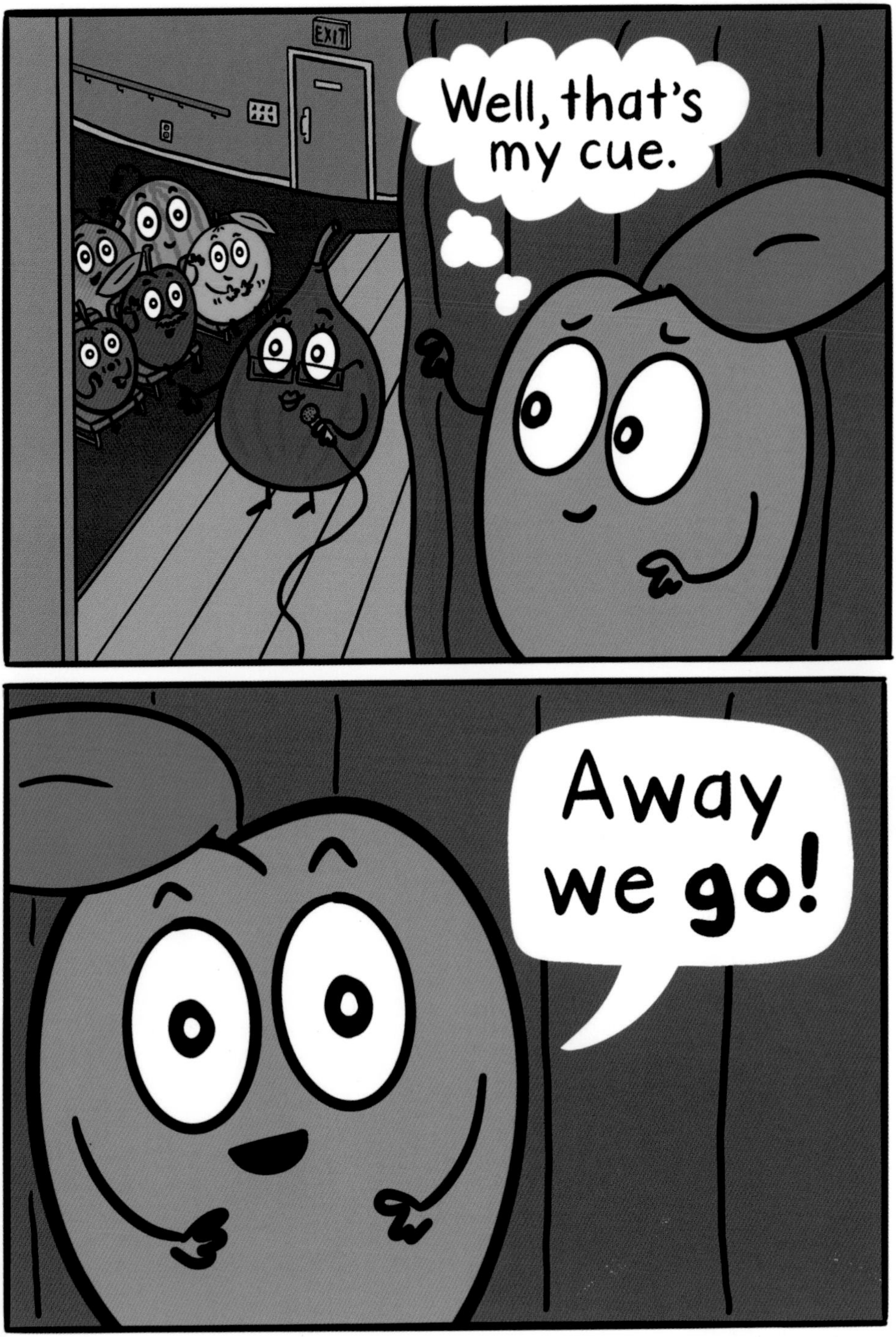
Well, that's my cue.
EXIT
Away we go!

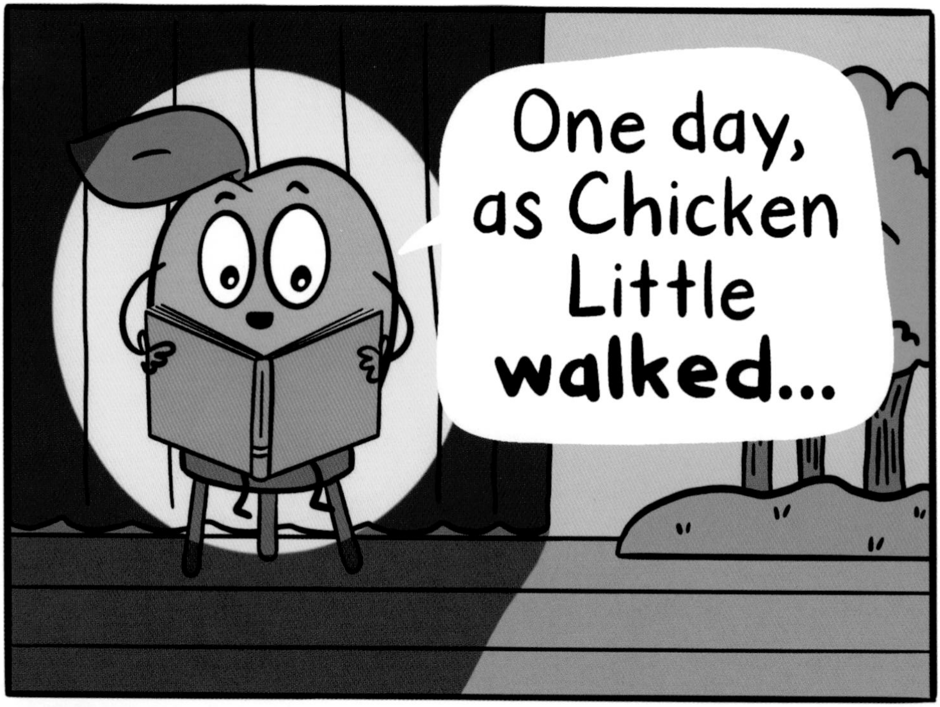
One day, as Chicken Little **walked...**

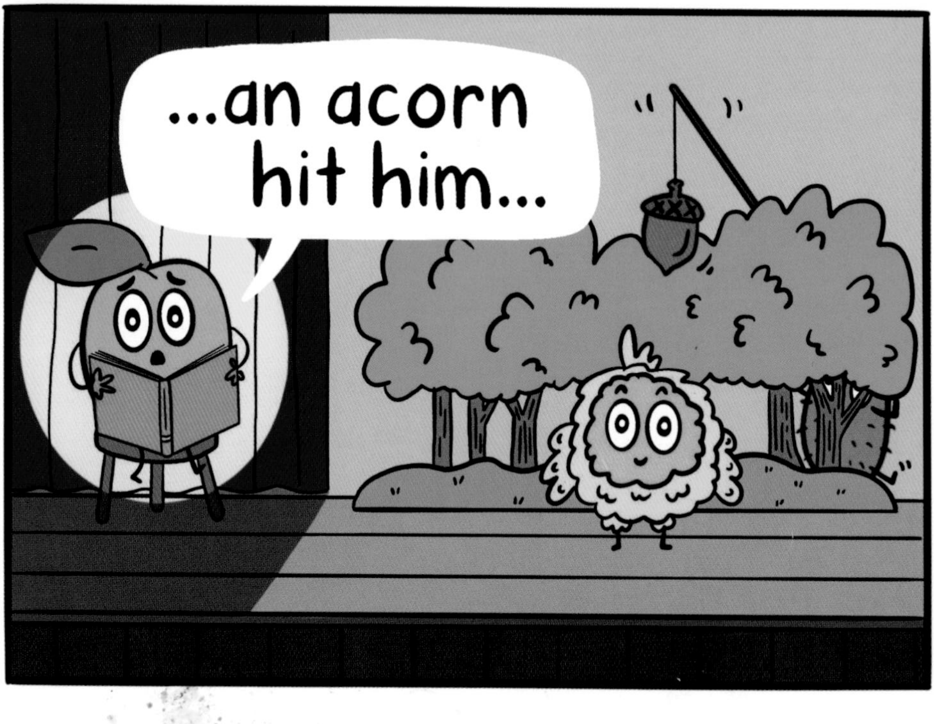
...an acorn hit him...

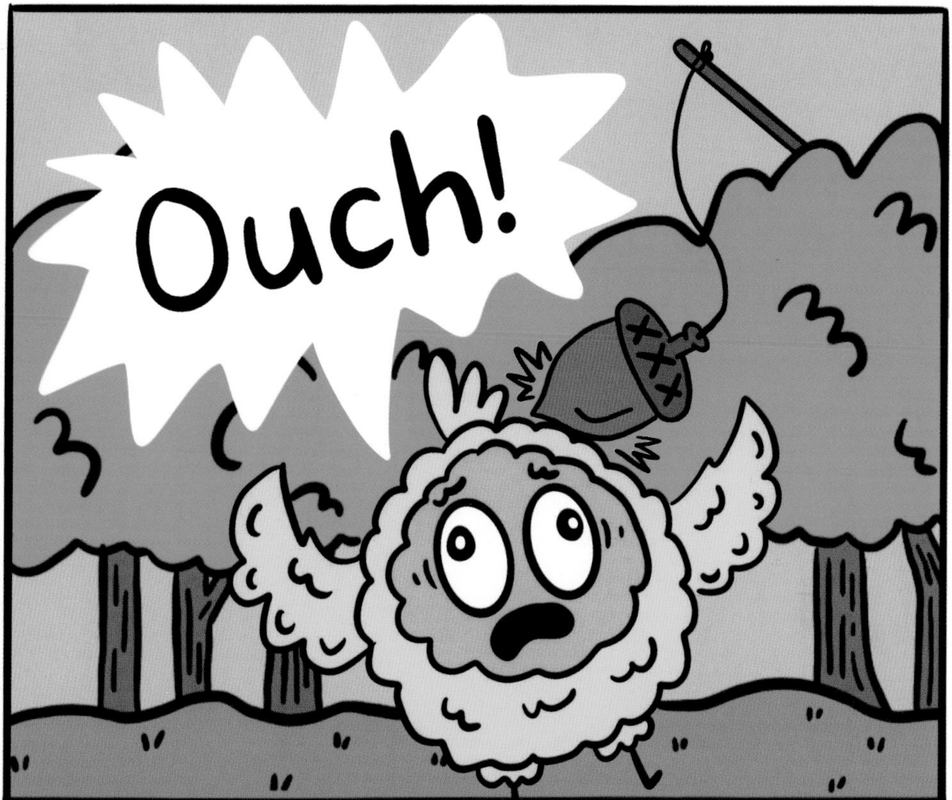
Ouch!

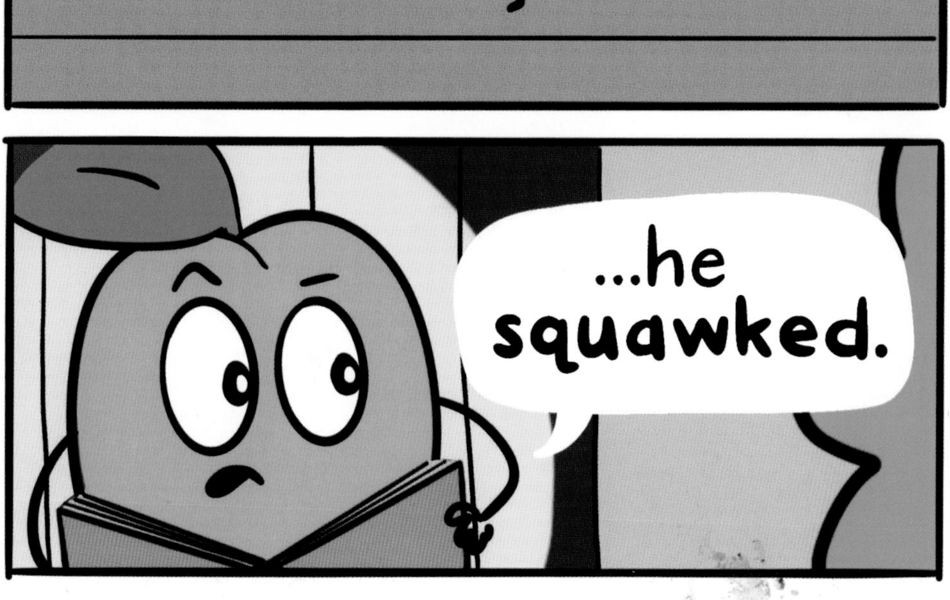
...he squawked.

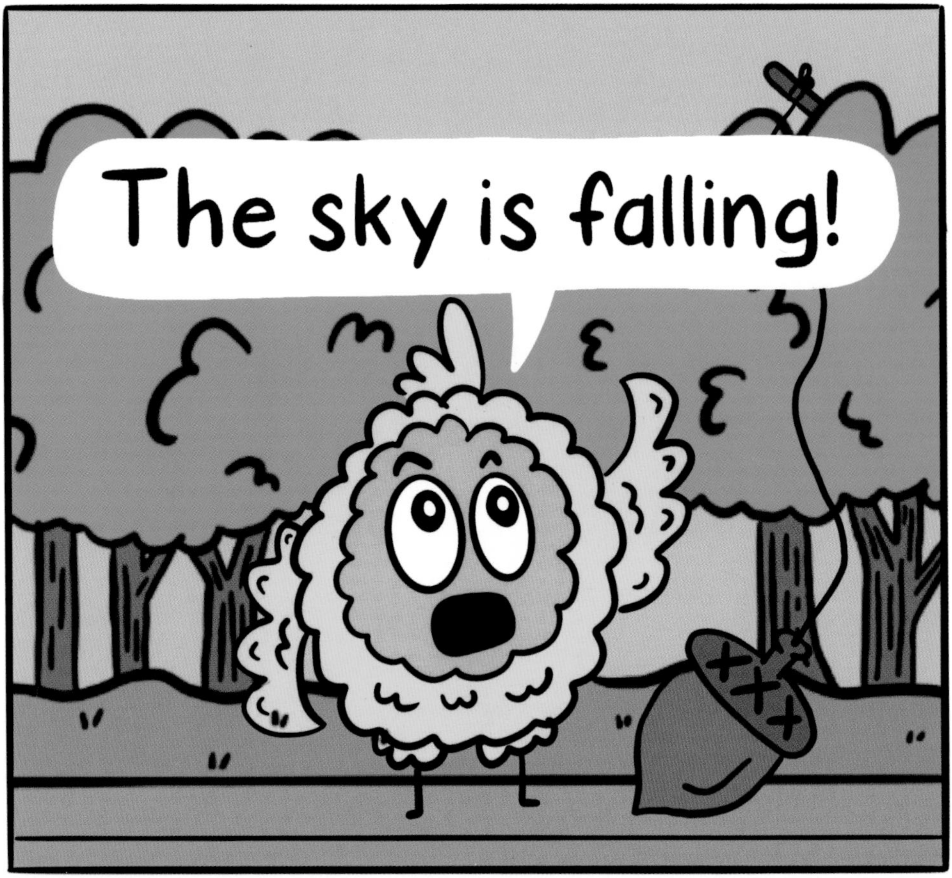
The sky is falling!

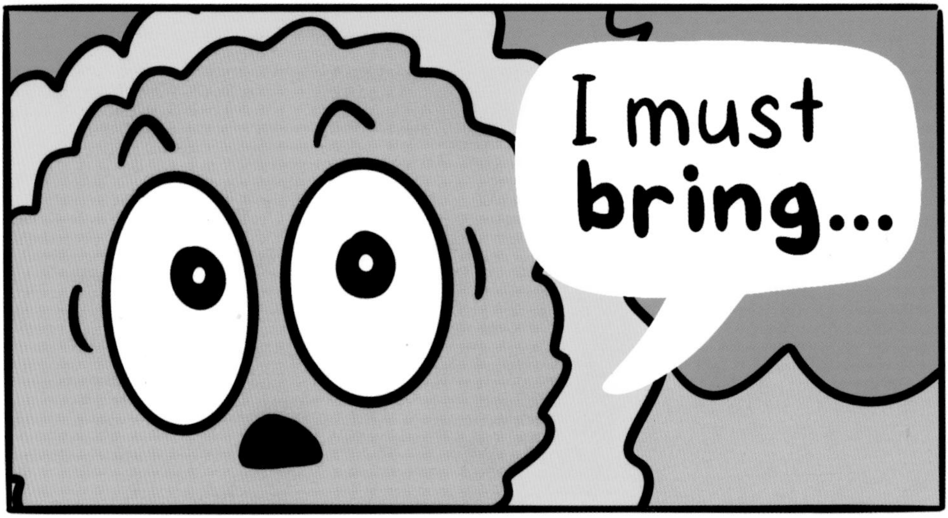
I must **bring...**

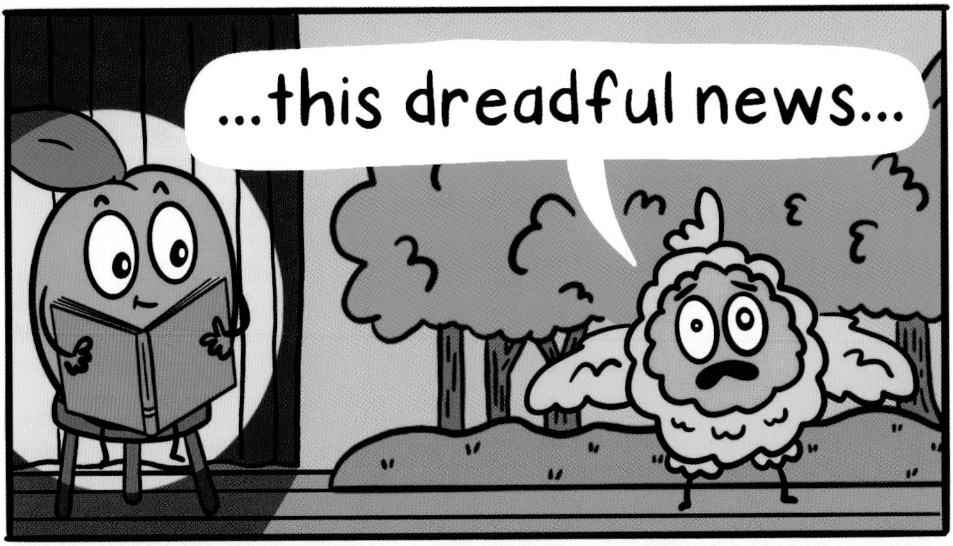
...this dreadful news...

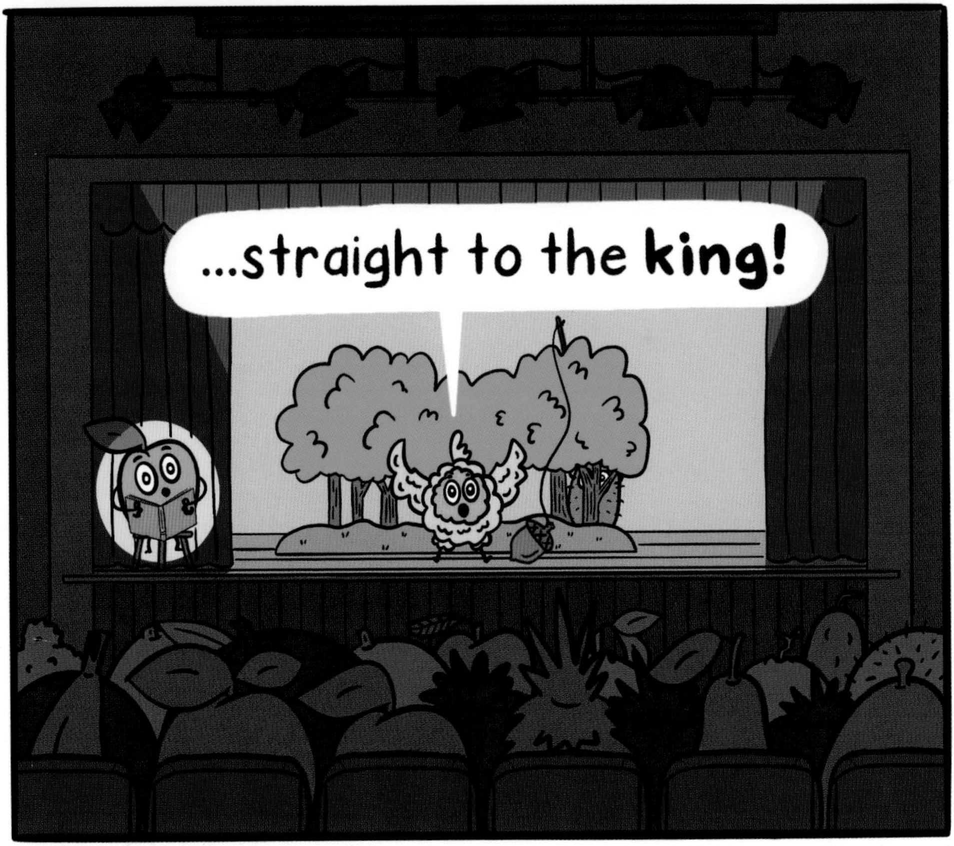
...straight to the **king!**

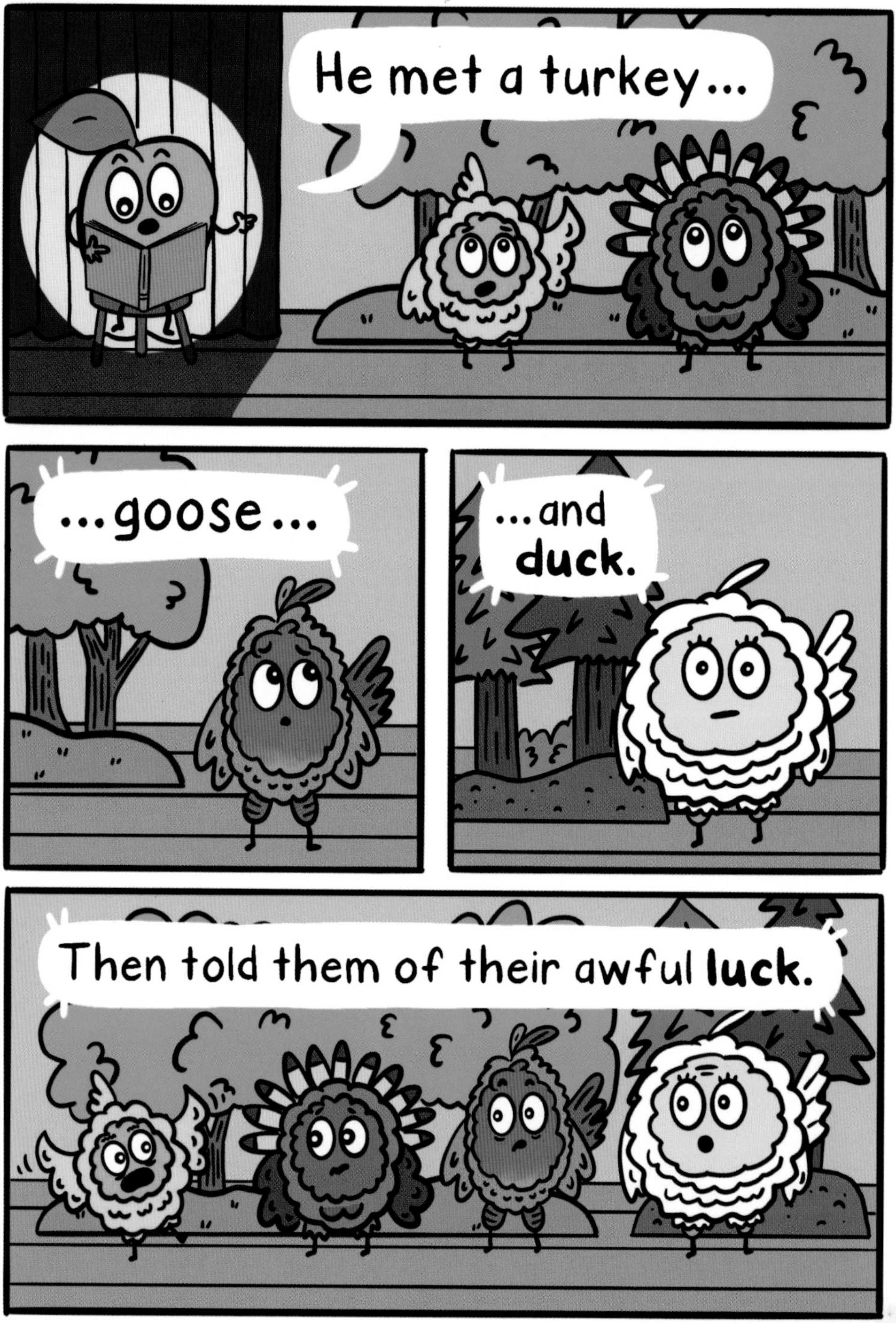
He met a turkey...
...goose...
...and duck.
Then told them of their awful luck.

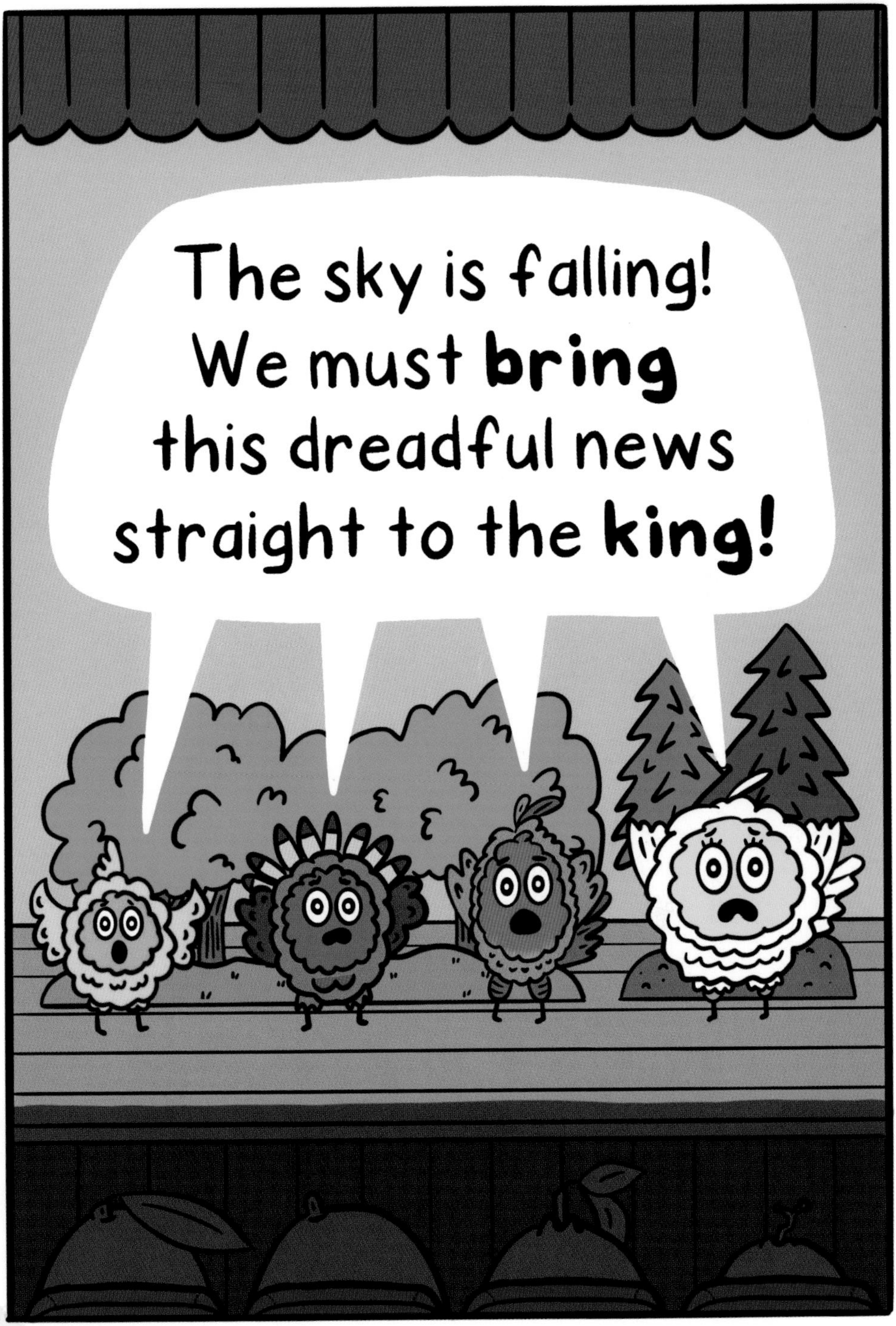
The sky is falling! We must **bring** this dreadful news straight to the **king!**

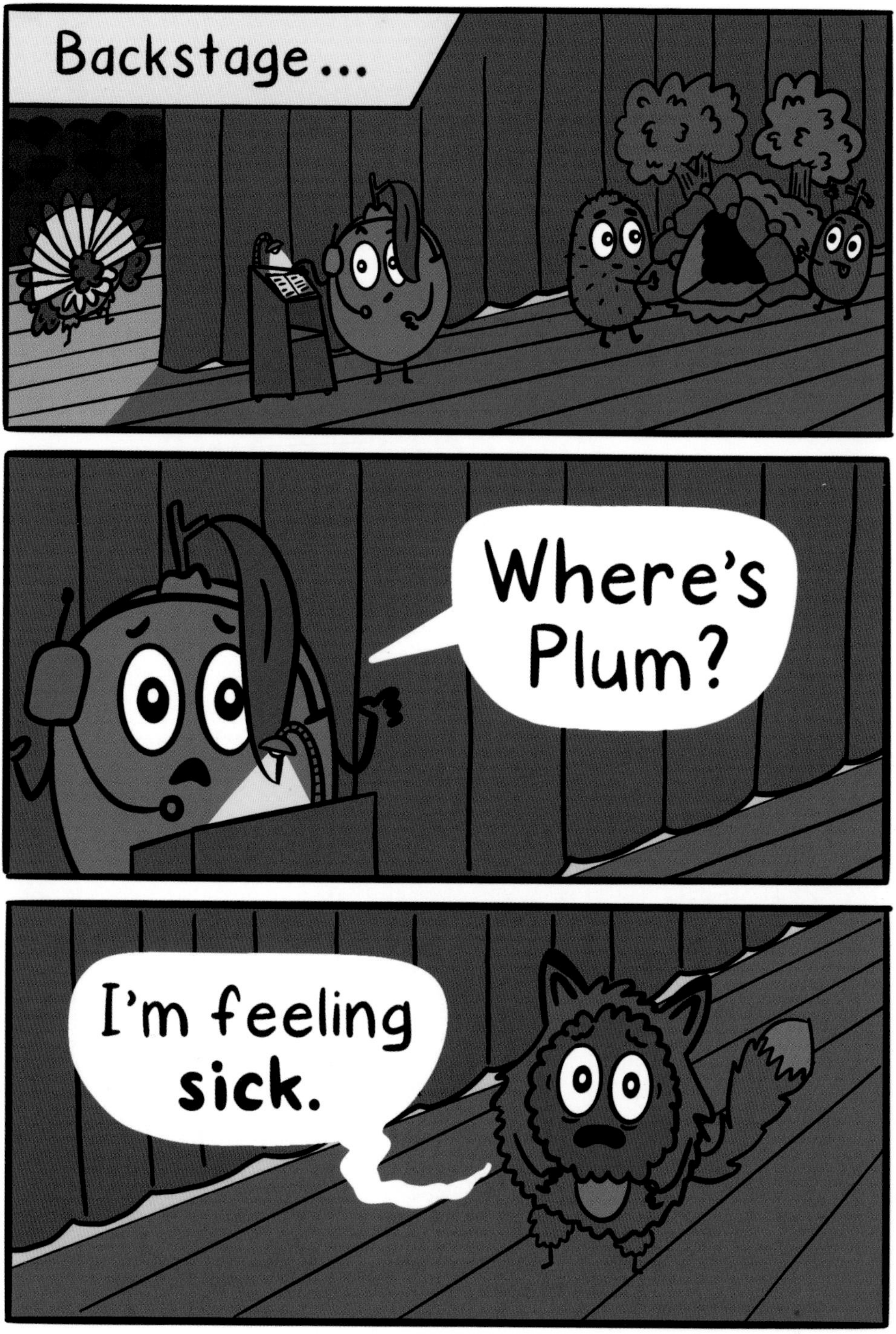
Backstage...
Where's Plum?
I'm feeling sick.

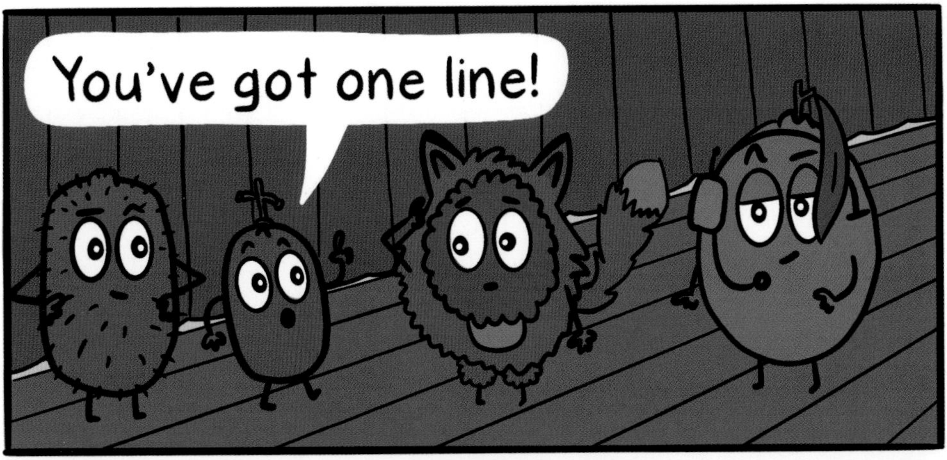
You've got one line!

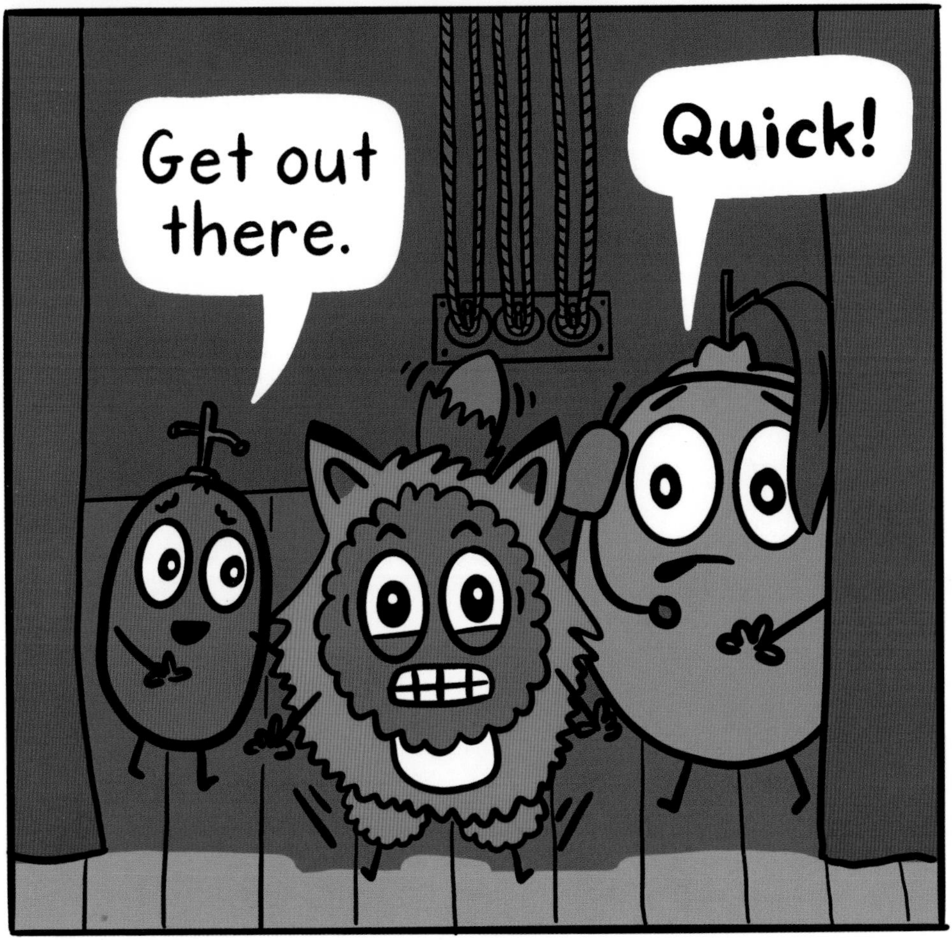
Get out there.
Quick!

Then Foxy Loxy said with **glee...**

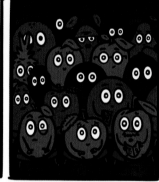

I know a shortcut. Follow **me!**

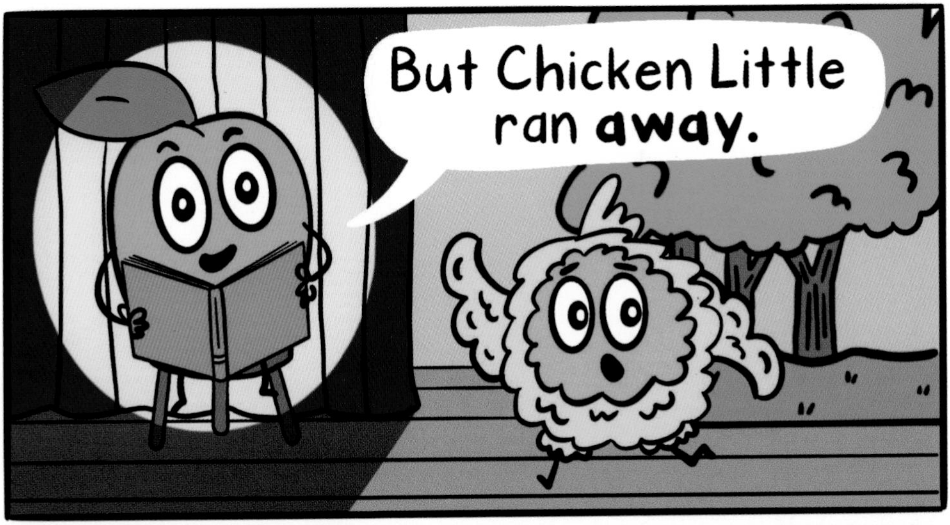
But Chicken Little ran away.

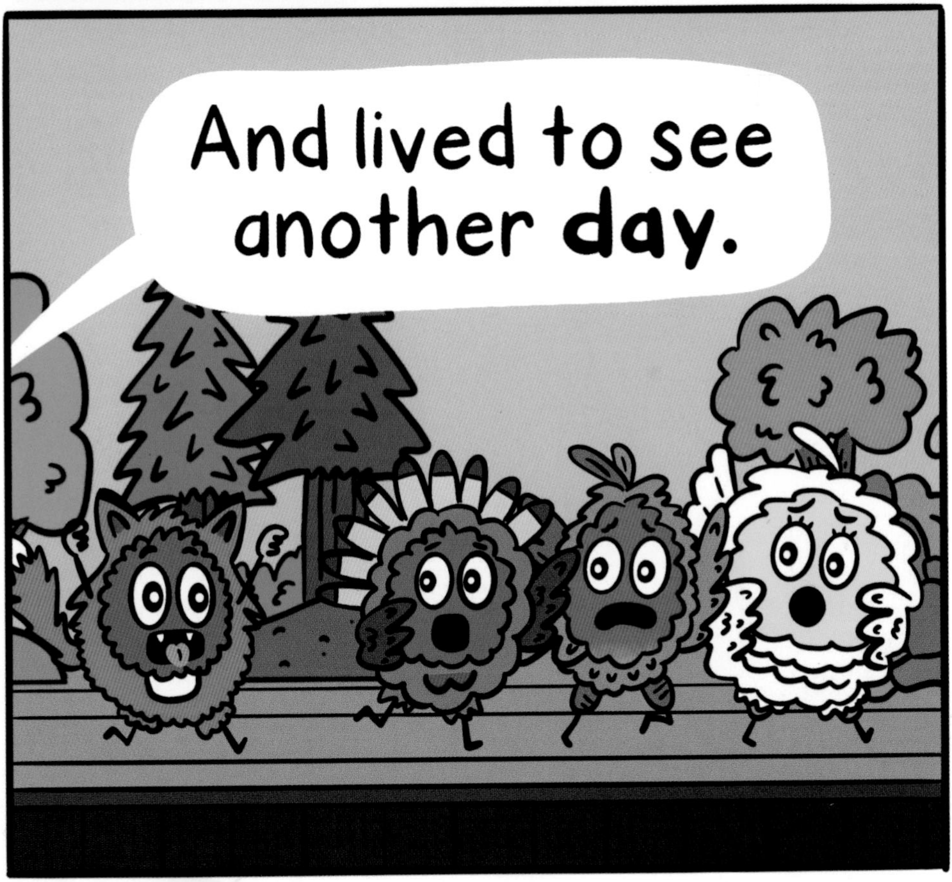
And lived to see another day.

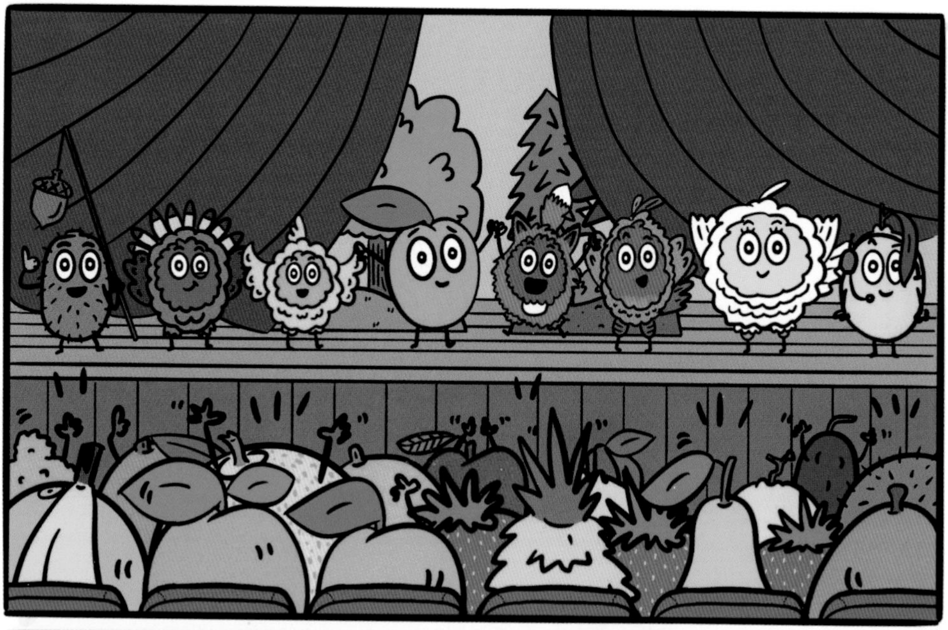

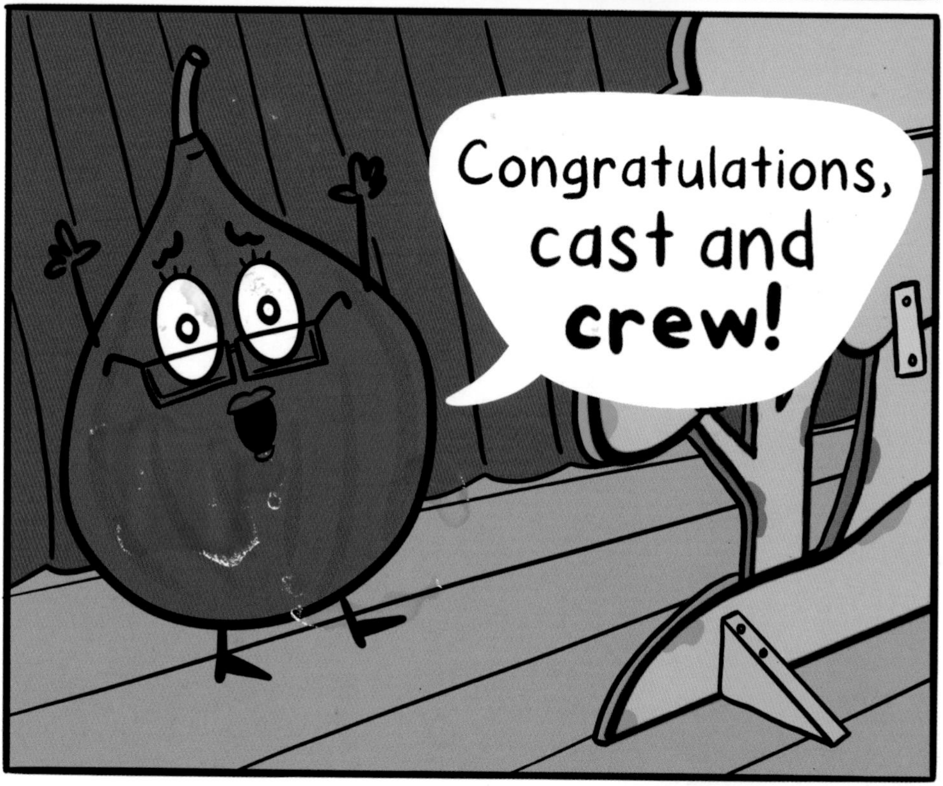
Congratulations, cast and crew!

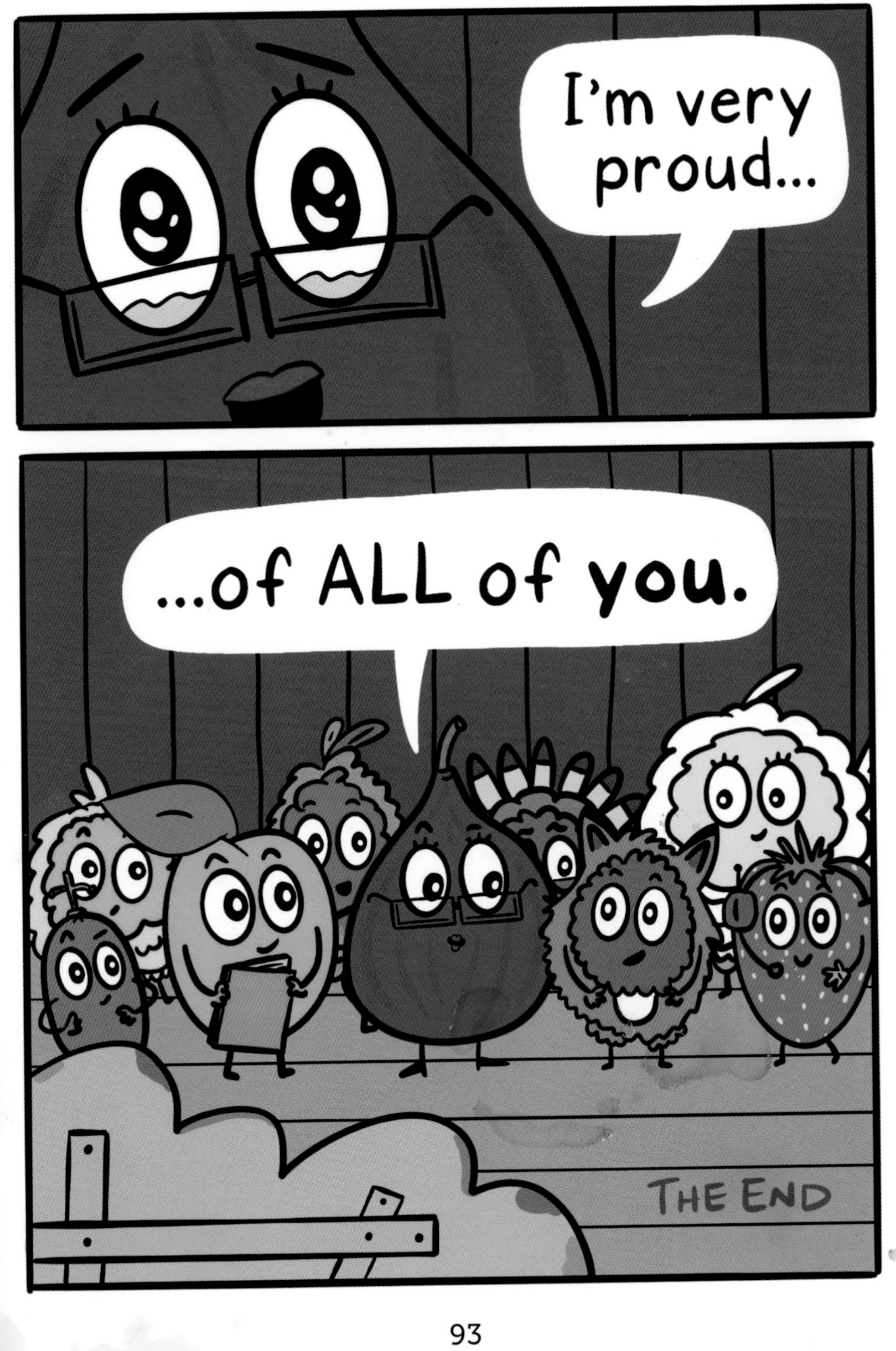
I'm very proud...
...of ALL of you.
THE END

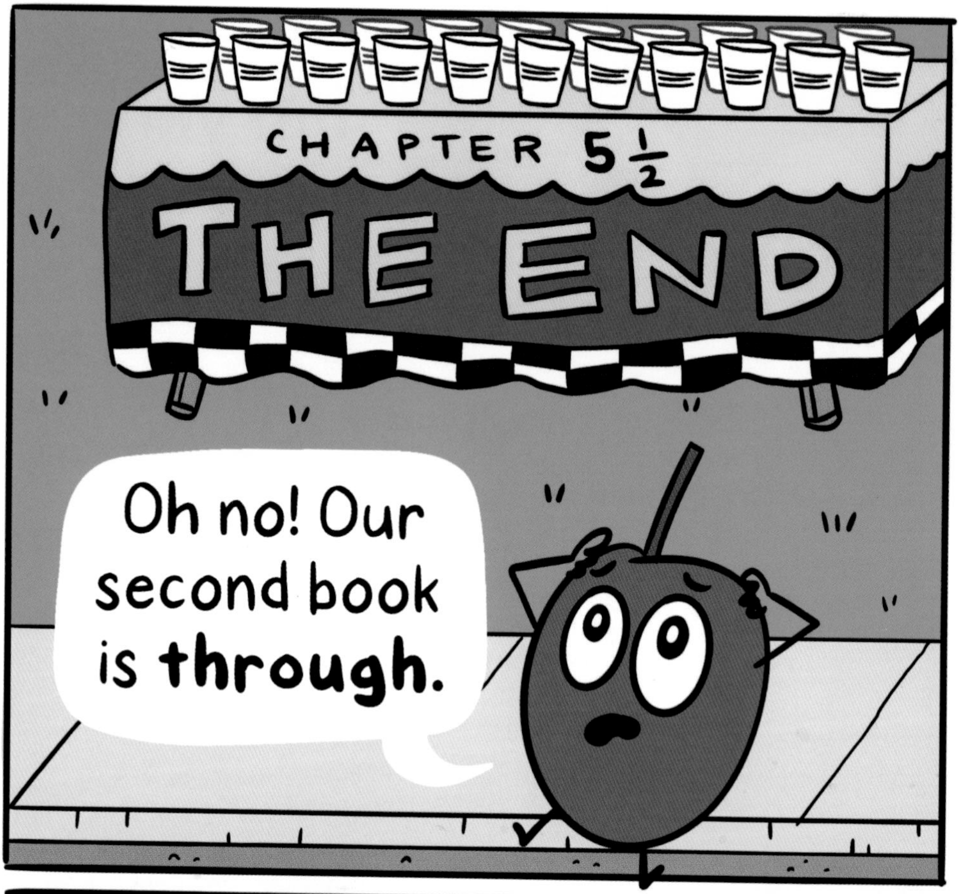
CHAPTER 5 1/2
THE END
Oh no! Our second book is **through.**

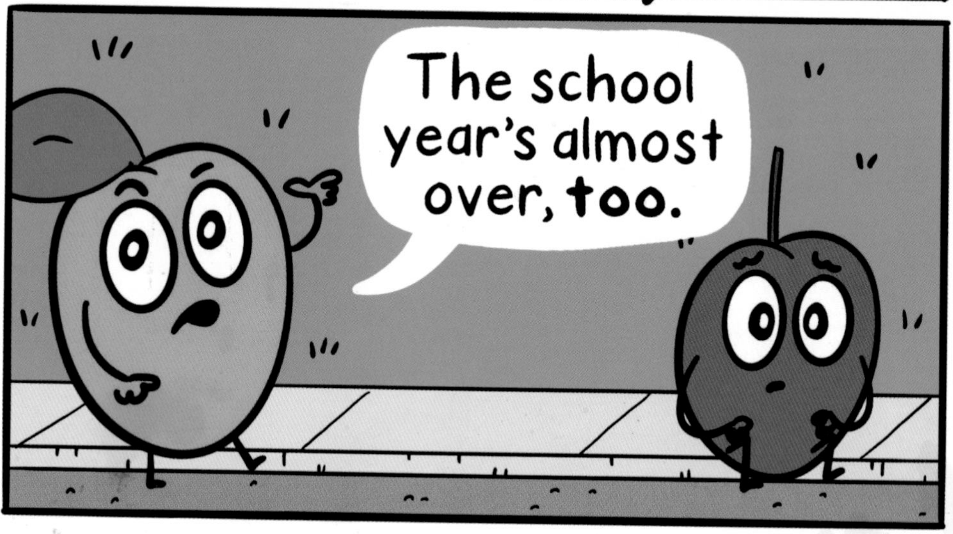
The school year's almost over, **too.**

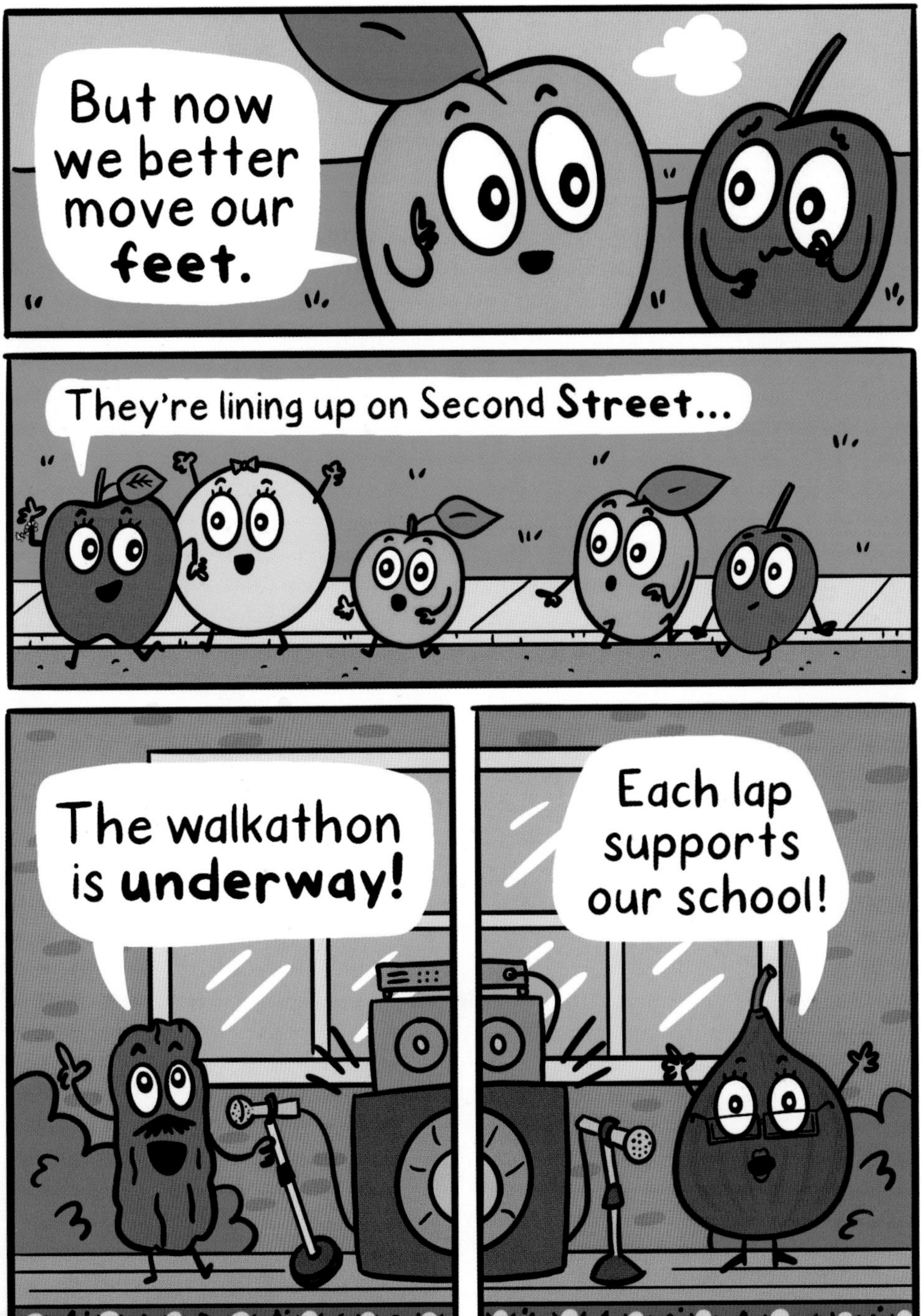
But now we better move our **feet.**
They're lining up on Second **Street...**
The walkathon is **underway!**
Each lap supports our school!

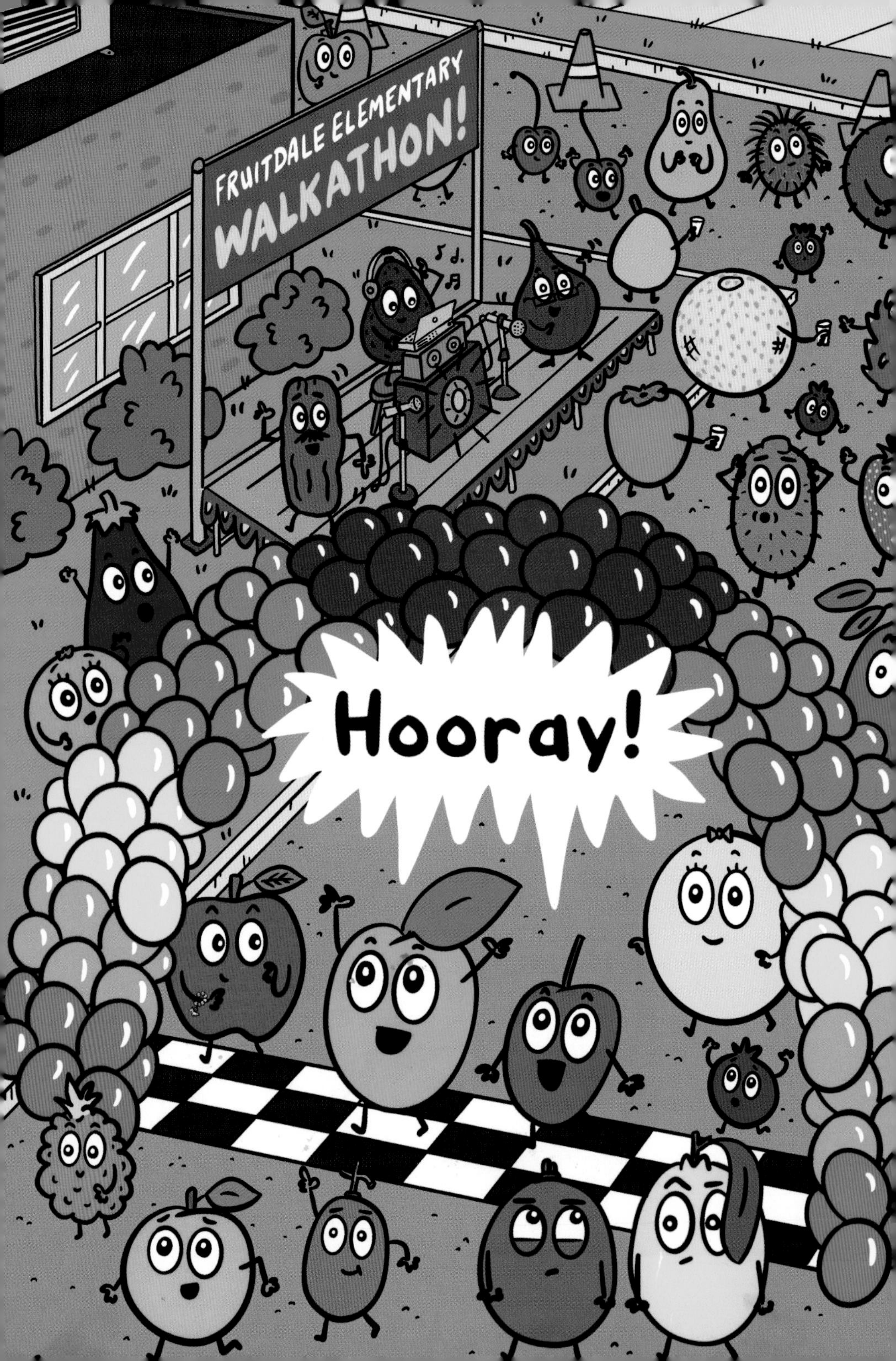
FRUITDALE ELEMENTARY
WALKATHON!
Hooray!